LoVE, FEAR, AND oTHER CoNSTELLATIONS

ALSO BY GANPY NATARAJ

TEXIT: A STAR ALONE

LOVE, FEAR, AND OTHER CONSTELLATIONS

STORIES

GANPY NATARAJ

MOYGA BOOKS

MOYGA BOOKS

MOYGA BOOKS

Copyright © 2025 by Ganpy Nataraj (Nataraj Ganapathy)

All rights reserved. Published in the United States by Moyga Books,

a division of Moyga Media LLC, Michigan.

The Library of Congress has catalogued the Moyga Books edition as follows:

Names: Nataraj, Ganpy, author.

Title: *Love, Fear, and Other Constellations* / Ganpy Nataraj

Description: Novi: Moyga Books, 2025

Identifiers (LCCN):

Library of Congress Control Number: 2025909804

Moyga Books Trade Paperback Edition ISBN: 979-8-9892435-3-2

eBook ISBN: 979-8-9892435-4-9

Cover and interior design by David Ter-Avanesyan/Ter33Design LLC

moygabooks.com

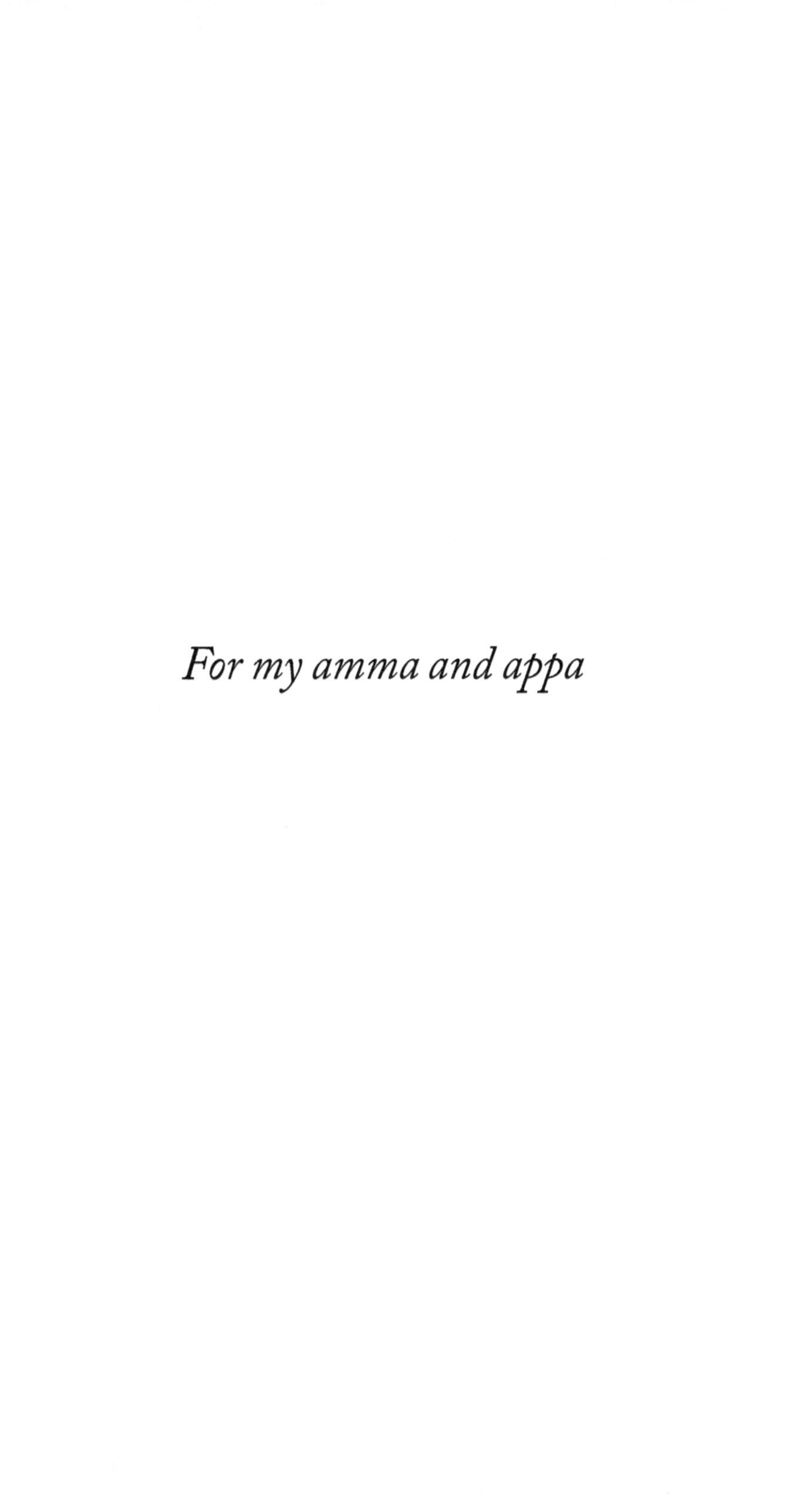

For my amma and appa

CONTENTS

It was inevitable. Waking up to the scent of fresh coffee, Gregory Morris couldn't hold back his smile, a smile that stretched his freckled cheeks, causing the dried tear marks to crack open. It was inevitable that Gregory Morris would look at his empty bedside and think of warm apple strudels for breakfast.

◆

All happy old couples are alike. And every unhappy old couple probably has a unique reason to be unhappy. Gregory and Margaret Morris had been married for a little over fifty-two years. Their companionship certainly had seen many bumpy rides during these fifty-two years. Gregory has not always been a caring husband, and Margaret has not always been a compassionate listener. But these days, more than ever, they sure were a happy couple.

No one knows what happened to their two adult children. The older son, Gregory Morris Jr., was an extremely intelligent student, way ahead of his peers in high school. He moved ahead very quickly in his academic pursuits and went on to invent a breakthrough diagnostic procedure for neural disorders, while still in medical school. The last anyone heard of him was that he was working for the World Health Organization in a major global initiative and had moved to Geneva, Switzerland. That was four years ago. The younger son, Michael Morris left home after he graduated from high school and has never come back to visit his parents since then. Greg and Margaret don't talk much about Michael, and it is a fair assumption that any attempt to ask about Michael would not only make them unhappy but also bring an air of discomfort to the relationship anyone has with the couple.

Gregory Morris was born in Richmond, Virginia, into a family of army veterans. He and Margaret went to the same high school. Gregory and Margaret were not meant to go out as a couple on that late spring prom night date in 1958, but as they say, life is nothing but a series of coincidences. Some may call it fate. The boy who had asked Margaret out on a date for the prom accidentally bumped into the girl, whom Gregory had asked out, earlier that morning at a bakery, and they decided to follow their hearts, even if it meant they broke other people's.

It was love at first sight. Gregory and Margaret knew on that very night that in a life full of coincidences, this was one coincidence they would never have wanted undone. They got married in the summer of 1964. The wedding was in Virginia Beach, right on the now-touristy boardwalk, which was simply a wooden boardwalk stretching hardly three to four blocks during that time. They chose that location because it was cheap, convenient, and they had a great many memories of hanging out together during their years of premarital courtship, when both were working in various small jobs in and around Virginia Beach.

◆

The house was built in 1971 in a neighborhood many call the "auto white-collar neighborhood" in the suburbs of Detroit. Gregory and Margaret moved into this house in 1976. They fell in love with everything about this neighborhood, and the day Margaret saw this house, she decided this was going to be their only home. So, it has been.

The house has a perfectly rectangular door, painted blue, with a shiny yellow brass knob exact halfway up. The door opens on to a wide foyer with very plush tilework leading up to the living room with its paneled walls and carpeted floors, complete with Victorian-style couches, impeccably arranged at right angles. The house has a beautiful front yard resembling miniature rolling meadows, and the back yard is large enough for a single family with two children. A white fence that separated their yard from their neighbor's not only added a touch of suburban elegance to the house but also gave a sense of privacy to the couple, which they seemed to value much more these days.

It had been more than a decade since Gregory retired, but he still went about every moment of his post-retirement life in a steadfast way. There had been a wave of change in the way he started living his life since his retirement. Margaret had always been his first love, but there comes a time in an adult man's life when he starts taking things for granted, starts sulking over his unattainable dreams, and goes on a tailwind chase behind certain fantasies. Gregory was no exception. There was a decade or two when he tried to pursue what then seemed like an ambitious career in a confounded corporate maze. But retirement had brought a sudden sense of purpose in his life.

◆

Every morning, Greg and Margaret started their day almost synchronously. At 5:25 a.m., one of them turned toward the other (it normally was Greg) and simply stared at the beauty of their beloved partner's face. A face that continued to shrink in its physical appearance with every passing year and yet continued to expand in its beauty while reminding the kind of anchor it offers to the other to be joyous for yet another day to indulge in requited love. This staring lasts for one or two minutes. But that is enough to wake the other person up. As soon as Margaret opens her eyes, Greg smiles at her. He leans toward her and kisses her, while he gently lifts his left arm from under the sheets to caress her face and to fix those few strands of hair that invariably get disoriented during the dark hours.

"Apple strudels or sesame bagels?" Greg asks with the curiosity of a high school boy.

"It's Monday. You shouldn't be able to spell anything but strudels today, darling!" Margaret says, mischievous as always, even if her eyes are not fully open.

"You look beautiful this morning, Maggie. More than ever. Good morning, darling!"

"And you, my dear, look more handsome than a man in his late seventies ever can be. Love you too. You just need to cut down on that sugar a bit. Look at that girth. I cannot even hug you completely anymore without having to go around at least once," Margaret says, fully awake now.

"I have no defense. At least I don't have to impress a new date tonight. Mm . . . the coffee has started brewing. Gosh! I love the smell of fresh coffee. Let's keep our appointment with the Panera bakers, shall we? Don't want to disappoint them by being the second customer of the morning." Greg gives one more peck on Margaret's cheek before he gets off the bed.

Before they go to bed every night, Margaret sets the timer on the coffee machine. At 5:45 a.m., the scent of fresh coffee wafts through the walls without fail. Greg and Margaret sit across from each other at their four-seater dining table in the kitchen, as they enjoy their fresh cups of coffee. Greg likes his coffee black with sugar, and Margaret drinks hers with two teaspoonfuls of half-and-half and no sugar. It has been this way forever.

At 6:10 a.m., they get into their car and start driving. They have a two-car garage. Greg's car, a 1995 Jeep Cherokee, which he gifted himself for his retirement, hasn't seen much mileage in the last three years, primarily because the Morrises don't drive much these days. For such trips, Greg prefers driving their cherry-red 1988 Oldsmobile, which Margaret used to drive when she was working. Margaret has't driven since she was diagnosed with amyotrophic lateral sclerosis a couple of years ago.

◆

To them, breakfast is a big deal. Not because breakfast is the most important meal of the day, but because they believe that as a couple, breakfast gives them an opportunity to commit their love and to reaffirm their care for each other every morning. Many unhappy marriages end every night after making love, and if they are not rebuilt over breakfast, they eventually fail. Greg and Margaret may be in their seventies, but they insist on sharing their dreams over plates of strudel or oatmeal or whole-grain toast and omelets, like they had just met in their teens.

You know you live in a small town when everyone knows what you eat for breakfast. Greg and Margaret don't live in a small town. But by homogenizing their breakfast routine, they have made sure their waitresses at Panera know what they eat for breakfast. More or less.

◆

"Morning, Jenny, how are you today?" Greg asks as he walks into Panera.

"Hey, morning, Mr. Morris. I am doing terrific. Thank you. You look radiant today. I am sure your wife did something special for you last night," Jenny says, trying to brighten his day.

"I'll tell you a secret, Jenny. Margaret is a good explorer, you know what I mean?" Greg winks at Jenny with a bit of difficulty a man in his seventies is expected to have when he tries to wink. He guffaws, and a burst of laughter erupts from his mouth quite involuntarily, like a burp peeking out after a sumptuous meal. Greg quickly realizes Margaret may have heard him teasing her, as he turns around to see if she is in already.

Margaret is still making her way inside. She insists on Greg not helping her as she walks from the car through the door. Greg understands how important these few moments of freedom and independence she enjoys are during these early morning hours at Panera. There is no other customer waiting for her to make her way in and embarrassing her for being slow, and if she accidentally trips, there is hardly anyone to notice. Greg simply knows what this beautiful dream of his, the woman he fell in love with fifty-eight years ago, on that bright spring evening, while dancing to Danny and the Juniors' "At the Hop" on the prom dance floor, would be ready to trade for just a few minutes of that dancing freedom. ALS is a debilitating disease that can suck the positivity out of you if you don't have the right person caring for you.

As Margaret walks at a sedentary but a rhythmic pace, one step followed by a wobbly second step, all Greg can see is the image of a petite seventy-eight-year-old girl dancing her way into Panera.

Jenny sees Greg's eyes getting a bit moist, and as if on cue, she plays "At the Hop" on the restaurant speakers.

"Greg, your table is ready. I think it's time to impress your lady with apple strudels." Jenny tries to break the daydream that was distracting Greg from doing more important things.

"All right, I will see you at the table, Jenny. Don't forget my coffee." Greg holds Margaret's hands and starts guiding her to their regular table.

As Margaret walks to the table, Gregory helps remove her coat and hangs it on the coat stand. The chair is already pulled away from the table to make room for Margaret to sit. Once she sits comfortably, Greg pushes the chair to the right position. There are things only a longtime companion would know. One is knowing exactly how many inches you should leave between the dining table and the chair.

"Gregory, dear, I have to tell you about the bittersweet dream I had last night." Margaret starts the conversation, while Greg is still busy adjusting the folds of his sweater right above his belt. A man has got to hide what he has got to hide.

"What was it?"

"Well. You remember the time Michael broke his right elbow during a soccer game?"

"Oh yeah . . . he must have been seven or eight? I was out of town, and you had to rush him to emergency."

"Oh, hey, Mrs. Morris, I love your blouse today. Is that new? You must have made Greg happy or something. Did he get this as a gift?" Jenny is at the table, leaving a fresh pot of coffee and two cups, while pretending she is ready to take their order.

"Yes, dear. This is new. But no, this is not a gift from Greg. He has stopped giving me gifts of late. This is a gift from my sister." Margaret is not one to miss a beat when it comes to taunting her husband.

"What should I get you two lovebirds to munch on this morning? Other than, of course, strudels?" Jenny asks.

"Let's start with that for now. Something tells me I am going to be a bit hungry today." Greg smiles at Jenny.

Jenny returns the smile with a wink and leaves the table, leaving the two to continue their conversation on love, loyalty, and everything in between.

"So, what happened?" Greg asks.

"What do you mean, what happened?" Margaret says, completely perplexed with the question as she pours coffee into her cup.

"Your dream . . ."

"Michael. Yes, Michael . . . I relived that day, those few minutes of his trauma in all the gory details. But the bizarre thing was I didn't take him to the hospital. I brought him home, and there you were. You gave me a hug and a kiss. And somehow, I stopped crying and started giggling. The next thing I remember, you and I were out in Venice, sailing on a gondola. Don't know what happened to Michael. But we were happy. We were singing, laughing, and we were just happy . . ." Margaret's eyes become a bit moist.

"Eat them while they are hot. As always, you guys get to taste the first batch," Jenny says at the table with two plates of really large apple strudels.

"Thank you, Jenny. They look lovely. You know how much we look forward to our breakfast here. This more than makes our day." Margaret touches Jenny's hands with a sense of gratitude, warmth, and something else, which Jenny would only realize much later.

The romance in Greg and Margaret's life is not about the complexities and mysteries, but it is all about the simplicities and platitudes. Love, if you ask them (and who better to ask than a couple who have been together for fifty-odd years), they would say is not a feeling of breathlessness or palpating excitement. Love is not about staying awake in bed imagining that you are being kissed all over your body and is certainly not the burning desire to see him or her while the stomach churns if you don't, but they would say, actually all of the above is what you experience when you are just beginning to fall in love. It's the beginning. But love is a residue of all that. It's what is left over after you experience all of the above.

Greg and Margaret have made their breakfast a ritual. Barring a few exceptions here and there, they have never missed going out for breakfast. Even on days when Margaret feels weak and doesn't feel like stepping out, Gregory makes sure she at least gives him company in the car. He would go to get their breakfast tray from Panera and bring it to the car. They would just sit in the parking lot, eat their breakfast, sip their coffees, and share their dreams of the night and the dreams of their future. They like extending those minutes of togetherness into hours if they can.

Jenny has worked at Panera for more than three years, and she has always taken care of Greg and Margaret, maybe because she prefers her early morning shifts. On those rare days when she doesn't see them at Panera at 6:30 a.m., she goes through moments of restlessness, calmed only by the next sighting of the couple.

◆

Today is another day.

It is inevitable that Gregory Morris would look at his bedside and think of warm apple strudels for breakfast. Greg gets into his car and starts driving on this cold morning. He has his long coat on, his gloves and a hat to battle the cold. He looks toward the passenger seat and gives a nod. There is a smile creeping up the corner of his mouth.

As the car pulls into the parking lot of Panera, he can see that the lights are not on yet. They open at 6:30 a.m. Did he get here early today? He checks his clock, which shows 6:20 a.m. And his watch shows 6:20 a.m. as well. How did he miss his timing? He has been doing this for more than ten years now. This new routine. He doesn't know how he missed his sense of time this morning. He patiently waits for the Panera employees to turn the lights on and to flip the sign board from "Closed" to "Open."

The lights are on now.

"Good morning, Mr. Morris! How are you doing on this cold November morning?" Jenny is still adjusting her apron, but she notices a very fidgety Greg.

"Morning, Jenny. How are you? Yeah . . . I know. It's a bit cold. Could do a lot better without that wind," Greg says, trying to sound cheerful.

Before Jenny can say anything, Greg starts walking to his regular table. He removes his coat, hangs it on the coat stand, and quickly takes his seat, not bothering to move the chair across the table from his for Margaret. He leaves what was in his left hand on the table, across from him.

"So, Mr. Morris, what can I get you today? We just baked some pecan braids, but I know it's a Monday and Mrs. Morris may be aching for those warm apple strudels," Jenny says, still a bit puzzled but not wanting to lose her poise.

"Of course, it's a Monday. You shouldn't have to ask us. Strudels it will be. If they are those pecans from South Carolina, then I will take one with me for the road. Shh . . . don't tell Margaret! She doesn't approve of me having that extra sugar." Greg is still itchy, but with a silly concern in his eyes.

Jenny notices that Greg's eyes show a sign of weariness. Almost like he never slept through the night.

"Mr. Morris, should I just bring one plate then?" Jenny pauses for a second and continues, "Guessing you are going to take the tray to the car and eat your breakfast there?"

"No. Just serve them here. We will eat here. We love the conversation we can have over strudels here. Right at this table. So just bring them here."

"Oh . . . B-b . . . u . . . t . . . where is Mrs. Morr . . . is? Is she joining you soon?"

"She is right here." Greg points to the other side of the table.

There sits a bouquet of pink chrysanthemums, beautifully tied together in white lace. Right next to it is an envelope, unsealed. Greg picks it up, opens the envelope, removes the letter that's inside, and shows it to Jenny.

Dear Margaret,

Was I too late to feel your love? But for the time we spent together, when I truly loved you, I hope that these precious feelings stay with me forever. I am just a normal man and not anyone special. My name will soon be forgotten. But I got lucky when I met you. When I leave, I hope that I gain the respect that, I have succeeded as pompously as anyone who's ever lived and to have loved another, with all my heart and soul, and to me, this will always be enough.

I am better today because of loving you. Your love has made me wiser. All alone, just by my soul, I can neither sleep, nor drink, nor eat. So, be with me while I eat. Always. I would like to share my dreams with you today, tomorrow, and every day. I hope I have earned that time from you.

I will miss you sharing your dreams with me.

Forever in Love,
Gregory Morris

Jenny holds Greg's hands. A stream of tears starts rolling down Greg's cheeks, and the drops start falling on the letter, making it shine under the light.

There is silence.

You could hear the voice of love under that silence.

Love does transcend and amaze all notions of time. It erases the memories of a beginning and eliminates the fear of an end.

◆

THE LOST MARBLE

It was just a game all right, but a defeat, big or small, would cloud any kind of rationality in him. Before it did, Arjun knew to walk away. However, Ramesh, his brother, would argue that Arjun didn't do it often enough just based on the times he had borne witness.

Saturday

The first rain of summer started coming down gently. The dust in the air began settling down, bringing out a not-so-pleasant smell from underneath the surface of the earth.

"It's all over, Arjun!" said Ramesh. "There's nothing you can do now. You lost. It's over. Better don't get into a fistfight. You can come back next week and take revenge!" Ramesh sounded very concerned.

"This was completely unfair. I don't know why I deserve this, Ramesh ..." Arjun said with a defeated look, looking for some sympathetic words from his brother.

Ramesh tried giving Arjun a loose hug, but apparently the feeble attempt of consolation from Ramesh failed to create its due effect, and Arjun pulled away with a jerking motion. Ramesh was used to such tantrums.

They started walking back home. It was a five-minute stroll down the street on any other day, but Arjun had decided he wanted to be home at his earliest that day. The rains hadn't picked any intensity. It was a very welcome change to be out and getting wet in that summer drizzle. Every drop on their sunburnt skin brought a sense of freedom that could only be described one way: orgasmic.

Among the residential buildings on this particular street in Tirunelveli,[1] there was something ancient and common to them all, great or small. All the houses were built in the early 1900s, before the First World War; some renovated and most not yet, but all uniquely bearing a character that can only be felt and seen, a character that is so uniquely South Indian, so uniquely Tamilian and all the same so uniquely portraying the early twentieth century architecture of Tirunelveli.

All the houses were lined up one after the other, with a small alley in between. Each house pompously announced to the passerby what the meal of the day was through its grand window and a doorway opening into its roadside kitchen, with a door made of the heaviest native wood (not teak) laid out on a very peculiar two-panel design, separated by three horizontal wooden bars bearing enough room for some decorations, should they wish to add. Perhaps the carpenters of the early twentieth century in Tirunelveli either lacked the right machinery or they fell short of finding enough inspiring ideas. These panels invariably ended up looking alike, house after house, with three brass domes, pervertedly shaped and yet wouldn't cause an itch in your eye if you looked past them.

The houses were usually linear. A kitchen with enough room to cook, enough room to move around, and a large floor-level sink—yes, one had to squat on the floor, quite literally, inside the sink to clean dirty utensils—a passage room (which usually acted as a storage space for huge items and occasionally as a changing room), and

---

[1] A city in the state of Tamil Nadu, India

a hall or living room. The living room opened into a small verandah, which then led you into an open courtyard. On the other side of the courtyard was usually another house with a reverse orientation, ending with a kitchen, opening into a back yard, with some coconut, neem, and mango trees, and in the corner were washrooms and toilets, sometimes shared by residents of both the houses, or sometimes a separate one each for each household.

Back Yard

That's where Arjun honed his marble skills. The back yard at their house was laid out not so conveniently for any sort of outdoor sport. Even for the kinds of marble games that Arjun wanted to play, the terrain was uneven and didn't have more than two feet of uninterrupted smooth dirt at a stretch. There were many bumps and too many large roots from trees that were more than forty years old, poking out of the ground. But Arjun managed to build his marble field in a creative way within the usable space, complete with three holes and all the boundaries.

Ramesh was not a natural at playing marbles. But like all younger siblings, he too was largely influenced by his older sibling, and he did things just because, and not because he had developed a special interest. Ramesh, who preferred riding his bike if he had to indulge in any outdoor activity, was more often forced to play cricket with Arjun. Marbles was really a weekend activity.

Arjun was a great cricketer. At twelve, he was already playing for his school team and was also part of many local teams comprising boys aged ten to fifteen. He would often go out on Saturdays for his school cricket matches, and he spent most of his weekday evenings playing cricket in the very small open courtyard that separated the two houses in their housing complex.

Marbles was considered a crude sport by the family, especially their mother. This perhaps could be attributed to the kind of neighborhood they lived in. Theirs was the most affluent family there. The only house with a telephone, a TV, and a car. Most of their neighbors belonged to the lower-middle-class section of society, and their children mostly went to schools that were not on par with the schools that Arjun and Ramesh went to. Arjun and Ramesh were very self-aware of the surroundings. Their mother often encouraged them to play cricket with a few selected neighborhood boys. For whatever reason, cricket cut the mark for her. But marbles with the neighborhood boys was taboo.

Marbles

Arjun loved the feeling of holding marbles in his hand. As he held more than one, he would involuntarily squish them together in a rotating motion while forming a fist. He derived a certain sense of pleasure as the marbles rubbed against one other and made a scratchy noise, while he focused on the task on his hand, be it reading a book or thinking about solving a sibling issue. The marbles were his stress buster.

Marbles had always fascinated Arjun. The fact that they came in many colors and yet all of them so unique made Arjun often wonder how they even made marbles. He wanted to visit one of those marble-making places. He wanted to be able to design his own marble. For him, a marble defined the beauty of universe. He would often hold a marble close to his heart, picturing himself traversing through the clouds, across continents.

His mind would often wander off, imagining marbles in many different colors. He was designing marbles in an abstract impressionist style.

"A narrow streak of yellow starting from one end of the sphere, waving its way across, and when it's about a quarter of the way through, it lends itself into a golden orange, which becomes a thick blood orange about halfway through, when it attains its maximum thickness. As the streak continues, it lightens its orange shade only to end the last fourth with a thickening band of red."

Arjun had a clear jar for his marbles, a jar that used to house homemade citron pickles. His mother had reluctantly parted ways with this jar because it wasn't large enough to hold her seasonal delicacies. She needed a taller one. The old jar had since then been thoroughly cleaned, sprayed with Father's leftover perfume, and dried in the sun for many days, before the first marble was placed in it.

Now there must have been about a hundred inside. He had collected these marbles over the past three to four years. Most of them were gifted to him by friends and cousins, while some he had won in marble competitions. But there were about twenty or so that he held very dear to his heart because he had bought them with his own pocket money, much to his mother's disappointment. Each marble cost him about five paise.[2] He vividly remembered each and every one of those twenty marbles he had bought. He could possibly even close his eyes and pick a marble at random from the jar

---

[2] Hundred paise equals one rupee (paise is the plural of paisa).

and identify if it was one of those twenty or not, just by holding the marble in his hands for a few seconds.

Yet, there was one marble, just one, that meant much more than any other marble in the jar. A green marble that was distinctively bold in its shade of green, offering very little color variation. It was shiny all around, except at one spot where there was a scratch, "a battle injury" as Arjun referred to it. That green marble was Arjun's favorite marble. He would ensure that the green marble was clearly visible from inside the jar from his bed. He kept the jar in his direct line of sight from the bed, and it was almost a habit for him that when he woke up, the second thing he looked at was his marble jar, after he had a chance to look at this huge poster of Kapil Dev[3] with a wide grin, holding the 1983 Prudential Cricket World Cup.

Both Arjun and Ramesh never really understood why their mother never let them play marbles. The hardest thing for children to understand is what their parents ask them not to do. Their mother was not a tiger mom. She was just trying to raise her children in the most acceptable way possible for her family. Although she perfectly accepted the house she lived in (where she had moved after her marriage) and everything that came with it, there were elements of the neighborhood that affected her dearly. Filth on the roads and even filth on the bodies were acceptable to her, while filth on the mouths repulsed her. There was no way she could have explained this in plain words to her children.

Marbles was a popular sport in the neighborhood. It was cheap

---

[3.] Kapil Dev— Captain of Indian cricket team, which won its first cricket world championship in 1983.

and didn't need any special playing ground. Not every child played the sport, but it was an integral part of every child who grew up there. Except for Arjun and Ramesh.

Next Saturday

Arjun was getting ready for his cricket match. His seventh-grade class team was playing the eighth-grade class team at their school grounds. The commute on a Saturday morning normally was a breeze. The roads were not busy, especially at 7:30 a.m. He had overslept that morning. He wanted to be out of his bed by 6:30 a.m. in order to be on the city bus by 7:30. But by the time the hidden sun's rays broke through his windows on that cloudy day, it was 7:00. Arjun was angry with himself, and he tried his best to make up for the lost time.

"Hey, Ramesh! Have you seen my gloves?" Arjun asked.

"No, I haven't. Did you check near the laundry hamper?" Ramesh was quite annoyed with Arjun for interrupting his sleep.

"Hmm … I don't see them there. You were playing with them the other day, weren't you?" Arjun moved next to his brother's bed with some anger.

It was very clear to Ramesh that Arjun was getting ready to blame him for the misplaced gloves. But he really didn't know where they were, and as far as he remembered, he kept them on the table right next to the spot where Arjun normally kept his practice cricket balls and hat.

"I did use them on Thursday, but I put them back on the table, right next to your hat."

"Well, they are not here. You are always careless with my things.

That's why I never like sharing my stuff with you." Arjun was almost ready to chew off Ramesh's ears.

The frantic search for those two soiled batting gloves continued for a couple more minutes. Ramesh couldn't lie down on his bed, for he feared that would show his absolute lack of empathy for his brother, nor did he want to get out of the bed to join the search party, for fear of how much worse an enraged Arjun would treat him.

7:28 a.m.

"Hey, Arjun, can you check on the other side of the hamper?" Ramesh spotted something on the floor, while still on his bed but in a half-seated posture.

"There. See, I told you. You never take good care of my things." Arjun picked up the gloves, stuffed them into his kit bag, and rushed out of the house without saying anything to his mother.

Arjun knew he was going to miss his 7:30 bus, but he wasn't going to let that fact make him spend ten extra minutes with his brother. He blamed Ramesh for everything that happened that morning, including his delay.

If I could get on the 7:50 bus, I think I may still make it for a few minutes of warm-up fielding. If I'm lucky, I may even get to hit a few balls, Arjun thought to himself as the pace of his stride increased. A gentle stream of sweat started flowing around his temples, making its way to his cheeks and eventually to his collarbone.

The next few hours of the day could be summarized as an unfulfilling, lonesome battle that Arjun gallantly waged to minimize the humiliation his team was being meted out by their school seniors. The cherry-red leather ball had caused more than a bruise on his right thigh, taking a couple of bad hits, but Arjun knew life was not meant to be made easier on a cricket field.

A defeat nevertheless.

The somber bus ride back home had offered nothing to cheer him up, except for a moment, when his eyes caught a poster on the wall. It was for an upcoming movie starring his favorite actor. As the bus made a sharp right turn, he barely caught the release date of the movie. He made a mental note to ask his parents about this movie.

The Marble Competition

At 4:30 p.m., Arjun ran out of his room to the kitchen to check if his mother was preparing any snacks for him. He saw Ramesh already seated there at the table, munching on what looked like pakoras.[4] Ramesh consciously avoided making eye contact with Arjun, and Arjun did the same.

Arjun helped himself to a plate of pakoras. He opened the refrigerator and grabbed a bottle of ketchup. As he tried to squeeze the last few drops out, he caught Ramesh looking at him through the corner of his eyes. The fury foaming inside him at that moment didn't know any bounds. That was exactly why that moment made him think how much he didn't appreciate having a younger brother.

He waved goodbye to his mother, who was not very happy that Arjun was going out to play marbles. By the time Arjun turned twelve, she had relaxed her restrictions on him playing marbles with the neighborhood boys. He was allowed to go play for an hour per

---

[4] Pakoras—chickpea flour fritters

day during the weekend. So, she didn't try to stop him because she could see the joy and excitement in Arjun's strides. Ramesh knew better than to accompany Arjun that evening.

When Arjun reached the venue, he put his right hand inside his pocket to look for the marbles he had brought from home for the evening's competition. He remembered that he was in a hurry to pick twenty marbles he wanted to bring for that evening. His hands were in the jar one moment, and the next moment, in what would have appeared as a reflex action to anyone who was watching, he grabbed twenty of them, counting them in fives as he squished them together in his palm. He was looking for his lucky marble, and he couldn't see it inside the jar. He was in a state of shock for a moment. But he didn't have time to shake up the jar or get all the marbles out onto his bed to locate his lucky green marble. He had no choice but to leave for the competition without his lucky marble. He wasn't happy.

He met the other seven boys who had gathered that evening to play. If he played reasonably well, he was sure he wouldn't lose any of his twenty marbles that day. Since he knew all of them very well and how well they played, he decided to strategize his techniques for that evening. He had picked two of the boys from those seven to be his high-risk opponents. His strategy worked that evening, and he actually ended up winning ten additional marbles.

While playing, the thought of his lucky marble kept nagging him. He wished he had the time to look for it before leaving home, but he was also focused on leaving the room before Ramesh came in. He truly wanted to avoid having a conversation with Ramesh.

Earlier that day, when he was on the bus ride home from the cricket match, he recalled that he was the last one who had used the batting gloves on Friday. When he brought them back to the room, he was trying to throw them one at a time, from his bed into the hamper, like basketball. Both the gloves didn't make the basket and ended up falling on the other side of the hamper. He was too lazy to get up right then, and he told himself that he would pick them up when he got out of his bed. He had completely forgotten this incident till Ramesh pointed out where the gloves were during his search. The feeling of guilt for going after Ramesh in the morning dragged his cheer down, so he rushed out of his room after quickly picking his marbles from the jar.

For the rest of the evening at the marble field, Arjun kept thinking about his green marble and was hoping it was safe inside the jar. After he waved goodbye to the boys, he started worrying about the marble again. He wanted to get home as soon as possible.

The walk back home seemed long. The anxiety of losing something precious and valuable was so disturbing to Arjun that even when he kept telling himself it was just a marble, he realized he had already let the sense of loss shake him.

As soon as he reached home, he removed his shoes and started running toward his room. He didn't bother to see or greet the houseguests being entertained by the family in the living room. He turned the lights on and looked at the jar.

There.

Only one marble was missing, his lucky marble, but to him, the whole jar seemed empty. The marble's absence went through him like thread through a needle. It felt like everything he would do would be stitched with its green.

A few minutes later, Ramesh walked into the room he and Arjun shared. Arjun was sitting at one edge of his bed, away from the door. He had tears in his eyes, with his head hung and completely oblivious to the moment of reality around him. The grief of losing his lucky marble pierced though his already emotionally drained day.

Ramesh went and sat right next to him. He wanted to put his arms around his sobbing brother, but instead, he hesitantly stretched his right arm around Arjun's back all the way to his right shoulder, while using his left palm to hold Arjun's left shoulder. A bit of an awkward hug. But there was enough warmth and concern in it that Arjun lifted his head and gave Ramesh a tight hug.

"I am sorry, Ramesh, for yelling at you this morning, for no fault of yours. I was the one who was careless with those stupid gloves. I just took out my anger at you. Like I always do . . . I am terribly sorry." Arjun was sobbing into Ramesh's shoulders.

"It's . . . all right . . . Arjun." Ramesh stammered to get these words out of his mouth, because he wasn't prepared to receive an apology from Arjun at that moment, but instead he had come into the room wanting to give one.

Then he blurted out in a trembling voice, "I am so sorry, Arjun. I wanted to hurt you. I really wanted to hurt you today after what happened in the morning. I wanted you to lose in the marble competition this evening . . . That's all I wanted."

Then he opened his right palm.

There it was. The lost marble.

It was Ramesh's turn to sob now, and he did that by covering his face with both his hands. Arjun put his hands around him. They both broke a smile. The sound of summer rain spattering on the window made for a celebratory music that moment demanded. The smell of freshly ground ginger, garlic, and a few other spices emanated from the kitchen, giving them a preview of what their mother was cooking for dinner. The green marble started rolling off the bed, onto the floor, till it stopped by the left edge of the doorway. And in the meantime, the brothers went back to being brothers, with a refined love and hate for each other.

How much do we take childhood for granted? Those trivial apologies, playful revenges, and somewhat meaningless moments. As adults, we seldom realize how much we rely on the ordinariness of everyday life. When we grow older and our childhood is gone, only then do we understand that those moments are what we live for.

DESOLATE FREEDOM

PROLOGUE

Justin wanted to do it. He now wishes he hadn't done it.

He may feel differently tomorrow.

The delirious visions he had may have been a result of the cocktail of drugs. And the voices he used to hear helped him construct a reality, conditioned by the rules and structures of his righteous world, in which very few could have survived.

Did isolation worsen the damage to his emotions? Or did he force himself into isolation because he couldn't maintain a normal relationship with the external world, including his immediate family?

If you had asked Justin, he would have said that he had simply removed his brain from the constraints of reality for a few minutes, in order to experience the weightlessness of being without tomorrow and yesterday.

As for what made him to do it . . .

Imagination.

CHAPTER 1

The evening downpour had subsided. For October, Santa Fe had been receiving a little more than its share of precipitation, but that's not saying much in 2008.

The gated community in which the Kinsleys lived was your typical Santa Fe suburban neighborhood, offering an affordable lifestyle to young and middle-aged families, who belonged to the New Mexican upper-middle-class tribe. The community itself bordered a golf course and was built at an elevation, giving its residents the least of its worries when it came to flooding. El Dorado was the suburb where many white-collar dreams were built, and a place those starting their aggressive careers use as a launchpad, before eyeing million-dollar homes in the Las Campanas area.

The houses in this particular community were all built in modern architectural style. That helped the building developers maintain uniformity in the community with a certain amount of ease, although one could drive around El Dorado and spot a few houses built in pueblo and adobe styles as well. Most of the houses in this community were built on a one-acre lot. In short, El Dorado offered that perfect mix of town and country living for families.

The Kinsleys had been living in this community since 1987. Russell and Kiera bought the house during the summer of 1987 and moved in within a month after they got married, with huge dreams that included raising a family of two children, a boy and a girl.

The Evening

The plan was that Russell would get home from work by 5:45 p.m., make sure Justin and Norah were home, plan their dinner, take a quick shower, change, and be out in his car by 6:45.

It would take approximately fifteen minutes to go pick up Melanie, and then another twenty minutes to drive to Geronimo in downtown Santa Fe. He had booked a table for two at 7:30 p.m. So, if they got there by 7:15, they would have just enough time to grab a drink at the bar before being seated. As for the rest of the evening, he had thought he would let the laws of spontaneity take care of it.

But Russell was running late that evening while returning from the college because he had to spend a few extra minutes with a student who had an urgent need. He was worried that he may be late for the 7:30 reservation, so he rushed into his room to change. He forgot to check on Justin and Norah. As he was changing, it quickly dawned on him that the children may not be home or may not have had their dinner plans sorted out.

It was 6:45 p.m.

The descent of the stairs, which he had mastered over the past twenty years, didn't take that long, and while he was coming down, he noticed Norah sitting at the dining table, doing her homework.

"Hey, Dad!"

"Hey, Norah. How are you, sweetie?"

"Good."

"When did you come home? Were you here when I ran upstairs?"

Norah nodded with a smirk on her face. "Yeah."

"Sorry, sweetie. I am in a rush. I am meeting someone for dinner tonight, and I am running a few minutes late."

"It's all right. It's not like …" Norah covered her mouth with one of her fists as she mumbled the rest of what she wanted to say.

"What? What did you say?"

"Nothing …"

"C'mon now!"

"It's all right, Dad. I understand. You should leave."

"What are you and Justin going to have for dinner? And where is Justin, by the way?"

"Justin is in his room. I am going to have the leftover pasta from last night. I think there should be enough for the two of us. I don't know if he is really in a mood to eat."

Russell started clearing his throat as if he was getting ready to shout.

"Hey, Just—"

"Dad, don't. I will check on him after a few minutes. You know better. Just leave."

Russell looked at Norah with a sense of pride, guilt, and affection. "You're too mature for your age, darling. And right now, that works for me. Thank you." Russell smiled.

"Bye, Dad. Have a good time!"

Russell walked up to the table and gripped Norah's shoulders tightly before walking out.

"Don't stay up too late. Tomorrow is school day. Love you!" Russell put on his blazer, waved at Norah, and jogged out of the door, letting it slam really loud, much to Norah's annoyance.

"Love you too," Norah mumbled to herself.

The drive to Melanie's house wasn't terrible. He got there at 7:05 p.m. He drove his car up to her empty driveway, put it in park, and let the engine idle. He turned the rearview mirror to his left and adjusted his seat a bit to see himself in the mirror. He checked his eyebrows and his collar. Russell took a deep sigh and smiled.

He was wondering if he should text Melanie to let her know that he was waiting outside or if he should walk to the door and just announce his arrival. In a flash, he decided he would go old school.

Russell let out a wolf whistle quickly, as it was his habit when he had to tell himself to just do it. He opened the car door and placed his left leg out of the car onto the driveway. And then, as he got both his legs out and stretched himself to a standing position, almost as an afterthought, he decided to leave his phone inside the cupholder, instead of putting it in his coat pocket. He bent and leaned inside the car to drop the phone. He had to stretch himself to reach the cupholder, and as he did, he failed the "breaking from your routine" test. The phone slipped and slid through the narrow gap between the driver's seat and the panel that holds the cupholder. Russell had already closed the door and started walking toward the main door without noticing it. He stopped by the main door and took another deep breath.

He hadn't felt like this in a very long long time. Almost twenty-two years.

Melanie Adler hadn't felt like this in a very long time either. Almost thirteen years.

On the other side, sitting on her couch, about fifteen feet from the main door, and anxiously looking at her phone in anticipation of a call or a text message, Melanie was beginning to feel hungry.

She was a forty-nine-year-old lead psychiatrist at CHRISTUS St. Vincent Behavioral Specialists. Melanie had become a creature of routine in the past twelve years since she started her tenure at CHRISTUS. It had nothing to do with the hospital but everything to do with her deliberate attempt to forget things. The trauma. Tonight was a change of routine, though. As much as she was looking forward to this evening, she was more anxious about what and when.

Russell rang the doorbell. Melanie got up from the couch, straightened her dress and hair, and walked toward the door. She took a look through the peephole, confirmed that it was Russell, and quietly opened the door.

"Good evening, Dr. Adler. How are you?"

"Good evening, Russ . . . Mr. Kinsley . . . I am doing well. Thank you. How about you?" She had an itchy smile gradually breaking from the corner of her mouth.

"I guess I am doing well, considering I haven't been on a first date like this in almost twenty-two years. By the way, is it okay if we cut through the formalities? May I call you Melanie?" Russell started laughing.

"That would be lovely . . . I think. I will let you know if you need to switch and call me Dr. Adler," Melanie said with a twinkle in her eye and continued. "I am ready to leave unless you want to come in and use the washroom or something."

"No. I mean yes. We can leave right away. I was running a few minutes late anyways. I think we can still be there before seven thirty, but I may miss an opportunity to woo this beautiful lady with a fancy cocktail before dinner."

They started walking to the car.

"That'll be all right. I am least impressed with men trying to woo me with a drink at the bar anyway. You wouldn't really miss any opportunity."

"I am relieved. Be careful, it's a bit slippery."

With that, Russell opened his car door and let Melanie in. He got into the driver's seat.

"That wasn't necessary, but thank you," said Melanie.

With smooth jazz filling in the quiet drive, they let the beautiful sight of a mild drizzle washing the skies painted in hues of sunset create the mood needed for the evening, instead of their small talk. They were going against the traffic at that time of the evening. So, within fifteen minutes, they were at Geronimo. Russell slowed down as he entered the parking lot and cruised slowly to the valet area, where he handed over his keys to the attendant. He jumped out to rush to the other side to hold the door open for Melanie. She didn't mind the chivalry but really wasn't going to judge a man based on these trivial acts and would rather count his respect toward women when and where it really mattered.

It was exactly 7:25 p.m. as they stepped in.

"Good evening, sir!"

"Good evening. We have a table reserved for two at 7:30 p.m. under the name of Russell Kinsley ..."

"Good evening, Mr. and Mrs. Kinsley. Your table is ready. If you would wait for just a minute, please, I will have Jonathon take you to your table."

Melanie wanted to correct him.

"Sure. Thank you," said Russell. He looked at Melanie apologetically as if to say, *Please don't mind the most annoying assumption.*"

"This way, sir and ma'am." Jonathon was directing them to their table, and they followed his cue.

Once they were seated, Melanie looked at Russell with a sheepish grin on her face. "You really thought I was offended?"

"Well, I would rather assume you were. An apology never goes to waste. Does it?"

"I have not been out . . . out like this with a man for a long time. So, I really haven't experienced these . . . these assumptions. I don't think I actually thought about it much in terms of getting offended. But more in . . ."

Russell interrupted. "You know, I am used to walking into restaurants and they calling out my reservation as 'Table for Mr. and Mrs. Kinsley is ready or something to that effect'? But to be honest, I haven't experienced this in a while as well. Five or six years maybe . . ."

Jonathon said, "Before I read out the specials for the evening, do you want to start with a cocktail, or do you want to go with our chef's recommended drink pairing for the evening?"

"Drink pairing sounds fun. Let's do that. Do you mind, Russell?"

"Absolutely. Surprise us, Jonathon. Surprise us to your glee."

"I will do my best, sir." Jonathon gave a nod and a smile before walking away from their table.

Russell looked around the dining area. He could tell that it was a busy evening, as it is here every evening.

"Kiera and I have been here once. The place hasn't changed much."

"I've never been here. Also, I haven't heard anyone say anything bad about this place. So, I am hoping I won't be the first one to do that." Melanie adjusted her napkin and took a sip from her water glass.

"Funny you should say that. Kiera didn't quite enjoy the service that evening when we were here. The food was top notch, though."

Jonathon brought their first drink and their first course of the meal.

CHAPTER 2

Norah rinsed her plate and stacked it on the draining board. She checked the blinking clock on the microwave oven, and it was way past Justin's dinnertime, 7:15 p.m.

"Hey, Justin! Aren't you eating supper?" she yelled from the kitchen.

She shook her head in disapproval as there was no response from upstairs.

"Justin! What the heck is wrong with you?" Norah started walking upstairs, heavy-footed, clearly intending to announce her arrival. "I've been screaming from the top of my lungs. Can't you fucking just respond?" She started knocking on the door. "Justin . . ."

"Fuck off!" Justin screamed from inside.

"That's a start."

"What do you want?"

"Are you going to have supper? If not, I am going to clean up the kitchen and then go finish my homework. I can't keep waiting for you."

"Then go do whatever the fuck you want to. Don't wait for me."

With that, Justin just increased the volume of his music. Norah could hear Justin sing along with the chorus of "Rage Against the Machine," raging "Now you do what they told ya."

Norah rushed downstairs, cleaned the kitchen counter in a couple of minutes, and stuffed all the leftovers in the refrigerator. Within five minutes, she was in her room, ready to give her case study a final whiff. She slammed the door as hard as she could, so Justin could hear that she was back in her room.

About thirty minutes later, Norah heard a knock on her door. It was a soft whisper, almost in an apologetic tone.

"Norah, can I come in? I am sorry about what happened earlier."

"What do you want?"

"I . . . I just want to talk to you."

"I am busy."

"Norah, please. I need to talk to you now."

"Justin, go away. You've pissed me off enough for the evening."

"No. I mean . . . I am sorry. I know I was rude. But I am in pain. I need you. I need your help."

"What happened?" There was a sudden shift in Norah's tone, as the sisterly concern erased all the ire.

Norah opened the door. She was shocked to see Justin completely disheveled and in shambles. She rushed to hold Justin, who was about to trip over a shoebox as he started walking toward her. He was shaking.

"Are you all right? Did you take your meds?"

"I can't. I can't take those meds. You know I hate them."

"Justin, we have had this conversation over and over. Dad's not home, and I am not going be able to physically force-feed you those pills. Please work with me. You will feel better if you take them."

"Do I really want to feel better? That's the million-dollar question. Ha ha."

"Not now, Justin."

"Do you really want me to feel better? Does that old man really want to see me better?" Justin's words began to feel a bit shaky.

"Just lay down on my bed. I will get you some water."

Norah helped Justin rest his back on her bed. She ran to the kitchen to fill a pitcher of water and to bring a glass with her. On her way back up, she stepped into Justin's room to look for the pills. The room was spotless. She stopped for a second to admire how organized the room was. She wished she had the same interest and motivation to keep her room as clean as Justin did. For a second, she was envious of her older brother in a proud manner.

She knew where Justin kept his medicines. There was a box of pills in the medicine cabinet in the bathroom, which he used on a regular basis for bipolar disorder, among other things. Then he also had an emergency supply box, which normally was on the top shelf of his book cabinet.

She found the box in the bathroom and found the lithium container. It was empty. The only other medication she knew he took for his condition was Latuda. But she didn't want to administer that without Dad's consent. She started frantically searching for any other related medications. The Valproate container was empty. As was the Aripiprazole container. By now, she started to feel nervous and a bit worried.

She took her phone from her pocket and paused for a second, before deciding to text.

"Dad, Justin hasn't taken his meds. He may be out of his meds. He is acting up. Pick up his meds on your way back. No need to call back. I will keep him under control."

As Norah walked to the book cabinet to look for the other box, she could hear Jusin mumbling, "Told ya. You don't want me to feel better!"

The other medicine box had only two pill containers, and she had no idea what they were for.

Maybe for his seizures. Maybe for his heart palpitations, she thought. She put the box back on top, grabbed the water pitcher and glass, and went back to her room.

"Here, have some water. What happened to your meds? They are empty. CVS calls about refills at least a week before …"

"I never had a doubt, Norah. The old man doesn't want me to feel better. He must have asked CVS not to do auto-refills anymore."

Justin didn't remember that in a spate of rage and delusion, he had flushed the next two weeks' supply of his regular medications down the toilet earlier in the afternoon.

"And why would he do that?"

"Because he is a fucking prick."

"Jesus, Justin. Chill. I know you don't think much of Dad. But he is concerned about you. About us. Every single day."

"Right …"

"What's that supposed to mean?"

"It's supposed to mean what it means, Norah. Look where he is now. Leaving his teenage daughter and a really sick son alone at home just so that he could chase some …"

"That's enough. Why don't you lie down? I have asked Dad to pick up your medicines on his way back. And I will try to finish my homework while you rest."

"Look at my bright sister. What kind of homework are you doing?"

"Political science. Comparative politics. A case study."

"You gotta be kidding. My favorite. So, what's this case study on?"

"Russian politics."

"Russia. The land where semi-presidentialism has given way to neo-patrimonialism. From Gorbachev to Putin. Look at the man Putin. He is every world leader's dream. Isn't he?"

"You mean nightmare?"

"No, dream. What world leader doesn't want to have the kind of unlimited power that Putin has?" Justin sat up, visible excitement on his face as he started talking about politics.

"Go on …"

"He wants to be a powerful czar of Russia, like Alexander III. I mean, just in a span of fifteen or sixteen years, the man has already become the czar of Russia from being an unemployed spy. It's just a matter of tightening the screws and securing his unlimited power. It will happen eventually."

"You admire him, don't you?"

"I don't know if I do. But …" Justin's eyes closed and he fell back on his bed, breathing heavily.

Norah looked at him and looked at her case study on the table. She smiled and continued to work on her case study with a renewed sense of purpose. Another second of envy passed her smiling face, as she now visibly showed how proud she was of her really smart brother.

CHAPTER 3

Somewhere on the car floor, about a foot or so from the driver's door and directly under the driver's seat, lay a Nokia 5800 phone that kept buzzing. There was an incoming text message.

"Dad, Justin hasn't taken his meds. He may be out of his meds. He is acting up. Pick up his meds on your way back. No need to call back. I will keep him under control."

CHAPTER 4

"So, how long have you been at the community college?" Melanie asked Russell.

"Ten years. I decided to switch to a more predictable work routine when things got a bit unpredictable at home," Russell said, wiping his mouth with the napkin. "This elk tastes so good. Very tender. How is yours?" He tried to steer the conversation somewhere else.

"The sea bass is amazing too. The best I have ever had. I guess I won't be the first one to give a bad review of this place, after all. So, you were saying … where were you before? Before the community college?"

"Los Alamos. I can't really say much more than that," Russell said with a naughty smile.

"If you are well educated with a STEM background and lived in Santa Fe, I guess your choices are only a handful. You know CHRISTUS is the largest employer in Santa Fe?" Melanie said, feeling slightly tipsy with the Chilean Carménère that was paired with the sea bass she was eating.

"Yeah, I know that. A hospital. Wow, impressive, isn't it? So, how long have you been there?"

"Mmm … maybe thirteen years. Twelve-plus years. Somewhere around there. You know my life … as long as I have been at CHRISTUS has been pretty much the same for all these years?"

"Some of us prefer routines more than others. Kiera was sort of like that. She worked at the Santa Fe Indian Hospital. She was in the family practice. And she loved it there."

"I have a couple of friends who still work there. Where did you meet Kiera?"

"In Santa Fe, at Albertson's. If someone were to compile a list of top ten bizarre places where you met your spouse for the first time, mine would certainly be on the list. I walked into the ladies' restroom by mistake. And Kiera . . . Kiera was standing by the hand dryer and staring at me . . ."

"That's hilarious."

"Then one thing led to another, and we both, two middle-twenties adults, decided to have our first dinner date at the Albertson's deli. We bought a three-course meal and brought the food out to the parking lot, and planned our future under the clear, starlit skies of New Mexico."

"That sounds so romantic."

"Hardly."

"And then . . .?"

"Well. We were married in the next two months. And we bought our first house, our only house to date . . . in 1987, within a month after our wedding."

Jonathon interrupted them. "Sorry to interrupt, sir. Are you ready for the next course?"

CHAPTER 5

Norah was almost done with her case study. She was trying to find the best way to summarize her analysis. She wrote something on her draft paper and then struck it out.

"Are you done with your case study?" Justin mumbled.

"Just about. How are you feeling?"

"I feel like dying . . ." Justin responded with his eyes still closed.

Norah quickly closed her notebook and got up. She touched Justin's forehead to feel his body temperature.

"Norah, I feel bad for you and Dad. You have no idea what's coming."

"What are you talking about? What's coming?" Norah was beginning to feel a bit uneasy.

"I mean it. After we lost Mom, Dad has had no clue what he has been doing. I remember he was in pain right after. But then, something changed. It was like he wanted to forget Mom . . ."

"All of us want to move on, don't we? That beautiful chapter of our lives is over. It was hard on you and me and Dad, of course."

"That's bullshit and you know it. You never felt anything for Mom. Dad probably felt sad because he had to take up more responsibilities. Not because he fucking felt for Mom's passing."

"We need to get your meds, Justin. Sometimes these images in your mind … they are scary. Why don't you get something to eat and then come back and lie down again?"

"Okay, I'll eat something. That sounds like a plan. I don't want you to feel the pain. I am sorry. I know I've been acting a bit strange since Mom died. But it's not like I know when I'm going to act strange." There was a marked change in the tone of Justin's voice as a teardrop slid down his cheek and fell on his wrist.

They started walking toward the stairs. Norah turned to Justin. "Hey, are you okay? Do you feel weak or something?"

"I'm fine."

As Norah started walking slightly faster, Justin slowed down.

"I feel what you are going through, Norah. I do."

Norah was already by the dining table. She was going to open the refrigerator to get the pasta out.

"Don't do what they tell ya. It makes you unhappy. It brings you more pain. It's enough that I am the only one who has to endure the pain." Justin collapsed when he was almost at the bottom of the stairs.

"Justin … Justin … are you okay?"

"I could be better." Justin was trying to smile.

Norah picked up her phone and started texting frantically. *Dad, I think I am losing control of Justin. He really needs his meds soon. Can you call me please?*

"Have some pasta. You can sleep right after you finish eating this. Come over here."

"Your dad is a selfish monster. I don't trust him to keep you safe. He will kill you, Norah. He will kill you before you turn twenty. You are already in pain, sweet sister, and I am sorry you don't know that."

"C'mon! Eat something first, okay? I think you are beginning to imagine too many things. Do you want to watch some TV?"

Justin started walking toward the dining table. His strides were steady, but his posture was still wobbly.

"I'm fine. I have more clarity than ever before. I can see things clearly. I can see what will set me free, and I need to protect you. I am the big brother, after all. Mom would be ashamed of me if I didn't protect you and set you free."

"Justin, you are beginning to scare me. Drink some water. Here!" Norah forcefully pushed a glass of water into Justin's mouth.

He drank a few sips and spat out the rest. Within a few seconds, he lost control of his bodily movements and collapsed again. His head hit the dining table as he fell on the floor into what looked like a deep state of slumber.

"Sorry to bother you again Dad. I have a strange feeling that Justin is going to hurt someone tonight Dad. Love you!!"

CHAPTER 6

The Nokia 5800 phone started buzzing again. There were two more incoming messages. The light that flashed lit up the car floor for a brief period.

"Dad, I think I am losing control of Justin. He really needs his meds soon. Can you call me please?"

"Sorry to bother you again Dad. I have a strange feeling that Justin is going to hurt someone tonight Dad. Love you!!"

CHAPTER 7

"We have rhubarb cheesecake with strawberry cream for dessert," Jonathon said while filling their drink glasses.

"And what is this you are pairing our cheesecake with?"

"This is Frambozen, a Belgian-style American raspberry beer with mild cocoa husks flavor, ma'am," Jonathon filled their dessert pairing drink glasses, which didn't look like beer glasses at all. Melanie gave the drink and the glass an amused look, smiled at Jonathon, and whispered, "Thank you."

"Tell me about your kids," Melanie said, adjusting her hair and taking a sip of Frambozen.

"Justin and Norah. Justin is nineteen, and he is sort of in a break year right now, and Norah is a junior in high school."

Russell's hand went into his coat pocket to look for his phone, and he couldn't find it. He displayed a brief but visible shocked reaction.

"So, you will be an empty-nester in a couple of years."

"Yes. Maybe. Well … to be honest, I don't know. I am sorry … I got distracted a bit. As soon as I talked about the kids, my hands went in search of my phone, and I couldn't find it. I must have left it in the car."

"Do you want to go get it?"

"It's all right. They are grown-up kids. Ah … where was I? Yes … Justin … Justin has been having some issues of late. I don't want to talk about it in detail right now. But he has been . . . you know . . . fighting some mental health issues since his junior year. Everything is fine right now. He has good doctors, good psychiatric treatment access." Russell paused for a second.

"I forgot. You may even know his doctors. Anyways, he is under meds and things are under control. He is a brilliant kid. We were sure he would be at the Columbia School of Journalism this year. He was always interested in geopolitics and sociocultural changes around the world. Can you believe it? My kid?" Russell guffawed with a mix of pride and self-humiliating satire.

"And Norah?"

"Norah is not into geopolitics. She is a science kid. She is into chemistry. Food chemistry to be specific. I am proud of them both."

"That's endearing to hear."

"We have not been the same together as a family since Kiera left us. Hard on all of us. I guess each one of us is trying to figure out how to accept what a huge void her passing has left on us. I think my grief has been the worst, and then I look around and see Justin and how his life has turned out in the past couple of years. It's . . ." Russell was trying to finish his sentence in a choking voice.

Melanie stretched her hand across the table and placed her palm on Russell's left fist, which was resting on the table, and gave it a tight hug.

"Russell, look here. I understand. Grief is very personal. There is no way you can compare your grief for the loss of Kiera with Justin's or Norah's grief for the loss of their mother. Grief is like fear. You have to face it and deal with it to overcome it. Cry, weep, yell, do whatever helps. But express it as much and as often you need to. That's the only way you can reduce the depth of your grief. I can help you . . . if you want to . . ." Melanie's grip on Russell's hands tightened, and she could feel a teardrop fall on her hand.

"Thank you, Melanie. That's so very kind of you to say that. This means a lot to me," Russell said, wiping his cheeks with the napkin quickly.

"I would love to meet Justin and Norah."

"I'd like that."

Jonathon quietly stopped by Melanie's chair. He sensed the mood of the table but didn't want to come across as inquisitive.

"Is everything all right, ma'am?

"Oh yes. Absolutely."

"Would you like me to bring your final drink for the evening? Gautier cognac?"

"That would be great."

CHAPTER 8

Justin was pacing up and down his room like a restless man on the brink of discovering something new. He was still shaky. His hands were cold and shivering. He had his head down, as if he was staring at his feet. There was no music. He could hear himself breathing heavily. He stopped near his work desk and looked at the magazine page that was open. He noticed some scribbling there. He was sure it was his, but he had no idea when he had done that. He tried hard to read his own scribbling. He could read only a few letters. He attempted to make sense of what he had written.

"L__th_ p_i_ e__ _ith me. I'__ ___e t_ ___te_t N__ah!"

He lifted the magazine with his hands and used his right hand to spread the page to remove the folds. He ended up covering most of his own scribbling with blood that still had not dried up.

Downstairs, not too far from the refrigerator, Norah lay in a pool of blood with knife wounds on her back, arms, and feet. There was an occasional whimper. Her broken phone lay shattered, a few feet away from her outstretched arms. Her right eye was open and blinking, while her left eye was covered in blood, facing the floor.

CHAPTER 9

"Thank you." Russell gave a ten-dollar bill to the valet as he got his car keys back. He unlocked the car and waited for a second to see how Melanie would react. There was a mischievous smile in Melanie's eyes, as she nodded as if to say, *Go ahead.* Russell ran to the other side of the car and opened the door for her. But before he could close the door, he saw the flashing lights from under his seat.

"There it is!"

Russell dropped his hand under the seat to grab his phone. He saw that there were five unread text messages, three from Norah, one from his mom, who lived in Phoenix, and one from his credit card company.

He got into the car and started the engine.

"Are you sure you should be driving?" Melanie asked.

"I think I should be fine. I didn't drink much."

"That's what we all say," Melanie said with a smile.

"Trust me. I am fine." Russell unlocked his phone.

The latest message was from American Express. An alert about his latest charge at Geronimo. And mom's message simply said, "Hi son."

He opened Norah's messages, and he immediately started to feel a bit queasy. His face was blushing red, and there was sweat trickling down his temples.

"Is everything all right?" Melanie asked with a worried look.

"No. I don't know." Russell sounded very concerned, with a bit of panic in his voice.

He picked up his phone and dialed Norah's number first. It rang once and immediately went to voicemail. He called the home number. The phone kept ringing.

"I hope they are okay," Russell said as he changed gear.

"Russell . . . look at me. They will be fine. Now, do you want me to ask the valet to find a driver for us? Or a cab maybe?"

"No, I will drive."

They both locked their seat belts, and they were on their way in no time. The cool breeze became cooler as it brushed the wet earth and brought a scintillating sensation on the skin. Perfect post-dinner weather for a couple on a first date. Except it wasn't so in Russell and Melanie's case.

Russell seemed like he was in control of the wheels, in spite of his anxiety and alcohol. He was driving under the speed limit, and he was sure he would get home by 10:00 p.m.

Melanie held his right hand with her left.

"You know, as soon as Kiera was diagnosed with cancer five years ago, she knew she didn't have much time left. The first thing she did was to plan a vacation for us." Russell smiled and turned toward Melanie.

Melanie gave a warm smile back.

"So, we traveled to Spain that summer. Malaga, Barcelona, and then finally Bilbao. Kiera wanted to soak in the Guggenheim Museum. I had no idea she was into art, let alone contemporary art." Russell laughed and continued. "But she was so particular that we left her alone at the Guggenheim for two full days. I mean, we were there, but not by her side for those two days. She was so happy. It felt like she found a closure for her life. And both Justin and Norah loved being around their mom during that trip. We all knew that was going to be our last happy vacation as a family of four. None of us spoke about that fact during the entire vacation. But we all felt it. We made full use of that trip and created so many lovely memories."

"You should share those pictures with me one of these days."

"Absolutely."

Russell kept an eye on the exit and on his phone. The traffic was pretty thin, as expected for that time of evening.

"By the way, I am so sorry that this evening has been all about me and my problems. I really had planned on spending more time with you. I hope you understand. I am so sorry." Russell fully realized how awkward it was for him not to be in a listening position. And then he thought of what Melanie did for a living.

"I completely understand, Russell. Let's make sure the kids are safe first."

Russell made a right into the El Dorado community entrance where he lived. He swiped his card, and the gate opened. Suddenly, it felt like they had entered a dead zone. An eerie quiet pervaded, as the residents had all settled in their respective houses for the evening, with minimal lights on.

The car pulled into the driveway, and Russell's heartbeat increased as he unbuckled his seat belt.

"Should I go with you . . . or do you want me to wait?" Melanie asked.

"Why don't you wait here for a few minutes, and I will make sure they are doing okay. And then I will come back and drop you at your place. I can go to CVS on my way home after dropping you off."

"Are you sure?"

"I am. Listen to some music or something while you wait." Russell waved as he walked toward the garage door.

CHAPTER 10

Russell typed the four-digit code on the keypad mounted on the wall, opened the garage door, and walked in. He unlocked the door that led him into the mud room, where he dropped his coat on the bench. He closed the door and rushed in screaming. He was nervous, frantic, and also angry.

"Justin! Norah! Where are you? I have been trying to call."

"Justin …"

The hallway from the mud room led through the kitchen to the main foyer area. Norah was lying on the other side of the counter, which Russell couldn't see as he was walking toward the staircase.

"Where is everyone?"

As he knocked on Justin's door and didn't get a response, he decided to bump open the door. It opened easily, as it wasn't locked from inside.

Justin was on the floor with his eyes closed.

"Hey, Justin, what happened? Is everything okay?"

Justin moved a bit and after a couple of seconds opened his eyes.

"Hey, Dad!"

"Are you all right?"

Justin could see his dad's lips move but couldn't hear what he was saying. His ears were ringing as if someone slapped his ears with a cooking pan. He tried reading his dad's lips.

"Yes. All good. In fact, all better. You look like you need some help too, Dad."

"Justin, where is Norah? She isn't picking up her phone."

By now, Justin's senses were back to normal, and he could hear his dad speak.

"Norah is doing better. Much better than when she was under your care. I hope to make you feel better too."

"What are you talking about? Was? What do you mean *was*?"

"Because it was in the past. She doesn't need you anymore. I don't need you anymore. Well, actually you don't have to put up with this pain anymore."

"Justin, Norah texted me you haven't taken your meds. How long have you been off meds?"

"That matters only if you want me to continue enduring the pain. Dad!"

"Let me go get your meds right now. Tell me where Norah is." Russell was trying to lift Justin by holding his arms. While he was doing that, the magazine with Justin's scribbling caught Russell's eyes. There was a smudge of blood on top of the scribbling. But Russell could read it better than Justin could.

"Let the pain end with me. I'll have to protect Norah!"

"Don't touch me, Dad. Let go of me. I will take you to Norah."

Justin got up, and as he wobbled, Russell stepped out of the room and started walking toward Norah's room.

"She isn't there," Justin yelled.

Justin started walking toward the stairs.

"You are useless as a dad. You know that? I feel sorry for you. You are absolutely useless."

Russell didn't respond. He wanted to make sure Norah was safe.

As they got down, Russell could see a pool of blood stretching beyond the counter.

"Norah!" he screamed.

"Don't worry, Dad. I relieved her off her pain. All of it. She was struggling to be a good sister and a good daughter. She didn't have to put up with the pain."

Russell ran toward Norah. He couldn't tell if she was still alive. As he got closer, he saw that her right eye was blinking to acknowledge that she recognized his presence.

"Norah . . . hang in there! Let me call the ambulance."

Russell picked up the phone and called Melanie.

"Pick up . . . Pick up . . . Hey . . ."

"Russell, is everything okay?"

"No. Can you please call 911 and give them my address right away? Please come in after that. I need your help. Norah has some stab wounds, and she needs to be taken to the hospital . . ."

"Will do, Russell."

Melanie didn't waste any time, as she had been trained to respond to emergencies. She called 911 and started giving the necessary details.

"I hate myself. I am such a loser. I couldn't help Norah. I failed her. Oh no!" Justin cried, realizing that Norah was still alive. He was in a state of bewilderment.

Russell didn't want to move Norah's body, as he wasn't sure where she had been stabbed and didn't want to make any injuries worse by moving her.

"Justin, I am not going to ask you what happened. But just let me know where you stabbed her."

Just as he was completing his question, Russell felt a deep pain in his back. A tingling sensation at first, which quickly transformed into a pricking sensation, followed by a deep scathing pain, knocking him unconscious.

"I hope I get it right this time, *Dad.*" Justin was standing right behind his dad with a meat cleaver. He continued to pierce into Russell's spinal cord with the focus of a butcher trying to get the best sirloin cut.

Russell stopped breathing within seconds.

Justin got up and rinsed the blood off his hands and dropped the cleaver in the kitchen sink. Then he heard footsteps.

This must be my dad's date, he thought to himself.

He got the cleaver ready again and waited for Melanie to show up. Instead, Melanie walked past the counter from the other side, directly to the staircase. She was running upstairs.

"Hi, Melanie. It's a pleasure meeting you. My dad hasn't spoken much about you. But I am sure he would have had a lot to say about you right now, if he were alive."

"Justin … what … Russell … what are you … are you … saying?" Melanie said in a complete state of shock.

"My father needed relief. And I did my duty as a son. Just as my mom would have wanted me to. That's all." Justin was pointing at his dad's dead body on the kitchen floor.

As Melanie came near, she saw two bodies. She presumed one must be Norah's, and she didn't know how to react.

"I apologize for creating not the best of circumstances to meet you. I know this is not how a date night is supposed to end. But …"

Justin collapsed on the kitchen floor, right next to Russell.

CHAPTER 11

Ten years later.

"Sometimes it's hard to differentiate what we see with our eyes and what we see with our brains. What we see with our brains is often under our control. It's our creation. When it comes to what your brain sees, let's call it imagination. Imagination is always within our control because we control the boundaries of our imagination. These boundaries can change every time we imagine. But we are in control every time. But hallucinations are a completely different ball game. We don't have any control over them because they are external. The danger is that hallucinations can mimic perception and imagination, and they often do. When someone can't tell the difference between hallucination and imagination, then that person needs help."

Melanie finished her last lecture of the day to a new group of interns. She got into her car and drove back home. She hadn't moved out of the house since that dreadful night. In fact, she hadn't changed her routine much since that night. The only change in her life was that she now had a dependent to care for.

Norah was sitting on her custom-designed wheelchair, with her head tilted to her left. She really couldn't move much without her button-activated wheelchair, which she could operate with her thumb and index fingers. She had lost vision in her left eye completely. Her olfactory and aural skills had not been affected much. And she could speak in a feeble voice.

Melanie threw her bag onto the foyer table after she entered her house and came toward Norah to give her a hug.

"How was your day, Norah?"

"Not bad. Finished the paper that was due today. Watched a cake bake-off show and now just chilling. How was yours?"

"My day was uneventful. Do you remember today is October 10? You know what we have to do. So come, let's get ready and go out."

In a few minutes, Melanie helped Norah freshen up, change, put on some light make-up, and wear her shoes. She herself got ready quickly. Then, Melanie pushed the wheelchair to her minivan and helped Norah get into the vehicle.

They started driving.

Since that tragic night in 2008, Melanie had been taking care of Norah. Norah had to spend almost nine months in the hospital. Her total body damages ranged from penetrating spinal cord injury to pelvic fracture, and then from ankle fracture, corneal abrasion, numbness in her legs, to a severe lung infection. She had lost vision in her left eye, and she could hardly raise her voice due to partial vocal cord hemorrhage. Her spinal cord and pelvic injuries may have left her wheelchair bound, but within six months after she got home, she started working as a part-time research writer for a Boston-based chemical laboratory. When she was not working, she could still entertain herself by reading, listening to music, and watching TV. Cooking channels topped her list.

Melanie decided to bring Norah to her home and become her

permanent caregiver. But the state laws deemed that she get consent from the most responsible surviving adult of the family because Norah was not eighteen yet.

The state assigned Norah a temporary guardian immediately after the attack, but a long-term decision had to go through family court. Melanie petitioned for full guardianship. There was no legal requirement to involve Justin—but she chose to. Not for the paperwork, but for the closure.

Reflection (Flashback—Melanie's First Visit After the Attack)

There was no legal requirement to involve Justin in the process—the courts would never seek consent from a mentally ill inmate serving time for attempted murder. But Melanie requested a visit anyway.

Not for legal reasons.

For moral ones.

She needed to see him. To understand what was left. To see if there was a person behind the psychotic break. To tell him what she intended to do for Norah.

But she was also meeting him as a psychologist—and perhaps, as a mother searching for any flicker of remorse in the boy who had nearly killed his sister.

The first meeting had been quiet. Justin hadn't raged or shouted. He had sat still, blinking, lucid for perhaps the first time in weeks. When Melanie told him she was seeking guardianship, he hadn't objected.

"She needs someone. Better it's you than no one," he'd said, almost whispering. "Tell her . . . I didn't mean to. Not really."

Justin's gentle behavior toward her and his equanimity for the entire duration of her interaction with her made her believe that Justin was on the right track. The prison authorities were given strict instructions to give Justin his meds at the right time at all cost. Before Melanie left the prison, she very distinctly remembered what Justin had asked her. As soon as Justin asked that question, she felt a sudden cloud of guilt shroud her mind.

"Are you thinking about becoming my caregiver as well? Even if you decide not to, can we meet again? This felt good. To have someone visit me. You know what I mean?"

Melanie was not prepared to engage in a conversation with Justin. Even knowing what she knew about his condition, she just hadn't come prepared. She tried hard not to let her professional instincts take over at that moment.

"I know. I know what you mean, Justin. I will try to come by next month. Okay? Bye for now. Thanks for signing this paperwork."

"That would be great. Bye. Bye, Melanie." Justin was relieved and happy.

"Take care now, Justin."

With that, Melanie stepped out of the penitentiary and back into the world that still spun, indifferent to the broken pieces she carried with her. True to her word, she returned to visit Justin the following month. One visit became another. Then another. For nearly seven years, she visited him every few months, a rhythm that felt both voluntary and involuntary—like a ritual she didn't fully understand but couldn't abandon.

In the early days, she kept the tone clinical. Guarded. She spoke only of Norah's recovery, asked basic questions about his health, and left a small box of his favorite macadamia nut cookies. She resisted the urge to analyze him, to interpret his fractured speech or defensive humor. She wasn't his counselor here—just a quiet messenger from a world he'd torn himself out of.

But somewhere along the way, the boundary softened. She couldn't say exactly when or how, but during one visit, she stopped filtering her curiosity. Their conversation drifted deeper, the way riverbanks erode over time. And she let the therapist inside her speak.

"No one really dies," Justin had said during one of those talks. "We just change state. A shift in consciousness. Death is an illusion, really. Just a new frame of perception."

Melanie didn't challenge the statement. She had learned not to. Instead, she began steering their exchanges gently toward memory— toward who he had been before the spiral. She never asked him directly about the night of the attack. She knew the question could break something, trigger something. They weren't in a hospital. There were no padded rooms, no safety teams. Only a thin pane of glass and the silence it held.

So she asked about childhood summers. About the songs their mother sang. She even shared fragments of her own life—stories she rarely told. Like the years she spent in a quietly abusive marriage, the creeping erosion of self-worth, and the slow climb out.

One afternoon, after a long pause between words, she asked him, "What would it take for you to feel . . . content? At peace?"

Justin looked at her, head tilted slightly, as if trying to see through her skin.

"If I can help everyone who touches my life," he said.

"What kind of help?" she asked, her voice calm but alert.

He smiled faintly.

"Relieve them of their pain."

The phrase stayed with her. Not because it was poetic—but because it was dangerous in its ambiguity.

Two months ago, during their most recent visit, Justin had asked if Norah might come see him someday. His voice was calm. Earnest. Almost childlike.

Melanie hesitated. Then said, "Maybe in October."

She told herself it was just a conversation.

She told herself it didn't mean anything.

But she also marked the date.

<h1 style="text-align:center">CHAPTER 12</h1>

Penitentiary of New Mexico—Secure Visitation Room (October 10, 2018)

"Do you think Justin will recognize me?" Norah asked as Melanie wheeled her into the facility. Her voice was a breath, more air than sound, but it carried the weight of years.

Melanie didn't answer immediately. She handed her license to the intake officer, passed over the paperwork, and returned to Norah, crouching next to her.

"He might. He might not. But you're not here to be recognized. You're here because you're strong enough to face him."

Norah gave a nod that looked more like a shrug.

The security protocol took fifteen minutes. Norah was scanned. Her wheelchair inspected. Melanie passed through a metal detector and surrendered her phone. They were escorted by a guard named Hastings, who gave Norah a kind smile.

"You'll be in Room C. Inmate is in a secure chair. Double restraints. No physical contact allowed. Duration: twenty minutes."

Melanie nodded. "We understand."

Here they were, Norah and Justin, siblings, carrying the weight of a meeting that neither of them truly understood. Norah's heart was a battleground of dread, guarded hope, and a desperate need for clarity. This wasn't excitement—it was the terrifying ache of unfinished business, of facing the face behind the memory that haunted her sleep.

Inside, the room was brighter than Norah expected. A two-way speaker system divided the room, along with a thick barrier of reinforced glass. Justin was already seated on the other side. His hands were cuffed to the metal loops on the armrests, but he wasn't struggling. He looked thinner than Norah remembered, his cheeks hollow, his hair longer, grayer. His eyes seemed both dead and electric.

Norah's fingers fidgeted near the corner of her chair. Her heart was pounding. The decision to come had taken months of therapy, sleepless nights, and finally, a reluctant whisper to Melanie: *"I think I want to see him."* It wasn't excitement. It was a volatile storm of emotions—fear, unresolved anger, reluctant hope, and the lingering ache of betrayal.

She felt sick with anticipation, not because she wanted a reunion, but because part of her needed to see the damage—face it, name it, and maybe, finally, set it down. This wasn't a path to forgiveness. It was a walk through fire to see if she could come out on the other side with anything left.

She didn't expect to find peace. But maybe she would find a piece of herself she had lost.

"Well, shit," Justin muttered as he saw them. "Didn't think you'd actually bring her."

Melanie took a deep breath and sat next to Norah, placing a gentle hand on her shoulder.

"Hello, Justin," she said into the mic.

"Hi," Norah added, her voice wavering.

Justin laughed. It was dry and cynical, echoing off the walls.

"Hi, she says. Like this is fucking Thanksgiving dinner. Like I didn't carve her up like a roast."

Melanie pressed the talk button. "Justin, she's here because she chose to be. Don't ruin this."

"Oh, I already ruined everything, doc. Let's not pretend this is a Hallmark reunion. Look at her. Look what I did. Look what YOU let me do."

Norah flinched. Melanie stiffened. The guard outside the door looked in but didn't move. Words alone weren't cause for intervention.

"Justin," Norah said, her finger on the mic, "I wanted to see you. I wanted to see if . . . anything inside you was still . . . human."

Justin sat back. He looked at the ceiling, then down at his lap.

"You want to know if I'm human? Ask the concrete walls I talk to every night. Ask the cockroach that visits my cell. He knows me better than you ever did."

Melanie leaned closer. "Justin, please. Try. Just talk. Not yell."

"I'M NOT YELLING," he snapped, then laughed again, harsher this time. "This is me calm. This is me medicated. You should see me when they forget the pills. You should see me in the dark, doc. That's where the real show is."

He turned to Norah.

"Did you come here hoping for a sorry? An apology? Well, fuck that. I don't remember stabbing you, Norah. Isn't that funny? I remember flushing the pills. I remember the music. I remember the blood. But not the moment I stuck the knife in. That part's gone. Like Mom. Like you should be."

Melanie reached for Norah's hand, but Norah pulled away. Her eyes were locked on Justin, tearless.

"You don't remember . . . but I do. I remember every second. I remember the look in your eyes. You weren't my brother that night. You were a monster."

Justin tilted his head. He smiled faintly.

"Maybe that's the real me. Maybe you just never saw it."

The speaker crackled. "Five minutes," a voice said.

Justin pressed forward as much as the restraints allowed.

"You want to know what solitary does? It eats the walls first. Then your memories. Then your voice. It chews your brain and spits out static. But the best part? The absolute best fucking part? It shows you truth. Raw. Undiluted. Truth like a bone through skin."

His voice dropped to a whisper.

"And the truth, Norah? The truth is I freed you that night. You didn't die, but I freed you. I cut out the part of you that still believed in Dad. In me. You should thank me."

Norah blinked. Her lips quivered.

"I did believe. Until tonight."

Justin sat back, a look of mock satisfaction on his face.

"There it is. The little light going out. That's what freedom looks like. Desolate, huh?"

Melanie stood. "This is over."

But Norah didn't move. She stared at her brother one last time.

"You're right about one thing, Justin. Something did die that night. But not the part of me that believes in people. Just the part that believed in you."

The door behind Justin opened. Guards entered to remove him. As they cuffed his ankles and wheeled him back, Justin turned one last time.

"You came here for closure? Here's your closure, sis: If they ever let me out, I'll finish what I started."

The guards shoved him forward. Norah didn't flinch. She looked at Melanie.

"Let's go."

Extended Epilogue —Reflections
Santa Fe—Present Day

Melanie sat by the window, sipping lukewarm tea from a mug Norah had once gifted her—"#1 Food Chemist," it said in fading block letters. The sun was diffused behind late-October clouds, casting a soft grey over the horizon.

The house was quiet now. Too quiet. No wheelchair hums. No late-night YouTube cake challenges playing from the living room. Just silence, and memory.

She opened her laptop and read the latest letter. It had come from Colorado State Psychiatric Facility, forwarded through official channels. The envelope bore no return name. The handwriting was unmistakable.

"Melanie, I have stopped measuring time in years. I measure it in shadows now. The ones that move across my cell. The ones that vanish. That's how I know I'm still here. I want to tell you something about Norah, even if you don't read this. I think I see her sometimes. In the corner of my mind. Not in pain. Just watching me. That part's worse. You think guilt is loud. It's not. It's silent. Like teeth clenching in your sleep. Or bleeding under your skin. I think I tried to help her. I don't know if I ever knew what help meant."

Melanie didn't respond to his letters anymore. But she kept them in a worn shoebox in her closet. She read them when her own guilt rose like static in her chest—when she questioned whether she should've ever let Norah go into that room with him. Whether any of them truly believed he had changed.

She remembered that visit too vividly. Norah, leaving the room without tears. Not angry. Just . . . hollow. That was the beginning of her emotional turning. The body had survived Justin's attack. But some parts of her spirit had not.

Melanie reached for her journal and wrote, not for anyone to read:

"I don't believe in monsters anymore. Only people. Hurt people. Sick people. People who are capable of unspeakable things and still ask for forgiveness. Sometimes I think healing is selfish—because it means choosing to go on when others don't get to. But I choose it anyway. Every day."

She closed the journal and looked out the window.

Colorado State Psychiatric Facility— Present Day

Justin sat on the floor of his cell, tracing a shape into the dust beside his cot. The nurses had given up trying to make him take the chair. He didn't mind the floor. It was closer to the ground. Honest.

"I don't like when the room is too clean," he wrote in his notebook. *"It makes the ghosts look out of place."*

He had good days. Days when he answered the doctors' questions and ate all his meals. He even participated in group therapy once— until someone said the word *forgiveness.*

That had sent him back to silence.

He remembered Norah's face that day. The light leaving her eyes.

Not in fear. Not in anger. In *resignation*. It haunted him more than her screams ever had.

"Melanie hasn't written. That's fair. I think she tried. I think she still sees me as someone buried under sickness. But what if this is the only version of me that was ever real?"

Sometimes, he would fold bits of paper into shapes. He had learned origami from a therapist years ago. He made a swan once and wrote Norah's name on its wings. Then he crushed it in his fist and flushed it, whispering: *"Be free."*

The cell door buzzed. Meds. Lights out in twenty.

Justin closed his notebook and scrawled one last line on the back cover.

"Freedom is not the absence of walls. It's the silence after you stop trying to tear them down."

He stared at that sentence for a long time, then closed his eyes.

Back in Santa Fe

Melanie lit a candle in the window that evening. She did it every October 10.

Not for justice.

Not for forgiveness.

But for remembrance.

• • •

According to a Yale Law School study in 2018, over 4,000 mentally ill prisoners in the United States are held in solitary confinement.

In the state of New Mexico, 64% of mentally ill inmates are in solitary, often without consistent psychiatric care.

These prisoners spend an average of 22 hours a day in isolation, in cells often smaller than a parking space—with limited human contact, minimal therapy, and few paths to recovery.

Solitary does not heal. It hides. And sometimes, it breaks what little is left unbroken.

Justin wasn't an outlier. He was a statistic—made flesh, made violent, made invisible.

And Norah was collateral damage.

❤

SURGICAL BIND

Marquette

"Get out of my way, you son of a bitch. We need to throw you all out of the country. You are like pests!" the man in a white hoodie yelled as he elbowed his way to grab a pint of ice cream from the freezer.

Majeed was shocked. This was his first night in Marquette, Michigan. His eyes froze for a few seconds as he stood still there. He mustered some courage after a moment to open his mouth, when the man in the hoodie slammed the freezer door on Majeed's hands.

"Ouch! That fucking hurts, dude. What's wrong with you?" Majeed said, writhing in pain.

"Nothing is wrong with me, you filthy bastard. You and your brown-skinned n***rs have everything wrong with you. You know who is in the house? You all will get ejected one day. Just leave the country before they send your dead bodies back to where you came from. This country belongs to my people!" the man shouted at Majeed while trying to land a punch on his face.

Majeed quickly swung his head away, and the man ended up punching the air over Majeed's shoulder.

Asha was looking for light soy sauce two aisles away. She thought she found the right one that the recipe she had read called for, but the ingredients made her put the bottle away.

How many brands of soy sauce do the people of Marquette really need? she thought to herself. In her mind, soy sauce was one of those condiments that has been around for hundreds of years, and there was very little need for experimentation. As she put the bottle away, she heard what she thought was Majeed's voice.

"I am going to call the police."

Asha knew immediately that something was wrong. His voice was trembling. She knew he spoke like that either when he got too emotional in an argument or when he was really panicking.

"This can't be good." She left the shopping cart right where she was and started running toward the direction where she heard Majeed's voice.

It didn't take too long to spot him, surrounded by three other men.

Asha ran toward Majeed as a bald man in a short-sleeved T-shirt was trying to pin Majeed by his shoulders, while the other two were laughing and getting ready to lift his legs up. She spotted the emergency button that the grocery store had at the corner of each aisle and quickly pressed it before continuing her sprint toward Majeed.

"Stop hitting him, you jerks!" Asha screamed.

She was only ten feet away from those four men now. She could see Majeed clearly from that specific point, and she could tell that there was no visible injury on his face, which had turned red. She was relieved for a moment.

"Ari, don't say anything. Keep quiet." Asha was able to make eye contact with him now.

"Well, well, well. Who do we have here?" the third man in the gang said, slamming his palms together as he took a few steps toward Asha.

"Another brown bitch who needs to be sent home." The man in hoodie laughed.

All of them could now hear the footsteps of the store security guards. They could also hear the security guards' radios opening a line of communication with the local emergency dispatcher.

They were now two aisles away.

"You get lucky tonight. I just wanted to break your hand and leave a little token of love for you. So you will remember to get out as soon as you can." The man in black T-shirt relaxed his grip on Majeed, while the other two signaled him to run toward the other side.

The three men dropped their shopping basket right there and ran in the opposite direction they heard the footsteps of security guards coming from. Within five seconds, they were out of sight.

"Are you all right, ma'am?" one of the security guards asked Asha, as he saw her slouching toward the floor.

"Yes. Yes, I am fine. I am trying to make sure my husband is all right."

Majeed was up on his feet by now. He was still a bit nervous but seemed to have recovered from the unexpected violent encounter. Asha lent him her shoulders as he tried to gain composure.

"Who were those guys?" asked Asha, wanting to know if they were residents of Marquette.

"We didn't quite see them, ma'am. But if you want, you can walk with us to our security control room, and we will be able to get some footage from our cameras, and maybe you can help us identify them. We'll expedite our follow-up with the law enforcement officials. If these guys are out-of-towners, we can stay one step ahead of them."

Majeed and Asha looked at each other. They knew the right thing to do would be to help the security guards identify the assailants. But they weren't sure if this was the kind of thing they should get involved with at that very moment, in a new town they had just moved to.

"Is it okay if we come by tomorrow morning? I mean, we were fortunate that nothing major happened. And there seems to be no visible injury. We would like to just get home and recover from the shock. We are new here. We moved here literally eight hours ago. We have hardly unpacked our suitcases. This … this was just a warm welcome," Majeed said, wiping the sweat on his forehead with his forearm.

"Sure. We understand, sir. The sooner the better."

"If you would excuse us now . . ." Asha pushed Majeed out and they started walking toward the exit with the cart.

"Your groceries are on the house, ma'am. One of the guards will check these out for you. You can wait in your car. We will bring them out for you. We apologize for what happened."

"Oh . . . that's not necessary. We will . . . well, thank you. That's kind of you."

"Hey, Ash. Your cart?"

"Soy sauce can wait," Asha said with a smile.

Asha and Majeed opened their car and settled down in their seats. It was August, and the Upper Peninsula in Michigan can get really humid on summer days. As a gentle breeze from Lake Superior wafted its way through the parking lot, Asha looked at Majeed and said, "There will be a day when these racist bastards will be at our mercy in the ER."

Majeed broke an uncomfortable smile, a smile that was meant to both acknowledge and disapprove at the same time, of what Asha just said.

The Asha he knew, he thought, didn't exactly mean that.

Dr. Majeed Marikar

Dr. Majeed Marikar was born in Batticaloa, Sri Lanka. His great-grandfather had migrated from the southern part of Kerala, India, to Sri Lanka when the timber trade was flourishing. His grandfather married a Sri Lankan Muslim woman of Tamil origin, leading to a multilingual generation in which Majeed was born. Majeed could understand enough Malayalam to survive in Thiruvananthapuram, but in Kanoor, he would be lost like a skunk with a yogurt cup stuck on his face. Majeed was more comfortable with Tamil, not because he spoke Tamil at home but because Tamil was a prominent language in Sri Lanka, and it was a matter of identity for him and for those few who were like Majeed. They attached themselves to the Sri Lankan Tamil diaspora. That provided a sense of belonging, and a sense of ethnic pride.

Even though a majority of today's Sri Lankan Muslims' origins can be traced back to "lower caste" Tamils who converted from Hinduism to Islam, there are a few who moved from Southeast Asia during the golden age of rubber and timber trading. These Sri Lankan Muslims of Malay origin form a very small portion of the Sri Lankan Muslim population, which is about 10 percent of the national population. Together, the Sri Lankan Muslims are known as Moors. It's hard to trace any Arabic roots for these Moors. But there has been a change in that equation of late, and some of that could be attributed to deliberate attempts by certain external elements to erase the Moors' Indian past and overwrite it with untraceable Arabic past.

Majeed went to the Faculty of Medicine of the University of Colombo and got his MBBS degree before moving to Michigan State University to work on his residency program in surgery. As his academic pursuits took him out of his home country, Majeed continued to stay in touch with his parents and his brother and made it a point to visit them at least once a year. The transformation from being a violent land when he was a teenager to a relatively incident-free land for a few years of late gave Majeed the opportunity to dream every now and then about returning to the beautiful hills of Ella and setting up a small hospital there.

His family, on the other hand, was happy that Majeed didn't have to deal with the growing Islamophobia in the country. The suicide bomb attack in a church in Negombo, not too far from where Majeed grew up, and other attacks in hotels in Colombo that happened on the same day, Easter Sunday, were all carried out by Muslim extremists, and that had generated turbulent dynamics for the Sri Lankan Muslim community. The family understood that life as they knew in Sri Lanka was not going to be the same again. They had already started talking about selling their lumber business off in the near future and had bought a house in the outskirts of Nagercoil, Tamil Nadu.

Majeed had been to Marquette before.

MSU has a partnership with the UP Health System in Marquette, and that's what connected Majeed to Marquette during this five-year residency program. He didn't think much of Marquette during his two-week stay back then. In fact, the only thing he remembered about Marquette from that stay was how his life changed forever for the better.

On the second day of his clinical rotation program at UP Health System, Majeed Marikar met Asha Ram.

Dr. Asha Ram

Dr. Asha Ram was a Midwesterner to the core. In fact, she had never lived outside the Midwest. Her parents moved to the United States about thirty years ago, and they found their financial footing in Chicago and had never felt the need to move anywhere else. As a company auditor, once you establish your credentials with the financial leaders of the company, the relationship almost always ends up lasting long term. The highly experienced CPAs they were, both Meenakshi Ram and Dinesh Ram, built a career for themselves as the founders of one of the leading auditing firms in the greater Chicago area for small businesses in the technology sector.

As a child, Asha was never drawn to math or technology. She wanted to pursue journalism until she reached her sophomore year in high school, when a magical switch triggered an obsessive interest toward biology and chemistry, resulting in Asha Ram becoming Dr. Asha Ram, with an MD degree from the College of Medicine at The University of Illinois. Her quest for understanding human bodies and her passion for surgical procedures to help ailing patients get better led her to enroll in the general residency surgery program from the same college.

Asha and her older sister, Nivetha, were both astute students. They were only two years apart in age, and yet Asha started commanding respect from Nivetha right from their middle school years. Some leadership skills are innate to a person. Nivetha, a more traditional second-generation Indian immigrant kid, excelling in academics during school years, started looking up to Asha from her middle school years, when Asha started developing a personality of her own that drew her friends to come and confide in her or to seek counseling from her. Asha was good academically, but she was also a very good athlete. She captained the high school track team for two years and had won many state-level medals in the four-hundred-meter and eight-hundred-meter races. In short, Nivetha knew her sister, Asha, would grow into doing bigger things than she ever would get to do for herself, and she was happy to be cheering for her little sister right from that age.

Meenakshi and Dinesh insisted on speaking only in Tamil with their daughters when they were home together. That habit at least ensured that both Nivetha and Asha could move around with familiarity when they visited their families in India during their summer holidays. They could speak Tamil fluently with rolled R and bent L sounds and could a keep a conversation going with their family members without showing any signs of losing interest in the topic. Asha even picked up a slight Madurai accent during one of her summer breaks in India, and it was not all that hard for her to blend with the locals. Madurai, where Meenakshi was from, is a southern city in Tamil Nadu, with veritable qualifications to be classified as a temple city. Dinesh was from Trichy, where no distinctive accent could be drawn. Otherwise, Asha may have had the opportunity to pick up another Tamil accent.

Asha was not especially excited about the rotation she had been assigned. She was familiar with Marquette and had vague memories of spending a night there during a long weekend trip with her family, when they got to see Pictured Rocks on Lake Superior. She had to spend two-and-a-half weeks as part of this rotation. The UP Health System in Marquette, at Marquette General Hospital, is a Level II trauma center, and she knew the experience she would gain from this institution would be very valuable for her.

Little did she know of other valuable life lessons she would end up getting in Marquette.

"Don't let anyone ever make you feel like you don't deserve what you want," Majeed whispered to himself.

"What did you say?" Asha asked.

"Nothing. I said . . . all I wanted was some ice cream, and I just happened to want it at the exact moment when those racist bastards wanted it. And in a few minutes, they made me feel guilty. For no goddamn reason," Majeed said with a frustrated anger in his tone.

"You want to go back in and get some of that ice cream?" Asha asked in a concerned yet playful tone.

"Nah. I am over the ice cream now. Let's just wait for the grocery bags to arrive, and we will head out of here. I think we have had more life lessons than what we could have bargained for on our first night as a professional couple in Marquette." Majeed tried to laugh.

Asha laughed.

"Hey . . . what you said earlier about not letting anyone ever make you feel like you don't deserve something . . . that was a pretty cool thing. I really like what it says to us. I mean, it's deep. If you internalize it well, nothing will get us down."

"That was Heath Ledger," Majeed said with a smile.

"What? That quote? Wow!" Asha said, shaking her head in amusement, as she was clearly impressed with her husband's ability to quote Heath Ledger a few minutes after a racist assault inside a grocery store.

They looked at each other. Majeed put his arms around Asha's shoulders and tugged her toward him. Asha leaned sideways and kissed his cheeks first. Majeed quickly placed his right palm on Asha's chin, as if he was holding it and giving it a gentle lift. He turned his face further toward her to plant a kiss on Asha's lips. She opened her lips to make it easy.

"Excuse me, ma'am . . . sir." The security guards were knocking on the driver's side window. "Your groceries."

Majeed released his hold on Asha's chin. Asha released herself from Majeed's grip and rolled down the window.

"Thank you so much." She collected the bags through the open window and placed them on the rear seat.

"You're welcome. Is there anything else we can do for you now, ma'am? We are very sorry for what happened."

"No. We are good for now. Thank you."

"Please come back tomorrow to see the security footage. Have a good night." The security guard started moving away from the car.

"We will," replied Majeed, as Asha slowly reversed the car.

"Ari, did you really see those guys' faces?"

"Sort of. I mean, I guess I will be able to remember only the face of the guy who started the altercation with me. The one with a hoodie. I don't remember seeing the other two guys. The only thing I remember about the man pinning me by my shoulders was that he had tattoos on both his arms. Forearm tattoos." Majeed was trying to recollect as much as he could, while Asha pulled onto the main road.

"It read **P-R-O-U-D B-O-Y**. That's the tattoo he had on both his forearms."

The house they had rented was a ten-minute drive from the

grocery store. There wasn't much traffic on the streets for a Friday evening.

They moved into Marquette on a Friday evening because they wanted to use the weekend to settle in. For both Asha and Majeed, coming back to Marquette after four years brought a weirdly excited feeling. Unlike the last time, this time around, they were both here out of their own choice and as a married couple.

As they kept thinking about the unexpected turn of events in the past hour or so on an otherwise perfectly normal moving day, Asha and Majeed were now starting to feel exhausted.

They should have been going home excited about the new career beginnings in a new city. They should have been thinking about the transformative roles they could play in the trauma center at UP Health System as lead surgeons. They should have been thinking about how to make use of their time effectively in a small town for their future research. And amid all this, if possible, they should have been seriously considering the pros and cons of bringing a new human being into the world and assess their general readiness as mature adults capable of playing the roles of responsible parents.

Instead, that night, they were both thinking about the changing tone of the American moral fiber and how racial intolerance no longer hid behind faux decency in a country that was supposed to be the model of tolerance, diversity, and equality.

The couple drove to their new house, which they soon would convert into their home. This small town, which was supposed to present them a welcome bowl that night with seeds of hope for a green future, instead offered them a welcome bowl with seeds and weeds.

Marquette is a beautiful small town with a reputation of being very welcoming. People consider Marquette one of the preferred cities in Michigan to raise young children. With a university to boast, Marquette is every bit a college town as it is a quiet Midwestern town. With a population of twenty-one thousand plus, the town offers amazing scenery all year round. From biking to hiking trails, from surfing to skiing, from snowmobiling to ice climbing, from art galleries to cool music concerts, this important port on Lake Superior is the go-to-place in the Upper Peninsula.

UP Health Systems or Marquette General Hospital is the biggest hospital in the Upper Peninsula. It is a 315-bed specialty-care hospital, and the hospital receives patients from across the UP and provides care across multiple specialties and subspecialties. The medical staff alone includes more than three hundred doctors among its three thousand-plus employees. The hospital cares for approximately twelve thousand inpatients per year and more than three hundred fifty thousand outpatients per year.

As a Level II trauma center, this hospital has a few special distinctions, such as Blue Distinction for spine surgery.

After their graduation, Majeed and Asha, who were already dating across Lake Michigan, had decided that they would work together in a big city for a couple of years before making a collective decision on their future together. That's what led them to working and living together in Chicago for two years before deciding to move to Marquette for the vast amount of possibilities that a career at UP Health Systems would give them.

In spite of a racially abusive start to their stay in Marquette, Majeed and Asha quickly settled into a routine, both personally and professionally. In the first month, they got to spend only one night together every week in the same bed, because of their shifts. As lead surgeons being assigned on ER duties for the first couple of months, they both worked twelve-hour shifts. Their shifts in the first couple of months were such that Asha would relieve Majeed and Majeed would relieve Asha. This cycle would continue for 144 hours a week, when they both would get to stay home for twenty-four hours together. This certainly was not how they envisioned their first months in the new town to be like. But given their strengths and training in trauma centers, and their interest in gaining additional experience in a Level II trauma center, they both opted to rough it out for the first few months.

It was one of those twenty-four-hour breaks.

Majeed was sleeping, and Asha had just come home from her shift. It was a typical ER night for her. Two blunt cases, neither life threatening, one appendicitis case, one chemical burn case, and a handful of usual ER cases. No surgical critical care cases for her that night. As soon as she got home, she dropped her coat on the dining table and walked into the bedroom quietly. She saw Majeed sleeping on his side, and his sharp jawline in the darkness presented an image of a chiseled Roman warrior. She went to the bathroom and undressed quickly to jump into the shower. After a five-minute warm shower, she felt clean and devoid of all the ER smell.

Asha crawled into the bed right next to Majeed without disturbing him and slowly extended her arm to wrap around him. The warmth of his body and the gentle breathing rhythm provided a sense of comfort for her. She fell asleep in no time.

Majeed woke first, in the early afternoon, and he turned around to see Asha's glowing face. He knew she would be waking up soon. He ran his hands under her silk top and unfastened the top buttons. She opened her eyes. He rested his head on her chest. Her hand touched his chest and began to fall in excruciating slow designs. Their flesh was innocent and warm. They both crumbled like sand into each other's hugs and touches.

It was half an hour before they fell apart, spent, and with a call for lunch.

"That was the best," Asha whispered into his ear.

"Expect nothing less from me," Majeed said with a naughty smile.

"How long before we do it again?" she asked with a wink.

"At the rate our professional lives are spanning out, I would say it would take approximately another 144 hours."

They both laughed.

After cleaning himself up, Majeed walked into the kitchen to take the leftovers from his previous night's meal. Some falafel and Mjadra went into the microwave oven.

"Hey, Ari, did you hear back from the security guys at the grocery store? It's more than a month already," Asha asked.

"No. As far as they are concerned, the case is closed. What are they going to do anyways? I couldn't identify a single one confidently from the security footage, and the one person I identified . . . sort of . . . was only a spotty guess at best based on the hoodie. I am not sure if this is going to go anywhere, Ash. Why do you ask all of a sudden?" Majeed turned toward Asha with a sense of bewilderment because they hadn't talked about this incident in almost three weeks.

"No particular reason. Just remembered our first night in Marquette. That's all."

"I forgot to mention this to you. I had a small incident at the gas station the other day." Majeed opened the microwave oven to get the food out.

"What do you mean?"

"Nothing really. I don't know . . . It was Wednesday, I think. I went inside the gas station at the corner of Seventh and Madison Avenue. I wanted to pick up some gum. And for two seconds, it almost felt like déjà vu. I saw a man in a hoodie. I can't tell for sure if it was the same guy or not. He gave me a quick stare as he walked past me to the door. He kinda stopped and looked at me again as if he was trying to confirm it was me." Majeed was calm as he explained what happened.

Asha was at the dining table now, serving some Mjadra for herself.

"And then, as he opened the door, he turned toward me and said, 'Let's see how long you get to stay here,' and walked out . . ."

"Did you call anyone?"

"No. It was quick. I just flipped the bird at him. I don't think he saw it."

"But you couldn't tell if it was the same guy who confronted you before?" Asha was a little frustrated with her husband's inability to recollect things.

"That's the thing. I thought the guy at the store had a beard. And this man didn't. I can't be sure." Majeed spoke with a piece of lentil stuck in his teeth, which Asha pointed out.

"Do you think we should talk to the cops, Ari?"

"Ummm. Maybe we should. I will try to stop by the police station on my way back from the hospital tomorrow." Majeed was at the sink now.

"Better do it. Please . . ."

"Yes. I will." Majeed came toward the table and stood behind the chair where Asha was sitting. He held her shoulders from the back and started rubbing them as if he was giving her a massage. Asha turned her head, and they kissed.

"Is it 144 hours already?"

130 Hours Later

Asha had two more hours left in her shift that night. It was midnight. Majeed's shift would start at 2 a.m., and he would relieve Asha.

This night was unusually quiet. Managing the trauma team that night, Asha decided to call her team for an impromptu knowledge exchange session. This was something that she started doing very recently. If she was able to gauge a slow shift, after ensuring that all her trauma team members had absolutely cleared off all their procedures, she would call them to a small makeshift conference room inside the ER facility. She had two to four trauma specialists from her team not attending these sessions, just to provide coverage in the few seconds it may need for all of them to assemble outside to attend a new patient, whenever they got admitted.

These were meant to be ten- to twenty-minute sessions. Someone was supposed to bring up a trauma research or trauma management and methodology-related topic for discussion and talk about it for not more than ten minutes. And then the rest of the attendees would spend another ten minutes discussing the topic. As the clinicians warmed up to the idea in a few days, she began to look forward to these sessions. Now into her sixth week, she must have called for at least twelve such sessions in this period, averaging about two per week.

These sessions became so popular that even Majeed was initially forced to take on this idea on nights when he was leading the trauma team.

On this particular night, one of the trauma team clinicians was talking about neck trauma and how most neck traumas result in hemorrhagic shock because of lacerations of major vessels. As the team discussed a few cases they had personally worked on at UP Health Trauma Center, one of them shared a unique case she worked on. A male patient in his fifties was brought into the trauma center with a neck injury. The cause of the injury made the trauma care team work very carefully around the lacerations caused before they found out that the patient had actually suffered a herniated cervical disc.

The patient had been out for a jog in a local park during dusk. While on a secluded trail, he was ambushed by three assailants who strangled him with an old, coiled telephone cord they had brought with them. That evening, luck was on his side. Just as the attackers believed they had snapped his neck and ended his life, they loosened their grip—coincidentally, at the very moment a small group of joggers passed nearby.

The attackers let the man slip to the ground and ran away. Eventually, the good samaritans the joggers were, they called for emergency help.

A coiled phone cord caused severe lacerations of major vessels and ended up causing neurological deficits in the patient.

The Phone Call

About thirty-six hours earlier, around noon, Asha received a phone call. It was a number she didn't recognize, and because she was not particularly good with area codes, she couldn't guess that 407 belonged to Orlando, Florida. Her mobile phone alarm was set to 1 p.m. That would have given her about thirty minutes to get ready and be at the hospital by 1:45 p.m. The usual ER check-in process would have given her the fifteen or so minutes to settle in before Majeed could be relieved.

But when her home phone rang at noon, that kind of changed the routine for Asha. She picked up the receiver and answered the phone.

"Give me one good reason why you are still in the country," the voice at the other end said.

"Who is this?" Asha said, half asleep and half shaken by the message.

"That is not what you should be worried about. Where is your brave Ali Baba? Ask that Hadji husband of yours to stop poking around in our business. We heard your brown mustard went to the police and talked about us . . . huh?" The voice on the other end was really angry now.

"What are you talking about?"

"Just let him know that we are here to do what the big man in da house wants us all to do. If your husband stops calling the cops about us, we will lie low. The moment he cracks a whisper, he is gone. You hear what I am saying? You both will be gone. You fucking subhuman pieces of shit."

With that, the man on the other end of the phone disconnected the call.

Asha was beginning to sweat a bit. She went into the kitchen and poured herself a glass of water. She looked at the clock and then grabbed the phone.

"Not urgent, Ari, but those guys called to threaten us. Have you been talking to the cops? About them? Be safe. Maybe we should stay away."

Asha sent a text to Majeed, knowing well that he may not see it unless he was having a quiet ER shift or at least till the end of his shift, by which time she could ask him the same question in person.

Majeed responded.

"Yes. Meaning to tell you. Store security called. Asked me to check additional footage. I was able to confirm one of them. Best guess. Then the cops wanted to talk to me."

"But you never told me all this."

"Nothing really came out of it. It was a quick ten-minute meeting with the cops. They asked some basic questions. I had told them I am available for further inquiries. That's all. Nothing to panic."

"I am worried. Let's talk about this in a day, when we both will be home together. Don't do anything before that. Love you.♥"

"Gotta go. Yes, we'll talk at home. Will be careful. I promise. Love you too. See you in a couple of hours when we change shifts."

Shift Change

In another hour, Asha would be done with her shift. She was looking forward to going home and getting some rest before Majeed arrived after his shift. It would be 144 hours in another thirteen hours. A gentle smile broke through the corner of her mouth when she thought about the silly calculations her mind was indulged in at that moment. But she was also thinking about the conversation she wanted to have with Majeed. They had to consider possibilities. The worst possibilities of being victims of racist attacks in this Midwestern American town and what that would mean to their future.

Asha walked back to her chamber. She started looking through the new cases who got admitted to ER in the past thirty minutes or so. There were two. One was an infant with flulike symptoms, and the other was an epileptic seizure-related case. She wasn't concerned about either of them. She put the notes aside and was beginning to check her emails on her tablet when her pager started buzzing. It was a pre-triage notification. It usually meant that the paramedics were prepping the ER staff about them bringing in a patient with potential trauma. Every single member of the trauma team usually got that notification.

The team assembled in one of the designated rooms. In about four minutes, they could see the patient being ushered in a stretcher.

"Accident?"

"Yes, and looks like some stab wounds as well."

"How bad is he bleeding?"

"We thought we arrested it a bit. His pulse is stable. But his blood pressure is beginning to drop …"

"Dr. Noel, prep the surgery team for potential abdominal or splenic rupture. Dr. Claire, can you get the transfusion set up ready?" Asha was completely in charge of the situation.

Asha was checking the vitals of the patient while giving instructions to her team.

"Where are the stab wounds?"

"One on his left shoulder and the other on his left chest."

Asha asked the nurse to prepare the patient for procedures, which usually involved undressing the injured patient in the most clinically safe way possible and preparing the patient for further treatment.

Asha noticed a tattoo on the patient's left arm. The sight of it gave her chills, and she immediately turned the patient's right arm for better visibility. Both forearms had a similar tattoo.

"P-R-O-U-D B-O-Y"

"I will evaluate the patient for blunt abdominal trauma when I come back. Team, keep his oxygen level optimal," said Asha hurriedly as she stepped out of the room to fill the trauma case log on her tablet. She knew the clinicians were in control. The tattoo had clearly upset her a bit, and she needed a few minutes to collect her thoughts to decide what to prescribe next. After a few minutes, she took a deep breath and went inside the room again.

Within the next hour, the trauma team continued to finish all the initial trauma management steps for the patient. He was not fully stable yet, but it was time to assess the next steps. Surgery was not an immediate need, as the splenic rupture was not very acute. There were more immediate and urgent needs.

Asha decided to take a break just to clear her mind. She took her tablet out to fill in some notes, and when she looked at the clock on her tablet, she was beginning to feel agitated.

2 a.m.

"Ari …" Asha's first thoughts were not so optimistic.

She pulled the phone out of her coat pocket to check if there was any text message from him. There was none.

She quickly sent him a text, checking to see where he was. It was very unusual for Majeed not to be there at least fifteen minutes before his shift started.

2:20 a.m.

Asha thought it was best that the team evaluated the patient for neurological trauma. Based on the symptoms and the way the patient was responding to the initial treatment, she had a suspicion that it could be an intracranial injury. Everyone else in the team thought that the patient needed to be rushed into abdominal surgery.

After a quick discussion, the team agreed that they would conduct a series of tests to assess brain injuries. Asha stepped out of the room again. All the while when she was inside the room discussing intracranial trauma with her team, her mind was thinking about Majeed.

There was no communication from him. She decided to call the ER director in charge of the night.

Dr. Paul Wilson, the director on duty that night, could sense the urgency of the situation, given how visibly shaken Asha was.

"Don't worry, Dr. Asha. I will send someone to check on Dr. Majeed. I understand this is rather unusual."

"Thank you, Doc," Asha said as she tried to smile.

2:45 a.m.

Dr. Noel was giving a quick summary to Asha, while complimenting his boss. "That was amazing, Dr. Asha. The patient did have an intracranial injury, and even though it was mild, we have alerted the neurosurgeon on call and moved the patient to specialty care. Based on their initial prognosis, the patient has minor lacerations and may have minor bone injuries. All vitals within permissible levels for surgery. If we had delayed getting him to them, we probably would be taking a different course. Good call. You saved him today."

"Thank you for the update, Dr. Noel. Glad to hear we are in the right direction. I am going to be at my desk. Let me know if you need anything. Dr. Majeed hasn't come in yet, so I am a bit concerned. I am waiting for Dr. Wilson to give me an update."

"Sounds good. Don't worry too much now. Dr. Majeed will be all right!"

Asha could see the reflected image of a walking Dr. Noel on the glass door outside her room.

Images

If one tried to project the flashes of images running through Asha's mind, the projector would have found it hard to keep pace. Images of meeting Ari for the first time in Marquette, their first coffee date, their first kiss, their first dinner date, the first time they made love, the grocery store altercation, the drive home, their conversations about their future together, images of an imaginary Ella that she had formed based on Ari's description of his beautiful country, images of white nationalists parading through the mall in Washington DC, the phone call, images of knives, phone cords, blood, Ari's face, a silhouette of a hooded man, the tattoo, Ari's face on the ground with eyes closed, blood, and the smiling face of Ari.

"Dr. Asha." Paul Wilson was by her desk.

"Dr. Paul. I am sorry I didn't notice you." Asha looked pale.

"That's all right. I have to … I am afraid … I am sorry. I am afraid I have some bad news for you."

Asha knew right then. She crumbled into her chair, and tears started flowing down her cheeks.

Just one more day … That's all I needed, Ari. Goddammit. Why? Asha made a fist with her right hand and stared to punch her thighs. Dr. Wilson could hear the sinking pain in her muffled cry.

"Where did they find him? And … and do you have an initial assessment on how long ago this may have happened?" Asha lifted her head to ask Dr. Wilson as she continued to wipe her tears.

It was as if Asha knew exactly what Dr. Wilson was going to say.

"In your kitchen. Gunshot wounds. I made sure your pager wasn't alerted when the paramedics brought him here a few minutes ago. It was too late by the time we brought him here. I am sorry, Dr. Asha. They say it must have happened within the last two hours. I know there are many questions to be answered, and this is a police case now. One thing my assistant who went to your house told me is that there was a knife on the kitchen floor with blood on it, but Dr. Majeed didn't have a single stab wound. I am sure the police will make note of it. But wanted you to hear this from me first." Dr. Wilson shared everything he knew about the crime scene.

"Thank you, Dr. Paul. I need a few minutes. Then I will go see him."

"Of course, Dr. Asha." Dr. Wilson left the room.

Asha was trying to process the tragedy, the crime, and the sequence of events.

Did Ari stab the killer to protect himself? And did the killer run away after shooting down Ari?

She felt like the pleasure of remembering things had suddenly been taken away from her. She had just lost the person with whom she liked to remember things. It was like losing her memory itself. She felt guilty for not being there for her Ari.

What was Ari thinking when he took his last breath? Was he angry with me for not being there with him?

She started to hope for a distant place where she could set the clock back, a place where she could have asked Majeed to go to the cops as soon as she received the phone call. She hoped that such a place really existed where everything was silent and there was nothing to lose. She couldn't accept that she deserved to lose the man she loved. She wanted to grieve, but she knew her grief had to wait.

Dr. Asha Ram got out of her chair and took her kit and started walking toward the trauma center area. She was still the lead surgeon in charge of the ER and trauma care team, as no one had relieved her yet. She smiled at Dr. Noel and other clinicians who were trying to make eye contact with her.

She knew what they were thinking. She knew what they wanted to say to her.

As she turned toward Dr. Noel to ask him where Majeed was, even before she could open her mouth to utter a word, Dr. Noel responded. "325".

"Thank you."

Asha stared walking down the east corridor that had all speciality care patients who came into ER and were waiting to be moved to surgery or ICU or in some cases waiting to be discharged as cured or dead.

She reached the room and stood outside the door for a few seconds. She closed her eyes. When she opened them, a few teardrops had gathered near the corner of her eyes. As she wiped them with the back of her hand, she looked at the chart that was hanging on the door. She wanted to ensure that she was entering the right room.

She took a deep breath and without knocking, she stepped inside the room.

The chart outside room 323 read:

Patient Information

Name: Jason Stevens	Home Phone:
Address: Unknown	Office Phone:
Patient ID: 0000-44444	Fax:
Birth Date: 07/07/1981	Status: Active
Gender: Male	Marital Status: Unknown
Contact By: N/A	Race: White
Soc Sec No: Unknown	Language: N/A
Resp Prov: Dr. Asha Ram	MRN: MR-901-1111

Problems

Trauma—Intracranial

Splenic Rupture

Stab Wounds (Chest)

Neurosurgery scheduled

Right next door, inside room 325 lay Dr. Majeed Marikar, lifeless, his body cold, his black hair crumpled, his eyes closed as if they were still dreaming of the wonderful future with Dr. Asha Ram, his stomach completely covered in dried blood, and his skin devoid of any glow.

The echoes of what Asha told Majeed on the night after their first altercation with their racist attackers at the grocery store reverberated through the thin walls of the UP Health System's ER building and reached his dead ears. *"There will be a day when these racist bastards will be at our mercy in the ER."*

But it may also be within my power to take a life; this awesome responsibility must be faced with great humbleness and awareness of my own frailty. Above all, I must not play at God.

A SPATIAL LOVE SONG

"You have no idea how long I have been wanting to do this."

"What if I told you I have been wanting to do this longer than you have been?"

"How do you know that for sure?"

"I just know."

With that, Carl ran a finger along Zoey's hairline till he reached her ear and tugged a lock of hair behind her ear ever so gently. She looked at him with her brown eyes wide open for a moment and then closed them in anticipation of what was to come.

With every breath he took, Carl thought he was smelling jasmine. He leaned closer toward her, moving a few inches, brought his mouth very close to hers, and stopped.

Zoey opened her eyes partially, and her eyes started fluttering. Heat rose from her stomach to her chest. She so wanted this. She could only focus on imagining how soft his firm lips might feel against hers and how addictively he was invading all her senses at that moment.

He stopped a few millimeters away from her mouth and could hear her heavy breathing as she began to part her lips slowly.

"How would you like to be kissed?" he whispered.

❖

She just hit "send" after carefully typing up a long email response to a coworker who had rebuked her for sending an email at 5:45 a.m. She wanted to give the coworker the benefit of doubt by assuming that his phone's notification settings may have woken him up after he received her email. But what put her off was the tone in his email response. Clearly, this was not the negative mood she wanted to start her day with.

She had planned on sending out a couple more email responses before she took her dog out for her morning walk in the neighborhood park. But this momentary anger made her realign her morning priorities. She really needed a breath of fresh air, and she told herself that those two emails could wait.

Entering the park, she could hear the mild rustling of leaves as a breeze set in. The flowers in the park this time of year were always bright and vast, covering the freshly cut grass. The trail around this small park was well laid out with asphalt, and there were decorative garden rocks on the side. The dog cherished this hour of the day.

She too enjoyed being in the park at this time of day, since it offered a variety of scenery, catering to her many senses, and the time she had for herself helped her clear her mind.

As the end of her walk neared, her mind was refreshed, and her body was energized for the day. At least it felt like that until she got back home.

Thoughts, unforeseen, always popped into her head during these walks, almost as frequently as how new answers to old problems unfolded.

New answers to old problems.

"Oh … shit! I forgot to block my calendar and get my pass. He will be waiting." She cursed herself and jogged back home in a rush.

❖

The tinny notes of the tireless wood thrushes perched on royal oak trees filled the air. Carl was standing underneath the tree, tapping his feet to the rhythmic birdsong. Unknown to him, his mind was humming a tune. He was leaning on the tree in a relaxed manner and looking to his left. His maroon-colored baseball hat gave some protection from the sun.

After about ten minutes, he broke a smile. There, about a hundred meters away, along the trail to his left, was the woman he was waiting for. Butterflies fluttered in his stomach, and his heart started racing in excitement with every step she took toward him. It was a deliciously magical feeling, this feeling of love, something Carl had once experienced twenty years ago, but now at forty-five, he felt that the magic hadn't been lost one bit, and he had the same sensation.

He could hear Zoey's boots clomp across the unpaved trail, crushing the tiny rocks underneath, from a hundred meters away. He imagined the smell of her hair from afar. He believed he could see Zoey smile behind her sunglasses. Dopamine rushed through his brain and his mind played a hundred symphonics at the same time. Zoey extended both her arms as she got closer. They locked themselves tightly in each other's arms to form a tight embrace for the next thirty seconds.

"Please don't tell me you've been waiting for a long time," she said.

"No. Maybe ten minutes max. I knew you'd be at least five minutes late. The usual." Carl still hadn't let go of Zoey and was holding her tight.

"You know, I almost missed getting my pass today for the park? You are lucky I was able to get one this morning." Zoey pinched his arm.

"I am the luckiest. Just to have you in my life, Zoey."

"Now, don't get all mushy!"

Carl and Zoey, now free from their embrace, moved a step back and were facing each other. The wood thrushes continued their singing. There was no one around in the park near those royal oaks, and that's precisely why Carl had suggested they meet there.

"So, how much time do you have really?" Carl asked.

"Well. Let's see. I guess I have fifty more minutes. Maybe add another five. I got to get home before the after-school chaos sets in the house," Zoey said with a frown.

"That sucks. I was really hoping I could take you to another spot today if you had another pass and maybe an extra hour. Someplace we have never been before. It's kind of boring to meet at the same two or three spots secretively. Don't you think? I want to spice it up a bit." Carl laughed.

"Tell me more. I will plan better the next time."

"No, I can't tell you. I want the new spot to be a surprise. Just let me know which day, and I will plan the rest."

"Let me think … ummm … How about next Wednesday? Same time? But I will make sure I have an extra hour," Zoey said.

"Fantastic. It's a deal then. And one more thing. This is a public place. So …"

"What? Meeting in public? Are you crazy?" Zoey was agitated.

"Relax, Zoey. Don't you trust me? I just want the world … err … okay … a hundred people … well … even if it's a hundred people … I want them to know that I am in love with this most amazing woman. I want them to see us. Just once. Maybe a few minutes, that's all. I will make sure this doesn't hurt us. They will all be strangers," Carl responded as if he was anticipating this reaction from Zoey.

"Too risky and precarious, I feel. But …" Zoey was only partially convinced.

"I know. Trust me." Carl held Zoey's hands tight and came closer.

"I trust you, Carl. Of course, I do. Look at me. A forty-six-year-old woman, with a husband, daughters, a family, and so many other established social connections. I am here with you. Am I not? I am living this other life with you. Because I so want this, Carl. I do love you. I do trust you. But I don't want to jeopardize this life because of one adventure. I just want this to go on forever. I want to love you and be with you for as long as you continue to love me the same way you do now."

"Zoey, I get it. I get that you have more at stake in this romance than I do. My other life … that's … that's mostly in the past. This feels like my only life. You, this feeling of love. This is all I think of all day. But …" Carl started choking.

"Hey! Look at me. Let's do it. Okay? I trust you to play it safe. I will go wherever you take me. I am ready for the adventure." Zoey kissed his moist eyes as he closed them.

There was nothing more Carl wanted at that moment. After a few minutes of silence, Carl decided to spread the picnic blanket he had brought with him. He opened the picnic basket and took out a bottle of wine.

"This all feels surreal. I didn't think you'd say yes when I asked you out for the first time two months back. I mean … you are single, and so many single women were always swarming around you. What were my chances?" Zoey sounded like she was still trying to come to terms with their romance.

"Are you kidding? Do you even realize what you are asking? If you ask any of our mutual friends, they would say you could do better than me. Err. Correction. You did do better than me. Damien. Your husband. And then something happened that you decided to ask me out."

"Let's not talk about him. I want this time I spend with you to be only about us. When I am with you, Carl, you know, I feel like I am starting anew. It's like this life feels more purposeful. Like I have a whole new future that awaits me, and I am dreaming of doing things with you … you know … just you and me. None of the baggage from my other life follows me here. You have no idea how happy I feel." Zoey was wide eyed as she explained what this time she got to spend with Carl meant to her.

"Maybe I do. Maybe I do have an idea of how happy you feel. Because I feel the same too. Every waking minute of my existence in the last two years has revolved around this future you are talking about."

"The future is here, baby." Zoey raised her glass of wine.

"But wait. You said two years. What do you mean?"

"Just because you didn't think about me until about two months ago doesn't mean I didn't think about you sooner." Carl gave a gentle tap on Zoey's lap.

"Two long years? I had waited about that long too for you to make the move. To ask me out. Or say something. But you never did. So, I just decided to ask you out."

"Really?" Carl's eyes gleamed and he blushed.

"Well. Even if we had said something to each other two years ago, do you think this would have been possible? Like what we are doing right now? I mean, I have the greatest luxury of living two lives."

"About that …" Carl stopped mid-sentence. He didn't want to remind her of her home, her family, Damien, among other things. This moment belonged to them. Only them.

"About what?"

"Never mind. Just wanted to remind you about our next rendezvous." Carl collected himself as he looked at his watch.

"It's time to go, I guess." Zoey reluctantly got up.

"I want to say, please don't go. But I won't. I can't. By the way, Zoey, remember the song I was talking about? It's almost done. I will be ready to record your voice for the song in a week or two."

"I can't wait. It's been way too long since I sang for an audience. Probably not since our college days. This should be fun. I am really looking forward to it. Just lower your bar of expectations, all right?" Zoey smiled and waved goodbye.

"Love you!"

"Love you too!"

Carl watched Zoey walk back in the direction she came from. He watched her denim skirt, denim jacket, boots, and her long, unbridled hair fade into the clouds.

❖

He was sitting quietly at his desk and staring through his window.

The dusk setting in the busy suburb had brought bicyclists and skaters onto the streets. There were occasional joggers and dog walkers. He saw the lady next door watering her plants. In the alley across from his window, there was a couple holding hands on the rooftop of a building, completely oblivious to their surroundings, and the well-planned suburban neighborhood was full of colors, thanks to seasonal flowers.

He was still in a state of jittery excitement after the meeting earlier that evening. He thought about their conversation, and as his mind raced to reflect on what had happened, he opened his computer and started typing.

> *We are like cities. Cities have streets, alleyways, small buildings, tall buildings, rooftops, gardens, sidewalks, hidden backyards, cracks on the roads and sidewalks, plants, tulips, daisies, and roses. People have them all too. When we present ourselves to the external world, we show only a snapshot of our pretty skyline, polished street corners, and well-groomed trees.*
>
> *Love changes all of that.*
>
> *When you fall in love, you find these hidden places in the other person, places even they didn't know existed in them. You find daisies sprouting out of a sidewalk crack, you see a rose bush leaning on a hidden fence, and you spot the graphical symmetry in the shadow of the two adjacent buildings under evening sun. When you are in love with someone, you really find beauty in all of them, even the ones they wouldn't have thought of calling beautiful themselves.*

He closed his laptop and rearranged the items on his table that had been disturbed during the course of the day. He picked up an amulet and smiled. This was his lucky one. Laura had given it to him on their sixth anniversary. The last anniversary they celebrated together. He held it in his right palm, looked at it longingly for a moment, and put it back where it belonged.

He got out of his work chair, walked a few feet to his studio desk, the one on the other side of the room and away from the window. It had already become dark outside. This studio desk was where he produced most of his music. From conceptualization to mastering, all his musical magic happened here.

Zoey was early today. She had planned her day better, was ahead of her planned schedule with most of her tasks, and her coworker was able to substitute for her at the last meeting of the day. Days like these in a management consultant's life were rare.

She arrived at the same spot. The wood thrushes were cooing, but they didn't reach Zoey's ears. She was looking forward to the next couple of hours, and her mind was filled with suspense.

Which public place has Carl thought of? Who is going to be the most likely person to see me there? If someone I know sees me, what kind of trouble will I get into? Will Damien stop loving me if he finds out? Who gets custody of the girls if we end up getting divorced? Oh, gosh … please … I don't want to divorce Damien. He is a great partner. He is a wonderful dad.

Thoughts were running so wild that she completely missed Carl's arrival.

"Nervous much?" Carl whispered near her right ear.

Zoey was startled for a second. "No … I mean a bit."

"Don't worry. I have it all planned out. Yes, there may be some surprises. But that's the sort of adventure we seek, right?"

"Not me. You are the one who wants to show off your new romantic interest."

"You are right. Listen, if you don't want to do it, that's fine. We don't have to do this."

"I'm in. I want to partake in the thrill. Come what may. We will deal with the consequences later."

Carl and Zoey sat on the picnic blanket. A bottle of zinfandel later, Carl alerted that it was time for them to start their adventure. He opened another bag he had brought with him. The bag had clothes for Zoey. "There is a spot over there. Behind those two trees. We are going to go there and change."

"You really have thought this through, haven't you?"

"I need you to record that song for me, honey. I can't wait to have you over at my studio. If that must happen, you and I know we need to do this. We need to."

❖

Funerals are just like weddings. In fact, they have more similarities than most notice. Both are emotional days marking a big milestone in the lives of friends and families. The environment during weddings and funerals includes both happy and sad moments with them overflowing and overlapping into each other throughout the day. They are not at opposite ends, as most seem to think. There are funny toasts and speeches, elaborate ceremonies and rituals, carefully selected food and drinks, and beautiful dresses and suits in both. Eventually, they both are about shifts in the membership of a family. A wedding formalizes adding someone physically to the family, while a funeral formalizes physically taking someone away. There is one big difference between the two, though. As much as a wedding is a real celebration of two loving individuals saying a vow to start a new life together, a funeral is all about real celebration of true love, and the joy for the bright hope of tomorrow. Funerals are where the reality of one's worldview and its validity are brought to bear. There is something pure about the love you experience at funerals.

"Black? Are we going to a funeral?" Zoey hadn't expected this.

"Yes, we are."

"Seriously?" Zoey was clearly amused but tried hard not to show it.

"Come on! I had to do a lot of homework to pick this funeral. It will be fun. I mean … not for the family. But for us. I read somewhere that weddings and funerals are more alike than we think. There's a ceremony, people show up dressed in uncomfortable clothes, there's food and awkward small talk. They both last a couple of hours. The big difference? At funerals, no one's judging you — not your outfit, not your plus-one, not your life choices. It's the one party where you can show up late, cry openly, and still be the second-most dramatic person in the room. Like … there is a sense of calmness all around. No one is going to look at you and try to guess who you are. They are going to look at your eyes with sympathy, like they think they know what we are going through because they too share our grief." Carl went on and on about how funerals are better than weddings.

"I get it, Carl. I get it. But will anyone be surprised to see us? Did you inform the family that we are coming?"

"I didn't. We are going to gatecrash. Like I said, no one is going to talk to us in that environment. No one will try to guess who we are. I'm guessing there'll be about 120 people. Seems about right for a gathering like this. We will quietly walk into the family home. Stand back. Grab a drink and some food when they open it up, slip way to the garden at the right moment, find a quiet place, and leave when our time's up." Carl really had thought it through.

"I can't believe we are really going to do this!"

"Let's go. We should be there within the next fifteen minutes if we start walking out of the south entrance." Carl held Zoey's hands tightly.

They walked away from the royal oak tree to the family home.

Since Mr. Johnson's funeral was taking place at his 2,500-square-foot family home, the whole atmosphere had a bit of an informal vibe. The funeral director was standing right outside the main door, greeting everyone as they walked in. Mr. Johnson lay in a solid-red cherry casket in the living room, close to the fireplace and mantel. The casket had beautiful carvings of musical notes all around. Mrs. Johnson and their two adult children were seated next to the casket, and there were four rows of seating provided for those who preferred to sit. Those who couldn't get a chair were standing. Zoey and Carl entered the house before the ceremonies began, and they quietly hid behind the tallest person in the last standing row.

A man in religious garb called the ceremony to order, and a couple of small children started singing some hymns. There was a middle-aged man playing the organ.

Zoey could see Mrs. Johnson wipe a tear off her right eye. She wondered how long they had been married.

"She looks like she is in her eighties. So, fifty-five to sixty years if this was their first marriage," she whispered to herself.

"Did you say something?" Carl reached out for her.

"I am sorry. I was just moved … by …"

"By the hymn?"

"Ahem … yeah … by the hymn."

"Didn't think you were the religious kind."

"I'm not. Just …" Zoey was stumbling and trying to make up something.

"I know you aren't. I was just kidding."

"I was just wondering how long they had been married. The Johnsons? Fifty-five years?"

"I have no idea. Maybe."

For the next forty minutes or so, it was all about Mr. Johnson. Sons, grandchildren, nieces, and nephews—they all came to the front and shared sentimentally moving and charmingly funny stories about Mr. Johnson. It was clear to Zoey and Carl that he had lived a full life, one that touched many others' lives, and he was and still is so loved by everyone who knew him.

"He was my orchestra conductor when I was playing for this city orchestra. Been a while."

"Wait. So, there could be people here who could recognize you?"

"Most likely not. Because I was in high school when I was playing in the orchestra. Look at me now!" Carl laughed.

They both were getting tired of whispering to each other.

"What's next?"

"The committal service should follow the hymn. So, there is more music, then all the guests pay their respects to the man, and then we are done. Drinks and hors d'oeuvres will be served in the other room for those who are not going to the committal service. If you are going, then you need to follow the hearse, and once the burial is over, you may come back here for lunch." The tall man standing in front of them turned back and blurted out the entire agenda like he was the funeral planner, which, in fact, he was.

"Thank you. That is helpful." Zoey was polite and yet showing her disinterest in prolonging the conversation. She was more worried about someone finding out they were there.

"How do you know Mr. Johnson?" the tall man asked.

Oh, no! It's happening … Zoey was freaking out in her mind.

"Umm … we are … he is … was … Mr. Johnson's student. Like from thirty years ago."

"He was a great teacher, wasn't he?" the tall man said.

"Yes. He was. We will all miss him," Zoey replied.

As soon as the tall man turned away from them and faced the front of the room, Carl held Zoey's wrists and whisked her away from the crowd to the dining room. They saw a banquet server standing with a tray of wine. They looked at him, and he started walking toward them. They each grabbed a glass of wine and smiled.

"What a thrill it has been!" Zoey pushed Carl to the corner of the dining room so the banquet servers were not forced to stare at them.

"Let's have a couple of glasses of wine and then …" Carl paused.

"Are you saying you have planned more thrills?"

"Listen. When the crowd disperses after the ceremony, will you follow me to the back yard? Through that patio door?"

"Sure."

They heard the same two familiar voices singing again.

"This must be the last hymn before Mr. Johnson leaves his home for the last time." Carl nodded.

"I feel terribly sorry for Mrs. Johnson. I can't imagine her pain." Zoey added sympathetically.

Carl felt a sudden sense of amusement when he realized the situation he had brought himself into and that made him chuckle. He quickly covered his mouth in mild embarrassment. The banquet servers turned toward them. "Everything all right, sir?"

"Yes. Yes. "Everything's fine, thank you," Carl said, his voice warm but edged with the awkwardness of their surroundings. "Except for Mr. Johnson, of course. This really isn't his ideal situation."

Both Carl and Zoey exchanged a glance, knowing this wasn't the place for their usual antics. But then again, when had that ever stopped them? They were fully aware of the gravity of the ceremony surrounding them, of the sacredness of the moment. Yet, they couldn't help but relish the absurdity of their little adventure. After all, it wasn't every day they had the chance to be in a public space where no one would judge them—just two souls secretly seeking a moment of freedom in the most unexpected of places.

"We are being mean," she whispered while trying to control her smile.

"Hey, the ceremony is over. I am quietly slipping to the back yard. Come with me." Carl slipped away from the dining room quickly.

When Zoey made it to the back yard, she saw him at the far corner standing between a fountain and the picket fence. There was no one else around.

"You look beautiful!" Carl said, seeing Zoey walk toward him.

"So, what are we doing here?"

"We have got twenty minutes before we leave this place. I just wanted to find a quiet place where I could spend some time with you and hear you talk. That's all."

"O … k-a-y …" a bewildered Zoey said.

"You know there's a reason why we are here."

"I do."

"Zoey, I am almost done with the song. The next time we meet, I will be able to tell you when you could come over to my studio."

"I can't wait. But …"

"What?"

"Nothing. Forget about it."

"Come on, Zoey! What is it?"

"Not a big deal. I will figure it out before we meet the next time."

"You can tell me now, Zoey. I may not have the answer. Why don't you try?"

"It's Damien, Carl. I have a feeling he knows. Or at least he suspects something."

"Hmmm …"

"The funny thing is, twenty years ago, he and I … Damien … He was the one who actually brought it up. You know the idea of being in love with someone else while he was with me and while he still loved me. He asked me how I would react."

"And?" Carl wanted to know more but wasn't sure how to show his inquisitiveness.

"Don't think we delved deep into the topic. It was … you know … one of those many conversations that didn't have a start and a logical end."

"So, how do you think he would react if he finds out you are seeing me?"

"How do you see this, Carl? Like … the woman you love is actually living another life. Spending time with another man. Perhaps loving him too. How do you process this? I don't think we have ever talked about this."

"Yeah … we have always tried to keep our other lives away when we are together."

"Correct."

"Here's the thing. I love you so much, Zoey, that I wish so many things had been different in our lives. So many. But then, that's all past. Believe me, I do think about this often. What if there was no Damien in our lives? In your life, that is. Just like there is no Laura in my life. What if? Then I become more pragmatic. It's not my choice to have Damien in your life or not. Is it? If you choose to have him but still give me the pleasure and satisfaction of knowing that you love me too, I guess I will have to keep reconciling my absolute desire to spend every minute of the rest of my life with you, with your desire to do what you want to do. Life's hard. Learning to appreciate your love is the thing I cherish most right now in my life, and that makes my life not as hard. So, yeah. That's the only thing I want to focus on. Appreciating and reciprocating your love. I am not going to waste my time analyzing the rights and the wrongs." Carl became a bit pensive.

"Wow. That's more insightful than what I could come up with, Carl. This means so much to me. I love you for a reason, and you reassured me why I would be a fool not to be in love with you for the rest of my life. Thank you." Zoey wiped her tears.

Carl sensed that the conversation had turned out a bit heavier, and he checked his watch.

"We got to go. To the park, change, and then leave. Before that, I must do something quick."

"What?"

"I wish I could explain how much you are tempting me. But I don't have time for that," Carl said.

It was clearly a rhetorical statement.

"So, if I may …"

His fingers traced slowly down Zoey's spine, his breath coming more quickly against her skin. Zoey was expecting this. And she was wanting this. Her hands went limp on his chest, and she felt light-headed for a couple of seconds again. He tilted his head slowly and touched his cool lips on hers, very carefully, parting them slightly. Shivers of pleasure shot through her body as he deepened the kiss, parting her lips further. She sparked alive and the rush of sensations crawling across through their bodies was maddening. Scary and thrilling. They were, after all making out at a funeral service and at a stranger's house.

Zoey kept wondering if Mr. Johnson would have approved of their romantic deeds in his back yard.

There is something pure about the love you experience at funerals.

Zoey quickened her pace as the clouds began to gather again. Droplets were dripping from the leaves from the earlier rain clouds that went over the park. For a few minutes now, the sky had been post-card perfect, despite the earlier rains, but it was changing. The beautiful cocktail-blue shade was beginning to darken into ashen gray. Large pillows of cloud were forming, blotting the sun's golden hue.

Carl had already taken shelter under the tree. He had an umbrella. A yellow one, blending with the seasonal leaf colors that seemed to have taken over the park. He was looking up to see if the oncoming rain would ruin their date. It had already been a week since he saw Zoey. Even though they had been exchanging messages regularly, this was different. The wood thrushes were not to be found, but he was still mumbling a tune.

"Talking to the clouds?" Zoey startled him.

He quickly recovered and took a deep breath. "You must not blame me if I do talk to the clouds," Carl raised both his hands and pointed them to the sky. He smiled at her with a sense of warmth that his face hadn't seen in more than a week.

The air above in the clouds was pure and fine, much like their love. Zoey and Carl hugged. There were so many words exchanged in those two minutes of silence. Suddenly, the gray clouds started to make way for the cocktail blue, while the wood thrushes flew back to their favorite spot.

"Do you even for a moment think about the morality of all this?" Zoey asked.

"This? This moment of happiness you and I experience when we are together? Where does morality come in here?"

"Carl, I have been struggling with it for the past few days. I thought I had more clarity when we started seeing each other. But the more I think about what if others find out, I am torn." Zoey looked deep into Carl's eyes.

"Babe, maybe because I am a man or maybe because I am single, I guess the consequences of what others think as right and wrong bear less on me. Besides …"

The wood thrushes above them started making cooing sounds to woo his mate. They could hear more cooing and fluttering of feathers.

Carl continued. "You know. I have stopped worrying about rights and wrongs. At least when it comes to love. If loving someone gives me happiness and does the same to the one being loved, then I believe I am right. It is right."

"Right …"

"What do you think, Zoey? Do you think what you … I mean we … are doing is wrong?"

"No. Everything in the world doesn't have to fall into these two categories, right and wrong. Does it? Perhaps that kind of a binary view works up to a certain age, so as a child you do not put yourself in danger. But as an adult, I have come to realize that most things in the world do not fall into the right and wrong categories. Really. Most everything in the world is just different. And there's nothing wrong with different. Maybe we all should learn to let things be different and not try to make them black or white, right or wrong. You know, we can let them be gray."

"I completely agree. Why are we talking about this now again?"

"Like I said, I wanted to make sure we shared the same view. When someone finds out, I don't want either of us to be under the pressure of being judged by others and make decisions that will hurt either of us. Because I truly and madly am in love with you, Carl. And this is very important to me."

"Then let's stop talking about it. And make use of this precious time we have."

Carl took a step in her direction. He could feel her accelerated pulse from a distance. Zoey was looking directly into Carl's eyes and didn't allow them to disarm her. She quickly moved forward to hold his head from the back and pushed it forward to kiss. Zoey's lips crushed on his unrestrained. She cupped his face with both hands as his fingers slid along her slender forearms to meet hers for a moment until she nudged him forward. Unlocking her lips from his, she gave a victorious smile.

"That … that was lovely." He was blushing.

"Your lips. They taste like maple syrup. And that stubble on your face … that was bothering me a bit."

"I thought that wouldn't make a difference and was too lazy to shave today. I was finishing up our song."

"That reminds me. Did our last public meeting help? Were you able to get the pass to get me to your studio? When can I visit you? When can we sing together and record the song? And more importantly, when can we do more of what we just did but on a bed?" Zoey winked at Carl.

"Trust me, I am ready to take you right now. But there is one last kink to be ironed out in the song. I should be done with it by tomorrow. So, the next time we meet, you could come directly to my house, and we can record the song. And do more, of course, you know to take care of all the unfinished business." Carl winked back.

When they said their goodbyes that evening before they left the park, Carl promised Zoey that he would message the song verses to her so she could familiarize herself with the words and the emotions. He mentioned that this was a poem he had started writing almost ten years ago but had the inspiration to complete it only after Zoey asked him out for the first time.

Carl also made a mental note of something that occurred to him when he was walking back home.

To fall in love is to become vulnerable. And you want to protect your love by carefully wrapping it and putting it in a safe of selfishness. Inside the safe, it will change—your love for someone will change and become impenetrable and unbreakable.

❖

Olivia was staring at her computer.

She thought she heard the front door open and her daughters walk in from school. But her mind was still in a daze. She put her headset away and rubbed the deep marks it had made on her forehead and temples. It was time to greet her daughters, get their evening snacks out, and take the dog out for a walk. She remembered Damien was going out for dinner with his team tonight, which meant she had to fix dinner only for the three of them.

She got up from her chair and was about to take a step when she heard a notification alert on her phone. It was from Bryce. She looked around before she opened the message. And then something on her computer screen caught her eye. She panicked for a second but was also relieved that she saw it before she left the room.

There, in the top corner, was her Metaverse avatar, "Zoey," doing cartwheels and reminding her she hadn't logged out completely.

She logged out.

Ensuring that there was no one around, she opened the message from Bryce.

"Hey, it's me. Let me know when you get your next pass. I will drop my studio coordinates a few minutes before it is time for you to come. BTW, here is the song. Hope you like it. XOXO.

Beyond time
Beyond space
There is a place I'll meet you there

Beyond right
Beyond wrong
There is a song you can sing along

—*Dana Dajani*

❖

808080

"Are we going to be slaves again, Momma?"

"What did you say? No. Never, my princess. Never. I ain't gonna let that happen. You hear me now, sweetheart? Why don't you close your eyes and just sleep tight as Mommy sings your favorite song for you?"

Alexis Lewis covered Nia with a maroon-and-gray checkered blanket and started humming a slightly modified version of an Ella Fitzgerald song, which almost always worked for Nia.

Good night, my love, the tired moon is descending
Good night, my Nia, the tired moon is descending

It was so heavenly, holding you close to me
It will be heavenly, to hold you again in my dream
The stars above have promised to meet us tomorrow

Good night, my love, your mommy is kneeling beside you
Good night, my love, to Dreamland the Sandman will guide you
Come now, you sleepy head, close your eyes, go to bed
My precious sleepy head, you mustn't play peek-a-boo

Nia smiled with her eyes closed, and Alexis wiped a teardrop that just fell on her right hand.

Precinct 16000
Southeast Zone

Placement Unit

Captain Foreman was busy keying in new data on his computer. He was sitting in a corner cubicle of the first floor of this newly commissioned building. He had a large window to peer outside if he chose to turn toward his left, but it would have merely provided him a gloomy view of an almost empty concrete parking lot, which someday could be filled with cars.

This placement office building was new for Precinct 16000. It was a two-story red building airing a rather stodgy style, a very common architectural approach taken by local administrative bodies of the time. And Captain Foreman was the first person to head this particular placement unit since its inception. The responsibilities of his job were evolving, as did the other jobs' responsibilities in all other units in the precinct. So, Foreman had the flexibility to define the basic framework of how his unit functioned.

He had three lieutenants, six sergeants, and twenty officers reporting to him in this unit. Almost double the team size he used to manage in his old role. His previous role wasn't the easiest, and Foreman was really looking forward to slipping into the new role and making it his own before the pressures of an established bureaucracy seeped in. He knew he had the opportunity to be the person establishing the new bureaucratic rules.

Foreman got off his seat and walked to the briefing room with a data card that updated itself in real time, even as he was walking. As he entered the briefing room, he quickly surveilled to ensure everyone who was to be there was there. He greeted everyone with a head nod and headed directly to the monitor and inserted his data card into a slot that opened up.

Within seconds, the monitor started displaying four different lists. Foreman could navigate through the lists simply using a hand-swipe motion, from about five feet away.

The first list was of all the Zeros who had ongoing placements, the second one was of all the Zeros who were ready for placements. The third one was of all the Zeros who were temporarily unavailable for placements while the fourth one was of all the newly arrived Zeros. For his Monday morning meetings, all Foreman needed was the second and third lists.

He called Lieutenant Cranshaw and asked him to walk through the second list. Cranshaw was in charge of new placements that week and would have already received this latest list by Friday night.

Cranshaw came prepared. He walked to the front of the room and quickly briefed everyone about his plan for the twenty-one people on the list for that week. Two of them were going to be placed at a poultry processing plant, the biggest one in the precinct, while four were being sent to the city planning office to help with some infrastructure projects, and the remaining fifteen were being sent to work at a retail chain store. All of them had placements confirmed for six weeks, beginning that Monday, which was the average placement duration for Zeros these days. Cranshaw also let Foreman know whom he had assigned for each of this group of placement journeys and introduced the sergeants and officers who were assigned to this group.

Captain Foreman asked all the assigned sergeants and officers to come forward and wait while he opened the third list. He was happy to see that this list had only two Zeros, and those two were not additions to the list, which meant they had already been accounted for all placement planning purposes. He now turned toward Lieutenant Cranshaw.

"Lieutenant, I hope your guys know the protocol. The equipment check, the medical check procedures, the drop-off and pick-up drill, etc. Anyone who hasn't done this before?"

"Sir, as a matter of fact, yes. We have a new officer who has joined us, and this will be his first week doing the placement rounds. Officer Raymond. He has completed all the training, and I've verified his credentials. He will be shadowing Officer Jules this week, sir. And Jules is a veteran in this, as you may know, sir."

"Welcome to Precinct 16000, Officer Raymond. I would like to have a word with you in private as soon as this meeting is dismissed. I am sure Lieutenant Cranshaw has prepped you well. Good luck!" said Captain Foreman with a firm voice.

"Yes, sir!," said Raymond, as he quietly watched his superiors exchange tactics for the week.

Foreman went on to discuss a few safety protocols, new guidelines issued by the Central Office for Zeros (COZ), and finally a quick update on his vision for the placement center before dismissing the meeting. The meeting lasted exactly twenty-four minutes, which was about the average duration a Foreman Monday morning briefing lasted.

Officer Raymond stayed in the room and waited for everyone else to leave.

"So, Officer, what brings you to 16000? I see it was a personal choice and not an operational transfer," Foreman said as he flipped through Raymond's personnel file.

"Captain, I requested a transfer to 16000 only to work in the placement unit. They say you run the best placement unit in the country, and nothing would give me more satisfaction than learning from the best," Raymond said without missing a beat, as if he knew exactly what Foreman was going to ask.

"That's a mighty flattering response, Officer. Flatter me once, shame on you, Flatter me twice, shame on me. Now, let's get you oriented quickly. No matter what you may have heard about my unit or about this precinct, remember this—we all are in this together. All precincts have a single objective. Burn the Zeros. Got that?"

"Yes, sir!"

"Remember, never trust a Zero. This job is thankless, as you know. And in this new role, unfortunately you don't have much time to learn. If you don't have any questions for me that Lieutenant Cranshaw can't answer, you are dismissed." Captain Foreman closed the file and exited.

"Yes, sir!" Raymond said.

Within twenty minutes, Raymond joined Jules in his vehicle with their test kits, equipment bags, and other operational essentials. The third one in the vehicle, the driver, was a medical doctor, Officer Barnes. They left the placement unit and drove directly to the residence quarters.

In precinct 16000, the largest precinct in the country, all Zeros resided in a single huge complex. With nine buildings just for residency purposes, one for training, one for medical and emergency supplies, one for food and related activities, and one relatively smaller building which housed the precinct's administrative unit, the residence was built on a seven-acre lot.

They pulled their vehicle in front of the training building.

Right outside the main entrance, there was a parking space exclusively for placement unit vehicles, and that's where they pulled in. As soon as the guard verified their identity, he went inside to alert his officers.

Six Zeros, two for poultry unit and four for city planning office, came outside with their placement trainer, and after the trainer verified a few data points on her handheld device, she shook hands with Officer Jules, who handed over his device to her, which she initialed to signal the transfer. This was a routine protocol.

The vehicle was large enough to carry at least thirty people. On this day, they were going to be driving it mostly empty. Once those six people got in and everyone was locked in their respective seats, the vehicle left the training building and went straight to the medical building, a four-minute drive.

Outside the medical building, there was a wait. It wasn't unusual for this time of day. The driver finally pulled into the designated parking space and was greeted by another guard, who asked for his identity. Once the formalities were sorted out, the six Zeros and three officers entered the building and walked quickly to room 101 on the ground floor.

Room 101 was where all gadget checks happened.

All Zeros, as soon as they arrived at a new precinct for the first time, were taken to the medical building for implants right away. "Gadgeting," as it was called, was an elaborate process. It took anywhere between eight and twenty-four hours, depending on the physical condition of the Zero being implanted.

A typical gadgeting process involved:

> Eye camera implant
> GPS tracker implant
> Body temp chip
> Vitals chip
> An arm motion sensor
> A feet sensor

Out of these, the eye camera implant was the most complicated procedure. But over the years, the medical professionals working for the administration had developed an advanced technology by which they could sense most of the complications even before the cameras were inserted. And yet, given the sensitivity of the organ, this was typically done at the end. So far, across all precincts, the success rate of eye camera implant had reached 96 percent, which had been a rapid improvement, given it was at 78 percent only about twelve months ago, when Zero-Sum Game (ZSG) became a federal policy and when it was officially launched.

But for Jules, Raymond, and Barnes, today's task was much simpler because they just had to do a quick status check of the implants on the six Zeros they were taking. Which was why they were in room 101.

As they waited there, Raymond looked up and saw a TV monitor showing a baseball game. He knew exactly which game it was as soon as he saw the collision near third base. A quick flash of memory rushed through his eyes, an image of him sitting in his living room with his friends watching this exact game live, game 4 of the 2017 World Series between Dodgers and Astros.

"Officer Jules …" a man in uniquely gaudy protective gear called out.

"Yes?"

"This way please." He led them all into a lab.

While the officers waited on the side of the lab where there were a few seats awkwardly laid out, the Zeros were asked to enter a moving bedlike chamber one by one. As they came out of the other side of the chamber, the machine beeped with the results on a screen right above, which the man in the gaudy suit was watching.

It took only ten minutes, and all six men were cleared. In other words, their implants were working as expected. Raymond and Jules had to initial a few screens on the device the medical professional handed over to them. Once the formalities in the medical building were done, it was time for drop-off, the last of their morning routine in the officers' placement journey.

The first stop was the poultry plant. Like other businesses that employed Zeros, this plant had a separate entrance for them, ensuring that all the protocols were duly followed. It also allowed the business to enforce proper security for Zeros while they were on their premises because they were responsible for the safety of these workers during regular working hours.

Jules walked with the two Zeros who were assigned at the poultry plant. He had to sign them in, as it was their first day at work, give some instructions to them, and most importantly provide direc-tions for their evening pick-up after work. Once they entered their temporary place of work, they worked like any other employee in that company and were totally under the discretion of their supervisors and managers as far as how they spent their workdays. While Jules was doing all that, he wanted Raymond to observe and take notes, which he did. The nervous duo clocked in and went into the poultry plant for their first day. From the next day onward, they knew they would be here an hour earlier, on time for the beginning of the general shift.

Jules and Raymond went back to their vehicle. The next stop was the city planning office. Jules asked Raymond to drop off the four Zeros who were scheduled to work there. Like a responsible mentor, he decided to observe Raymond from a distance. To his surprise, Raymond was very confident in the way he handled all the steps, and he didn't seem to give the impression to anyone at the city planning office that he may had been on his first day at this job. It took him just ten minutes to drop them off. And with the drop-offs complete, the three of them got into their vehicle. They soon got busy with some data entry on their respective devices before heading back to their offices inside the placement unit.

It had been exactly twelve months since ZSG was launched nationwide. No one in these precincts, especially no one inside the special units, debated the ZSG program anymore. It was the law of the land, and they were all there, implementing it within the power granted to them by the administration. No one inside the precincts would talk about the deplorable ethics behind ZSG, the regressive nature of the program, and the absolute inhumanity of it all anymore. It was something they all signed up for proudly and passionately. In some cases, they even convinced themselves they were doing it patriotically.

But Raymond? He may have been an exception.

ZSG

When ZSG was announced by the president in the year 2038, for all practical purposes, Black Americans had already lost many of their basic rights for almost a decade, albeit gradually. Things were being given a formal shape in 2038 through ZSG. The debate over formalizing a program like ZSG was not a nationwide one, as the white minority would never let go of their control.

Just like how the country had been constitutionally framed from day one, it was not the tyranny of majority that they were worried about but the popular democracy. That fear showed in the way the power distribution, electoral processes, and even judicial selection had been designed with the white minority always having the upper hand no matter what the overall demographic distribution of the country was. Implementing ZSG was never a question of *if* under this president but was always a simple question of how long it was going to take to cross those bureaucratic hurdles in the respective legislative bodies around the country.

Even though ZSG was a federal program all states were mandated to participate in, there were a few states that still had the power within the constitutional framework to chart out their own course to join ZSG under their own mutually agreed-upon timelines with the federal government. This meant the white minority who held the majority federal power had to patiently work within the system for more than ten years to plant their stooges in these states in order to manipulate the decisions that demographically had more reasons not to participate in ZSG.

If one had to summarize ZSG, it was a federal program launched to strip all the citizenship rights of Black Americans, separate them into various precincts, provide them basic living arrangements, find employment opportunities for them so they could continue to be beneficial to the white business owners and to be profitable for the government as long as they were alive, and support them till they either died or became completely unemployable.

The ultimate objective of ZSG was not openly discussed or disclosed, though everyone knew what it was. A majority of White Americans seemed to be on board with ZSG, if the president's approval ratings were any indication.

Precinct 14000

Midwest Zone

Residence Quarters

Precinct 14000 was the only precinct in the Midwest zone for Zeros. There was a historic reason for this, and that had everything to do with the population of Zeros in the area.

Even though ZSG as a program was only a year old, the program had successfully managed to admit about 85 percent of the country's overall Zeros population as per the last census. There were processes in place and laws in motion in each state on how the authorities closed in on each of their target individuals or a target family to induct them into the program. They gave a voluntary registration option for the first thirty days, and only 15 percent of the population took advantage of that. So, they had to start forcefully inducting the rest. It was only getting harder and harder as the days went by, because the remaining Zeros who hadn't yet been admitted to the program were really trying to escape from the program. The president had announced that his administration's goal was a net 99 percent admission rate within the next three months and 100 percent within the next six months.

When Zeros were rounded up by state authorities, they worked with the central ZSG unit to start the process of formally inducting them into the program. Only after they had initiated a request would a formal allocation happen. Once the central ZSG unit assigned a specific precinct for a Zero, the state authorities usually had about five to seven days to bring the Zeros to the respective precinct. And a Zero's first introduction to ZSG began at the Residence Quarters, usually at an admission unit situated somewhere inside the quarters.

On this dreary Tuesday, Captain Williams, who had been running this residence quarters from day one of ZSG, was unusually agitated, and he was not having the time of his day to listen to the excuses a couple of his lieutenants were giving for the sudden increase in the number of disabled Zeros in their precinct. Anytime a precinct had a new Zero medically marked as "disabled," it meant the Zero couldn't be employed and hence, from that point onward, that Zero would become a cost center for the precinct instead of being a profit center. So, it was in the precinct's best interest to have a plan for the disabled Zeros. If temporary disability was somewhat manageable, it was permanent disability that initiated a highly inhumane journey for that Zero, eventually resulting in "termination." Again, given that ZSG was a relatively nascent program, each precinct followed its own discretionary principles when it came to termination.

Captain Williams was one of those precinct heads who waited a tad longer than most of his contemporaries in other precincts before going down the path of termination. Maybe because he had fewer Zeros to deal with or maybe because he really believed in human miracles, Williams always said "Two more weeks and I am going to send you to the workshop to lift some heavy pipes. Get ready now!" or something encouraging along these lines when he met a disabled Zero. Such a raw and subtle humane tone was a bit of a misnomer among his peers and his unit officers, but Williams never cared for such misrepresentations, as he knew he could get way with being a bit lenient here. He still had the country's highest profitability ratio per Zero, thus making every other precinct captain envious of him.

"All right, Captain, then I will mark these two as perm, and I will put together a plan for them by tomorrow and take them off this temp list," Lieutenant Samuels said.

"Lieutenant, I think we are done here. You may go now. I need to receive the new admissions arriving." Captain Williams got off his chair and walked hurriedly to the reception area.

Williams was merely there in the reception area because he wanted to take a break. He had been discussing the disability cases with his team for more than an hour. He really was looking forward to getting out of his office and stretching his arms and legs a bit.

A green-and-yellow ZSG vehicle arrived right outside the front entrance. The officer who was sitting in the front jumped out of the vehicle and rushed inside the admission unit reception area. He ran to the registration desk to get his badge verified. Within a few minutes, all thirty-two new Zeros were bought inside the building. No one had a smile on their face. Williams was observing them and thinking to himself what on earth would be going through their minds at that very moment when their lives were going to be altered for the worse forever. The medical staff came and did a quick vitals check on all. There definitely was a frenzy of activity going on in that reception area, and Williams was just watching it all pensively.

Soon, the skills officer walked to the reception area with his handheld tablet. This initial assessment done by the skills officer was critical for the placement unit. The placement unit would get this assessment information right away, and they would work on placement opportunities from the next day onward. This whole cycle of how and when the skills officers did the initial assessment to how the placement units put together placement plans by coordinating with the training units to schedule required job training sessions before the Zeros stared their work was very well tested across all precincts.

It took approximately forty-five minutes for the skills officer to complete his work, and as he was about to leave, he spotted Captain Williams standing a few feet away.

"Good to see you here, Captain," Officer Peddleton said.

"Mr. Peddleton. A very good morning to you. Did we get a useful batch for you this time? Anything we need to know?" Williams was curious to know how this new batch of Zeros would perform in the professional world. The one mattered to him the most.

"All good, Captain. Except we may have one special case. I mean, we may have a Zero who has a unique skill or a couple of special skills actually, which I don't think our precinct can quite put to use. I recommend we do a follow-up on him and see if we need to transfer him to another precinct where his skill could be put to better use."

"Not bad, Officer. You were able to make that assessment quickly. Do you mind sending me that report when you get a chance?"

"Sure, Captain. As soon as I finalize this report, I will send it to you."

Transfers like these, although not very common, were not completely unheard of.

Precinct 12000

Central Zone

Residence Quarters

Alexis Lewis was already awake but was staring at the ceiling when the siren went off. It was the morning siren on weekdays. She shared her apartment with two other women. They all worked in the same area, but not for the same employer. Alexis and her roommates had one hour and fifteen minutes to get ready and be outside their building. They had one washroom and some essentials in their apartment, which let them have a quick breakfast before heading out. Lunch was usually provided by the employer, or the Zeros were given a brown-bag lunch on the vehicle that dropped them off, in case their employers didn't provide lunch.

Alexis looked at the single clock in their living room. She still had twenty minutes, and Shawanda was still in the shower, getting ready. Alexis thought about Nia and wondered for a moment if she should just not bother saying hello to her in the morning and instead meet her in the evening. She changed her mind quickly and opened her apartment door. She walked along the corridor for two hundred feet or so and stopped in front of apartment 493. She knocked.

"Is that Alexis?" came a voice from inside.

"Yes, it is, Denise. Can I quickly say hello to Nia, please?" Alexis was almost pleading.

"All right, only if you promise you'll be done in five minutes or less."

These five minutes were the most precious of Alexis's morning. Because all working people in the quarters couldn't live in the same apartment units with their children on weekdays. Alexis had all the freedom she needed to spend time with Nia after she got home from work, which was usually after 6 p.m. and on weekends. But Nia, and children like Nia, stayed in a separate apartment, typically within the same building, with a caregiver like Denise on weekdays. Alexis noticed Nia was still fast asleep. She quietly sneaked right between Nia and another girl sleeping to her right. She adjusted the maroon-and-gray checkered blanket, which lay crumpled and strewn.

"Good morning, Nia! Mommy is going to go to work. Just want to say how much I love you. I will see you in the evening, okay? Maybe you could teach me the new game you said you've just learned from your friends. What is it called?" Alexis was whispering while she kissed Nia on her cheeks.

"Guess my wish," Nia mumbled with a smile. Her eyes were still closed.

"That's right, I forgot the game's name. Guess my wish. Behave while Momma is gone, okay? Do your reading and writing practice lessons. Have fun and help your friends if you can." Alexis planted another kiss on Nia's cheek.

"Have a good day, Momma! I love you," Nia said through half-opened eyes.

Alexis got up and wiped a tear that had just formed in her right eye. She thanked Denise on her way out and rushed to her apartment. Both Shawanda and Tamara were ready by then. They had seven more minutes. Alexis thought she could have a small cup of coffee before they left. She ran to the kitchen and threw a spoon of instant coffee into her cup, added hot water, stirred it quickly, and gulped it down—all in two minutes.

When the vehicle arrived outside their building, they had already checked out in the monitor outside. Both Shawanda and Tamara would get lunch at their companies, while Alexis had to carry hers. Before she boarded her vehicle, the driver handed a brown bag to Alexis. Once the door closed, the seventeen passengers inside the bus looked at one another and exchanged muted smiles, as if to indicate and acknowledge the passage of one more bleak day. The mood inside the bus was just like it was yesterday and just like how it would be tomorrow.

"Alexis Lewis," the driver, a portly man in his fifties, called out. "Your stop is here!" he yelled.

Alexis worked at a very small electronics store. The owner, Mr. Hishem, a man in his sixties, had applied for one employee for his store when the ZSG employer lottery system opened up in his precinct, and he was lucky that he got allocated one, and that turned out to be Alexis. Alexis had retail experience in her pre-ZSG life, and this job was not a very stressful one for her at all. She occasionally had to play the role of salesperson, but mostly served as a cashier. Hishem didn't want to hire anyone else, so it was just Alexis and him all day. He usually got in after 11 a.m. and stayed till 8 p.m., the closing time, while Alexis got in at 8 a.m. and stayed till 5 p.m..

The eye cameras along with the GPS tracker installed inside her would capture a GPS code with an image and alert the placement unit that she had arrived at her place of work as soon as she walked into the store. There was a monitoring room inside each placement unit that kept track of all the Zeros' activities. They literally could track everything. Right from what they were seeing through their eyes to what their hand movements could mean, there were all kinds of images running through the screens. Each Zero had his or her data displayed on a specific screen inside the monitoring room. Algorithms were built to alert when unexpected behavior was encountered.

It was a rather quiet Tuesday morning at the store, and no sales were made until Hishem arrived. This was not very unusual for a weekday, as most of their buying customers visited only after noon.

"Alexis, how are you? Can you run the cash report for last week for me?" Hishem dropped his bag under his table as he settled down in his chair.

"Sure, Mr. Hishem." Alexis started generating a new report.

A customer walked into the store, looking tired. Alexis lifted her head from her monitor to look at the customer, and they made eye contact.

At the same time, inside the monitoring room, there was an alert.

"Look who is here trying to impress Alexis!"

"Is that Watterson?"

"Indeed it is. He already has put in an application for Alexis. He knows he is going to get approved. So, this is his way of softening things with her? Horny bastard!" a loud roar of laughter erupted in the monitoring room.

One of the dark sides of programs such as ZSG was the unintended but cruel side effects. Unknown to the federal command, a few precincts had started finding creative ways to generate some revenue on the side. For example, in precinct 12000, Captain Williams had approved a limited loaner scheme.

Every month, the precinct would pick ten female Zeros in their twenties or thirties and would rent them out to male suitors who wanted to pay for them. These male members of the society would have to apply, and if approved, they would get to have the company of one woman, once a week, for four hours. Depending on how many men applied in that particular month, a selected Zero could end up spending every evening with some man. It had never happened to any woman in this precinct yet, as this shady program was still new and being tested out. Only a very few people in the unit knew about this.

Alexis had been selected as one of the ten women for the following month. She had no idea about any of this, as the precinct authorities would share this with her only on the day of, if everything went as planned and her male suitor was found to be a trouble-free member of the society.

"Look at him, he is here clearly there to check her out. I bet he didn't go there to buy any phone."

"You are right!"

Hishem was getting a bit unsettled with the way Watterson was roaming around the store. He didn't want to offend any customers visiting his store, but on the other hand, he didn't want any loiterers. He kept staring at Watterson as he paced. After a few minutes, Watterson just left the store. It was one a bizarre experience. But before Watterson left, he dropped a small piece of paper, apparently intentionally. Hishem, from where he was sitting, didn't notice the paper being dropped, while Alexis noticed through the corner of her eyes—almost impossible for her eye camera to have alerted the monitoring room, as eye cameras didn't have a 360-degree range.

Alexis told herself that she would pick it up at the right time, when

Hishem moved to the other side of the store. She was also aware of how she was being monitored through all the implants in her body.

When Hishem actually strolled to the other side to do some inventory, Alexis rushed to the spot where Watterson had dropped the piece of paper and hovered over it with her feet without using her eyes to look at it so much. Once she felt the piece of paper with her feet, she quickly slipped her shoe off, grabbed the paper with her curled toes, and tossed it inside her shoe, slid her foot back in, and walked back to her seat behind the counter.

Precinct 16000
Southeast Zone

Raymond, Barnes, and Jules were having lunch. The morning had gone by uneventfully, and with no more briefings scheduled for the afternoon, the evening was going to be a regular affair as well for these officers. Just a couple of visits to the companies for a surprise inspection, filing the inspection reports, and finally completing their daily training exercise in their main office building were the sort of tasks Raymond was used to by then, after having spent two weeks on his new job.

"Hey, Barnes, do you mind if I ask you a question?" Jules said, grabbing a french fry from his plate.

"Not at all."

"Your record shows that you joined the police force just as ZSG was getting launched. I mean … some of us had no choice, and some of us like Raymond here were accidental. You know what I mean?"

"I'll be honest with you, Jules. I was thrilled to be part of this force. I had always wanted the police force to have complete control over how we treated them nig- … I mean Zeros. President after president, we had been hearing the same old BS. Didn't we? Finally, here is someone who is actually doing it. I was like … yes. This is exactly what I want my country to do. This is my calling. My patriotic calling. So, yeah, I wanted in. I would've done anything to be here. Turns out I was not alone. As you know, there were 120,000 new job applicants on the day before ZSG went official. Talk about patriotism." Barnes was not mincing any words, while comfortably munching on his burger.

Raymond was squirming in his seat but didn't make it very visible. He wanted to say something before Jules interrupted his train of thought.

"So, Raymond, I know you moved here exclusively to work under Captain Foreman. But what's your story? We haven't had much time to catch up since you joined. What's it like in your old precinct? Give us the scoop, Officer," Jules said in a curiously mocking tone.

Before moving to precinct 16000 in the Southeast Zone, Officer Raymond used to work at precinct 13000 in the Northeast Zone, where he was a residence warden.

As the rumor mill inside the police circle in precinct 13000 went, after ZSG was launched, Raymond either had some help inside the lab that certified his negative Zero results, or he just got lucky. It was open knowledge in the town he grew up in that Raymond's maternal grandmother was a slave descendant from an Alabama plantation. Raymond never openly had to defend or discuss his lab results with anyone inside the police force because he had a reputation for being an efficient officer. Being in the Northeast meant that the racial clashes were few, and Officer Raymond never had to be involved in a situation where he had to choose between his alleged slave ancestry and the prevailing police white supremacy.

"Well, Officer Jules, what you already know. I am not used to the aggressive nature of a program like ZSG. But I got along well with my folks in the residence quarters, you know. It was sort of mundane and yet was very satisfying to get these people situated … you know, people who came completely lost, with no hope in their eyes. In an odd way, it felt good to give them some purpose in life. That's what you folks at the placement units want. I mean we folks, now that I am one among you." Raymond paused for a second and smiled.

"You are right, Raymond. We need our profit centers to be fully productive, and for that, their mental state is critical. Can you pass me that ketchup please, Barnes?" Jules said.

"Sure." Barnes passed the ketchup to Jules and continued.

"But here is the thing, Raymond. We have seen presidents before. Haven't we? All trying to tiptoe around their whiteness but eventually winning elections only through the power of passive whiteness. Here we have someone, breaking the amulet open … finally. We are after all, going back to form, who we were, and not necessarily creating a new national order or something. Once you understand that aspect of our history, then ZSG won't seem like an aggressive program to you. Aren't you happy that we have someone who not only recognizes the symbol of whiteness but actually understands the power of it? This is not rewriting history. This is just … I don't know … this is just erasing a few dark pages in between," an animated Barnes said.

Raymond was about to respond to Barnes, but just then, another officer walked up to Raymond and stopped behind his chair. Raymond could sense that someone was hovering over his shoulder.

"Officer Raymond?" the other officer asked.

"Yes, that would be me." Raymond tried hard to read the badge on the other officer's shirt. "Officer Stevens, how may I help you?"

"Sir, I think Sergeant Kregs is looking for you. He said it is an urgent matter, and he needs to see you in his office within the next thirty minutes. He is heading out to a meeting soon. Like I said, it's apparently urgent."

"Sure. Thank you for passing the information, Officer."

He took a tissue, wiped his hands and around the corners of his mouth, cleaned up his plate and silverware, and arranged them all in the bluish-green tray.

"Well, gentlemen, I guess we have to continue this conversation some other time. It was a pleasure having your company over today's lunch. I enjoyed it thoroughly." Raymond stood.

"Likewise, Raymond. We'll see you later in the evening or tomorrow morning during drop-off. Behave now." Jules waved at Raymond as he walked toward the cafeteria door.

"Very interesting man, isn't he?" Barnes looked up and was curious to know what Jules thought.

"Aren't we all, Barnes? Sure, he comes from another zone with different demographics. He will get used to us. He has to. We will make him do that. This, after all, is the heart of America. Heart of ZSG. Raymond has to understand what this program truly represents. And where the country is truly heading. Yanks like him sometimes need sudden ice-water dips like these to shock their systems. You know. I really hope they transfer more kids from up there. We could teach them mushy hearts a lot about being strong. Being macho. Being a real American man." Jules flexed his arm, smiled, and went on.

"Couldn't agree more, Officer." Barnes flexed his arm too.

They fist-bumped each other. Loud laughter followed.

Meanwhile, Raymond had already reached the third floor and was waiting outside Sergeant Kregs's office. Within thirty seconds, he was ushered in by the administrative assistant.

"Good afternoon, Sergeant. This is Officer Raymond, reporting per your command."

"Oh! Afternoon, Officer. Thank you for making it so quickly. It's a matter of urgency only because I am not going to be available for the rest of the day." Kregs offered a weak smile.

Sergeant Kregs got up from his seat and walked toward the TV monitor on the other side of the wall. He pressed a few buttons, and it launched a new application that read "Transfer Protocol."

"Officer, I want you to watch this. I don't think you have ever done this before. And not many officers usually get to do this. We have a situation. Very uncommon. We need to transfer a Zero from 14000. That's in the Midwest Zone. It's not a security transfer. It's just an operational transfer, which usually means that our precinct needs this special skill or skills that this Zero has, for which precinct 14000 has no use currently. So, it's a win-win for all. With me?"

"Yes, sir."

"The way it works is simple. We need you to drive to precinct 14000 within the next forty-eight hours and complete the transfer papers, let my office know once it's done, and then we will transfer the negotiated purchase amount. Once they validate that, they will release the Zero to you. Remember, between the time they release the Zero and you bring him here and check him in at our administrative unit, the Zero is entirely your responsibility. This is why we chose you. We want someone who is honest, reliable, and strong. Someone who can defuse unfriendly situations in case they arise and effect a judicious resolution. After the Zero is handed over to you, you have about sixty hours to check him in here. With me till now, Officer?" Kregs knew he was throwing a lot of information at Raymond.

"I am with you, sir. I am honored that you've entrusted me with this responsibility. I will not let you or the precinct down." Raymond was truly thrilled about this opportunity, although he had no idea what he was getting himself into.

"All right then. My administrative assistant will put together a package for you, which you can pick up before you leave work this evening. A good evening reading assignment for you. Oh … you have to complete an online quiz after you finish reading that. It will help you mentally prepare for what's in store. Good luck! See you soon, Officer." Kregs walked back to his seat as he saw Raymond leave his office with a gentle nod.

The administrative assistant had the transfer package ready, which she handed over to Raymond. A data card and a safety kit, neatly packed inside an orange bag. Raymond peered into the bag as if to confirm that he received everything and waved goodbye to the administrative assistant before walking back to his office.

Precinct 14000
Midwest Zone

Residence Quarters

It was past 5:30 p.m. when Raymond's car pulled up in front of the administrative unit. Raymond drove six hours straight without any extended breaks. But he seemed strangely fresh and ready to go, like a man on a mission who had just been recharged. He walked past the main door after completing the formal check-in. The building layout looked familiar to him, as he had been working at the residence quarters in his previous job. He walked directly to the reception counter.

"Hello, my name is Officer Raymond. I am here to meet the sergeant in charge of transfers. I don't have an appointment, but I was told this didn't need an appointment. I hope I made it before your cutoff time for the day."

"Hello. Welcome to precinct 14000, Officer. Our cutoff time is 7 p.m. for transfers, so you have plenty of time. Let me check with Sergeant Mattis's office quickly while you wait." The receptionist picked up another device to place a call.

Within two minutes, she was addressing Raymond again. "All right, Officer. Sergeant Mattis is sending someone to check your credentials and the request. Once that passes, he says he would meet you."

As the receptionist indicated, there was someone from the transfer department meeting Raymond in the waiting area within a few minutes. All he needed was a data card and Raymond's badge credentials. He asked Raymond a couple of questions, and even before

Raymond could finish answering, the tablet flashed, "All checks complete. Transfer can proceed."

"That was quick," Raymond said, surprised.

"It was. It's all clean as far as I know. Let me send this to Sergeant Mattis right away," the officer said.

In fifteen minutes, Raymond entered Sergeant Mattis's office after being escorted by the officer who had come down to check his transfer data. Raymond walked into the office, and as soon as he stepped in, he had an eerie feeling.

Wow. This place is so much like Sergeant Kregs's office, he thought to himself.

"Welcome, Officer Raymond, to our precinct," Mattis said.

"Thank you for the warm welcome, sir."

"I don't like to waste our time. Let's get started with a few questions. I want to know a little bit about you, your record, and then we can complete the transfer formalities. As you know, it's an operational transfer. So, it's going to be quick," Mattis said in a commanding voice, getting up from his seat to walk to the mini-fridge.

"Listen, I can't offer officers any drinks in my office. I'd love to, as you are my guest. But I can't. I am sorry. I am permitted to open this mini-fridge only after 5 p.m., so, I've been waiting for this. Excuse me, if you don't mind."

Sergeant Mattis poured himself a frothy lager and took a big sip. He went on to ask a few questions about Raymond's police record. He was not just satisfied, but seemed impressed. Raymond was more than happy to share any information about his record, as he was always proud of his accomplishments.

It was time to start the transfer formalities. Mattis punched a few buttons on his large tablet to request the officer who escorted Raymond to come back to his office. When he gave Mattis the transfer data card from precinct 16000, Mattis quickly inserted that into his computer and looked at the huge monitor on the wall. Having handled these kinds of requests daily, Mattis was satisfied with the data. He initiated the approval process immediately.

"You may let your guy know we are ready!"

Raymond pulled out his mobile phone from his coat pocket and punched a few keys. Within seconds, he got a message that said, *click on this and open the wire transfer request.* After he launched the application, he just had to wait for a few seconds. Money was being transferred from one account to another in real time. The last step in this wire transfer process was to get an authorized signatory to accept from the recipient's end. Raymond let Mattis know that he should expect an alert soon. Mattis's tablet buzzed in about five seconds. He looked at the screen and quickly accepted the wire.

That was it. For ten thousand dollars, this Zero who would accompany Raymond in his car for at least six hours, after being sold from one precinct to another. Raymond tried to digest the uncomfortable thought that clouded his mind. Ghosts of his maternal grandmother's ancestry, whose fables he was familiar with, rushed through his mind.

What am I being part of right now? What am I doing here enabling the sale of a human being from one human being to another? The painful thought started nagging him.

"With that, Officer Raymond, I think we are done. You have a long drive ahead of you. If you go downstairs with the officer who escorted you here, he will let you know what the next steps are. Have a safe drive back home, Officer. And do let Kregs know he still owes me one for the bet he lost against me last year. Let's see if that son of a bitch still remembers." Mattis got up from his seat again.

Raymond stood and collected all his belongings from the table.

"Pleasure doing business with you, Officer Raymond!"

Raymond was accompanied by Officer James back to the ground floor.

"As you know, we have a guest house on the other side of the building. If you would like to spend the night here and head out tomorrow, let me know. I will have you taken care of by the guest services here. But if you are in a hurry, I will let the apartment warden know. Jamar will be here in less than twenty minutes," James briefed Raymond.

Raymond was tempted for a moment to take up the offer of spending the night and getting a good night's rest before driving again. But he dismissed his own whim.

"Thank you for the generous offer. I think I am going to be driving back home tonight. So, no need for any lodging."

"Perfect then. Just wait over there, and someone will see you within twenty minutes and hand you over your new property. It was good meeting you. You have a good night now, sir." James smiled and left.

Raymond moved slowly to the waiting area. That painful, uncomfortable thought was still nagging him. He picked up a digital magazine from the coffee table and started scrolling down. He didn't know how tired he was.

Twenty minutes later, someone was trying to wake Raymond up by tapping on his shoulder. "Officer Raymond."

"What? Who? … I am sorry. I must have dozed off." Raymond rubbed his eyes as he looked at the woman standing in front of him.

"Sir, Jamar Lewis, your transfer subject, is waiting outside with a guard. Whenever you are ready, you can head out and meet him."

"Wow, is it twenty minutes already? That's crazy. Thank you. I will see myself out. I will take care of the rest … ummm … Miss …"

"Drew. Have a good night."

"Night, Miss Drew. Thank you again!"

With that, Raymond was off to meet Jamar Alexis.

Alexis stood six-feet-four, lanky, with a well-trimmed beard, and was wearing a black shirt, blue jeans, and a pair of dark-blue Nike sneakers. Nothing distinctive about him. He looked like he was in his thirties.

As Raymond approached Jamar, who was standing near Raymond's car, a security guard approached Raymond.

"Sir, you may initial this, and you are all good to go. I will be happy to drop the Zero's bag in your trunk if you'd like."

"Sure." Raymond opened the trunk while simultaneously printing his initials on the tablet.

Jamar and Raymond exchanged an awkward smile. Raymond nodded as if to ask Jamar to get into the car. Jamar hesitated for a second if he should open the front passenger door or the rear door and decided to play it safe. He was about to open the rear door.

"Just hop into the front, Jamar," Raymond insisted. That made Jamar feel a bit relaxed. He got into the car and adjusted his seat back so his long legs could rest comfortably under the dashboard. Raymond settled in his seat, and they both put on their seatbelts.

They didn't exchange any words for the next forty-five minutes as the car left the cityscapes and entered the classical Midwestern landscape enveloped by kissing cornfields on both sides of the highway.

"Are you hungry?" Raymond asked Jamar without taking his eyes off the road. "Hey, man … are you asleep?" Raymond turned toward Jamar for a second. The thing about the highways in the Midwest is that you could afford to take your eyes off the road for a couple of seconds because the roads run straight for the most part.

That's when Jamar realized that they had been driving for forty-five minutes in absolute silence. No music. No audiobooks or podcasts. Absolute silence. But Jamar didn't think about it because he was thinking about his family. He was wondering how they were doing and if he would ever get to meet them.

"I am sorry, Officer. I guess I was just lost in my own world."

"No problem. Do you want to stop somewhere and grab a bite? I see a rest area coming up in the next five miles."

"Sure."

Jamar was really hungry. Within the next fifteen minutes, they were inside the food court with two trays of chicken sandwiches. They started looking for a corner table to sit. Jamar kept his tray on a vacant table and walked to get his drink. Raymond followed. They both filled their cups with fizzy drinks and settled on the plush cushions. The moon was almost full, and the sky was clear enough for them to see the moon through the window against which they were sitting. A few scattered stars made an appearance.

"So, Jamar, I hear you have some special skills," Raymond said, taking a bite out of his sandwich.

"Oh, that? I guess this whole human sale is for those skills. Am I right, Officer? I used to be in the United States Air Force. Wing commander. I've flown combat planes and the whole shtick, you could say. But I wonder if that's what you are buying me for." Jamar's voice had a tone of dry despair.

"Hey, man, listen. I am not your friend. Sitting with you here inside a restaurant in itself is a breach of protocol. I won't be surprised if I get an alert from my boss. You saw a few folks around here rolling their eyes when we walked in. So, I am not going to respond to your question. Also, that's the sort of question only folks above my pay grade would know about."

"Fair enough, Officer. I don't know what I am being traded for. Is it for my combat skills, my flying skills, or … I don't know. I would much rather stay in the Midwest Zone, closer to my family, you know." Jamar sniffled.

"What other skills do you have?"

"I used to work in the data maintenance team while I was in the air force. I know a few things about some special software programs the Pentagon uses."

"That might explain it then," Raymond said, finishing his sandwich. "So, where is your family?"

"They are in the Central Zone. Precinct 12000, the last I heard. I really miss them. My daughter is an angel. She must have turned seven last month." Jamar's eyes were beginning to well up.

"Why were you split up? Don't they try to keep the family together?" Raymond was genuinely curious.

"Must have got something to do with my encounters with the police in the recent past," Jamar said.

"What kind?" Raymond asked.

"From the point of view of the police, I guess I was going to assassinate an entire battalion of armed cops or some shit like that. From my perspective, though, I was walking outside a grocery store and accidentally bumped into a white customer, causing him to spill his beer case, which made him call the cops on me, and then that sort of made me flee the scene. They rounded me up. I resisted. I may have accidentally punched a couple of cops on their faces with my elbows as I tried to find my way out of their chokeholds. The kind of stuff that happens to every Black man in the country. Used to happen, I should correct myself. Now you … you all have put an end to this. Right? Successfully. Z … S … G. Z fucking S … G. No more unarmed Black man being shot to death kinda news. Well done."

"Wow." Raymond wasn't sure how else to react.

"I almost died. Then I got arrested. Was remanded in custody for three full weeks. Imagine if this was what happened to a veteran like me …" Jamar left the question rhetorically hanging for Raymond to complete it in his mind.

They picked up their trays and deposited them on the shelf. Raymond and Jamar quietly walked back to the car, both briefly lost in their thoughts. Raymond was thinking about Jamar's ordeal with his peers, while Jamar was mentally sending his goodnight wishes to his daughter.

After Raymond started the car, he turned toward Jamar again. "So, do you want to take a detour to go visit your family real quick before we head to our precinct?" Raymond completely caught himself with surprise with that question, and more importantly, with that line of thought.

"What are you talking about, Officer? Seriously. What are you talking about?"

"I am serious. It's against my code of conduct. I could get fired if I got caught doing this. But I checked the location of 12000 as we were walking back to the car, and it's going to be a short detour—like three or four hours tops. And I don't know how long we'd have to wait to find the right time to catch them. My guess is you could spend up to thirty minutes with your family before all alert systems get notified. As long as you keep your meeting under thirty minutes, we will be— we should be safe." Raymond was serious about the offer.

"Wow. I can't believe this. Absolutely, Officer. I will follow your instructions to the T and make sure I don't get caught or cause any trouble to you." Jamar was getting a bit excited and also a bit nervous.

"Give me two minutes, and I will initiate communication with my connections there!"

In the next ten minutes, Raymond had a plan. He didn't share any details with Jamar. He started driving. Now that the ice had been broken between the two men, the atmosphere in the car was a bit relaxed. Raymond turned his media player on, and out came smooth jazz. The notes kept them afloat, and it felt like they were sailing through the moonlit night.

Halfway into the drive to precinct 12000, Raymond wanted to check if Jamar was awake.

He was.

"I am not supposed to be asking this, but why did you voluntarily turn yourself in for ZSG?"

"I didn't, Officer. I didn't have a choice. They had my wife and daughter. They threatened to kill them if I didn't turn myself in. So, the choice was easy," Jamar replied.

"Sorry."

"It's all right. My people are used to this. Been used to this for a while now. Y'all have been training us for this day. We have been preparing ourselves for this destiny. We also have been prepping for what happens from here. We ain't giving up. Uh-hun. Not now. Not ever, sir."

"How was your life before all this? Let's say twelve to fifteen years ago. When you were with the air force?"

"It was better. It's an irony to say it was better. The thing with being us, Officer, is that we … our people have gone through so much for so many years. Centuries, really. We have always been the marginalized lot. From slaves to low-class citizens. Right? Heck, we fought for centuries to be even recognized as human beings. Then came our fight to have some basic rights to live as human beings. Your ancestors weren't easy. Was a hell of a fight. We eventually got that taken care of. Then we asked to be considered equal … I guess the day we started to fight for equality, that's when it hit the nerve of the next generations of your lot. Am I right? We had to constantly prove why we are worthy to be your equal and why we don't deserve what we deserve because you were all mocking us for our shitty lives after the so called equal rights were granted. Humiliating us constantly. The pressure was on us marginalized people all the time to be better and kinder than our oppressors. I mean, this is a form of structural violence designed to keep people nice and to keep people like us exhausted. I am not going to lie. We are exhausted, Officer. We are terribly exhausted. But if I quit because I am exhausted, who will guarantee some sort of a life with hope for my daughter, whose memory is all filled just with this precinct life right now?" Jamar was eloquent, precise, and poignant in venting out his thoughts. He hadn't had an opportunity to sit one-on-one with someone from the opposite side of the political spectrum, an oppressor, no less, in this case, and be able to freely share his thoughts.

Raymond was restlessly absorbing it all. He didn't say anything. He couldn't say anything even if he wanted to. He knew he just had to listen.

"Thank you, Officer, for letting me express my thoughts and feelings. I hope this stays here. Just here."

"Not a problem, Jamar. You have my word. I heard you."

The car continued to traverse in a straight line. The navigator on the device dashboard showed they had another one hundred miles to go. The moon was still bright. The kissing cornfields on both sides of the road had now been replaced by soybean fields. The rest of the landscape was mostly unaltered. They drove for another forty minutes in total silence. No smooth jazz to accompany them for these minutes.

"Jamar, I thought about what you said. I mean, I am still thinking about it. If I asked this in good faith, I am not sure how much you are going to trust me and answer. But I am going to try. What is your plan? How are you all planning to fight this regime? This ZSG? You gotta start somewhere …"

"Ha ha … Officer Raymond, is that a trick question?" Jamar laughed out loud. "Because if it is, I don't know the answer to that. If not, then I am not sure why I should be sharing that with you."

"Like I said, if you don't trust me, I can't help it. But …"

"Officer, let me ask you this question, if you don't mind. In good faith. Do you have any Black ancestry in your blood?" Jamar was straight and pointed with that question, which Raymond was not prepared for.

"What? What did you just ask? Why would you ask that?"

"Well, for starters, it's just an intuition. I can't put my fingers on exactly why I asked the question. Something tells me you just may have a soft corner for our cause. That maybe why I thought. Just an intuition. Never mind."

"I am not going to answer that question because I don't know the answer to that myself. The second part of your assessment is true. I may have a soft corner for your cause, and this entire road trip has been such a revelation of that side of me to myself. It feels almost therapeutic to say that out loud," Raymond said, smiling but without making eye contact with Jamar.

"Aha! Well, that's a start, Officer, isn't it? Soft corner is good. I am all for soft corners." Jamar laughed.

"Okay, will you answer my question then?" Raymond was really interested in knowing if Jamar had any serious plans.

"In that case, let me share with you what I can right now. Only in good faith. It's all in the beginning stages. Our first goal is to orga-nize." Jamar was looking at Raymond in his eyes while stressing the *organize* part.

For the next fifteen minutes, Jamar explained the details of his involvement with the anti-regime movement and things he was doing till then to help the movement. Raymond understood why Jamar's technical skills were so special and so unique. He also understood how the knowledge, precision planning, and thoughtfulness of someone like Jamar was critical to the success of the movement.

The navigator showed thirty more miles to their destination. Raymond took an exit ramp to pull the car into a rest area. He picked up his phone and pulled out a messaging application. He typed something in it and waited for a response. As soon as he saw the message, he turned toward Jamar and asked, "Are these your wife and daughter?"

Jamar looked at the picture. "Yes. That's Alexis, my wife, and Nia, my precious."

A few more exchanges later, Raymond once again looked at Jamar. "Well … we have a small situation. My contact says it's best we wait till at least late in the evening. When Alexis would be done with her workday. It means we have almost ten hours to kill. I suggest we sleep it off because there's nothing much we can safely do till then, in any case."

"As I said before, Officer, I will follow your instructions to the T. You are already putting yourself at risk by doing this. So, whatever you think is best and safe."

"Since I have your ears now, let me also tell you that we have a slight change in our plan. Before we sleep, I want you to hear it." Raymond went on to whisper the new plan.

Jamar was shocked, but he was getting more and more engaged. He animatedly explained something to Raymond, and within a few seconds, Raymond was on the phone again. As Jamar talked, Raymond stared at him and said something over the phone. Raymond continued to talk. When he was done, he hung up and took a deep breath.

"Now, we wait."

The two of them then pushed a couple of buttons on the device panel and waited for their seats to convert into a bed. The window screens came down automatically. And just like that, the interior of the car now turned into a comfortable Tokyo City hotel room-like setup.

Both men started snoring.

Precinct 12000
Central Zone

Inside the monitoring room.

"Hey, Pedro, did you see that arm movement alert from A718?"

A718 was the code for a specific employer who had employed Zeros.

"Yup. That's Alexis Lewis. She is the only one at A718. I am looking into it."

After a couple of minutes, Pedro confirmed that there were indeed some unusual feet and arm movements tracked. With no more details available at that point, Pedro took a call and just pinned it for future follow-up.

"Nothing alarming, as far as I can tell. But I pinned it. So, we'll keep an eye."

Inside the store, Alexis was contemplating how she was going to see what was on the piece of paper. She only had a hunch that the customer dropped it intentionally for her because if it was meant for Hishem, there probably were better ways to deliver whatever it was. And she was absolutely sure that it was deliberate on the part of that customer to drop it, not an accident at all. Her choices were limited. Another customer walked in and started enquiring about a new model that the store had started selling that week. It was a typical sales interaction. The customer completed the purchase within ten minutes and walked away. She hadn't seen these kinds of pleasant sales on a daily basis. Hishem smiled at Alexis as soon as the customer walked away.

Alexis decided to take a bathroom break. She convinced herself that was her best shot. Hishem, perhaps because of the small operation he was running, was more liberal with his only Zero employee, compared to other employers who employed Zeros around the country. He didn't have any special protocols for such bathroom breaks. Alexis turned toward Hishem, who was sitting twenty feet way on his chair, and let him know.

"Mr. Hishem, I will be back in a few. Is that okay?"

"Sure, Miss."

Alexis closed the bathroom door and sat on the toilet. The next task was to pull out the paper from her shoe without alerting the monitoring room. She had already guessed that her earlier movement to pick that piece of paper up from the floor would have sent alerts. These were common knowledge among the Zeros. And the officers didn't have a problem with the Zeros knowing how the monitoring room operated and what sort of actions triggered alerts; that's how they thought the Zeros could be kept in check. Alexis's main challenge was going to be how quickly she could read what was in it, if it really was anything relevant for her. She knew whatever she read would be recorded through her eye cameras in the monitoring room.

Just like Hishem, Alexis too felt curious about Watterson's actions inside the store. He definitely was not there to buy anything. Alexis was also conscious of not making any eye contact with Watterson because of the eye cameras. So, when Watterson left the store by dropping that piece of paper, Alexis was convinced that he had come into the store only to deliver a message, and it had to be for her.

She closed her eyes and pulled out the paper that was caught between her right foot and her shoe. Intuitively, she tried to feel the paper first. There was a sudden rush of thrill.

She thought to herself, *This is from Jamar!"*

Images of their beach trip from two summers ago flashed across her mind. She smiled.

That was the best weekend ever, she thought and smiled again.

She knew she had to open her eyes to read the message. The protrusion marks on the paper were simply to indicate who the message was from. Something Jamar and Alexis had planned for. They had discussed how they would reach out to each other in case they were separated. She decided to read the content very quickly and was hoping it would be in the simple code using the animals from the Chinese zodiac signs that she and Jamar had worked on in preparation for situations like these.

She opened her eyes and looked at the paper very quickly. It took her a while to read the zodiac signs used. Alexis didn't decipher the message immediately, nor did she want to. Instead, she memorized the signs so she could decipher it later by decoding it internally from her memory. This way, her eye cameras would capture what was on the paper only for the briefest moment. She tried to read the message again with her eyes half open, hoping the blurry image would make it harder for the cameras to capture the message with clarity. In the end, she also knew it didn't matter, as there was going to be an alert because she would be brought in for questioning if they got suspicious, no matter what. She needed an alternative story, an alibi of sorts for this, in the event of such an interrogation, and told herself she could work on that later.

Alexis quietly dropped the paper on the floor, picked it up with her feet, slid it inside her shoe, and walked out of the bathroom. It didn't take that long for her to get back to her seat, so Hishem didn't see anything abnormal. For the next hour or so, she kept repeating the symbols in her mind to make sure she didn't forget the order. And she was also trying to decode it mentally. She told herself there shouldn't be any more visual trace of this.

There was another alert in the monitoring room. Because it was related to the pinned alert, Pedro was already looking into it. He went through the eye camera footage slowly and saw nothing alarming. It was just a woman taking a bio break. And then for the last few seconds inside the bathroom, he noticed the eye camera sensing something out of the ordinary, causing the alert. He saw a blurry vision of a piece of paper. It was not very clear what was on it. He called his supervisor.

Four from the alert monitoring team assembled behind Pedro's desk as he paused and replayed the last few seconds. They zoomed in to it to see what it was. All they could make out was animal images. Horse, monkey, ox, snake, mouse, etc. They really couldn't make any sense out of it, but whatever it was, it definitely didn't look like a zodiac sheet. Pedro was the first one who came up with the theory.

"What if it's a code? Someone was trying to pass it to our Zero there?"

"Watterson. That son of a bitch!" Pedro's supervisor exclaimed.

Meanwhile, Alexis was smiling to herself. She had just decoded the message that Jamar had sent her.

"Denise to bring Nia to hospital. Green. Go on Dixon Street to pick up vehicle. Unity plan."

Outside Precinct 12000

"Jamar, it's time. We have an hour and a half to get there," Raymond said, slowly waking up and stretching his arms. He turned the alarm off on his watch.

"Officer. Wow. I fell asleep. Really deep. Hadn't slept like this in a while. How long was I gone?"

"Don't know. Maybe five hours. Listen, we have to be there before 5 p.m. So, if we need to grab something to eat and buy some essentials, we do that right now and keep moving."

"Sounds like a plan, Officer."

The car was back on the Midwestern highway, heading into the city.

Precinct 12000

A718

"Anything else before I clock out, Mr. Hishem?" Alexis asked.

"I can't think of anything. I think it was a good day for us, don't you?"

"Indeed, Mr. Hishem. Thank you for another good day. See you tomorrow."

With that, Alexis packed her bag and left the store exactly at 5:01 p.m.

Hishem had another three hours before he closed his doors for business. He wished the precinct would allow Alexis to work for a couple more hours because he was used to seeing a short spike in his customer traffic between 5:30 p.m. and 7 p.m.

Alexis started walking out of the store and made a right onto Sixth Street like she normally did. She would have to walk three blocks north and make a right on Grant Street and then walk about a half block or so to catch her pick-up vehicle. If she walked only two blocks and made a right, she would be on Dixon Street. She was nervous. She wasn't sure yet if she was going to meet Jamar himself or someone else.

As she approached Dixon Street, for a second, she thought about the alert the monitoring team would receive as soon as she made that right. But then, what other choice did she have? She had never stepped on Dixon Street before. She took one deep breath and made a right on Dixon Street.

Alexis was walking briskly. She felt freer with every new step, and she found a sudden spring in her steps. A few seconds later, she heard a deep male voice from behind.

"Do not turn back. Just follow my instructions, which will be very brief. Walk 250 meters. Walk straight. You will see a neon-green car parked on your left. As soon as you spot that car, keep looking at it. Don't take your eyes off the license plate. Once you go near the car, close your eyes. Don't stop walking. Walk a few more meters. Till I say stop. Keep your eyes closed till further instructions."

Alexis felt weirdly thrilled as soon as she got those instructions. She took this up as her first mission of Unity Plan. She was looking for the neon-green car. She spotted it about a hundred meters way. She kept her eyes on the car. Suddenly, images of Nia and Jamar flashed in front of her eyes; they had rented a similar-looking car during their trip to Nia's favorite amusement park when she was three. Alexis kept looking at the car. As she got close enough, she stared at the license plate and didn't take her eyes off. There was nothing special about the plate. She tried to memorize it just in case. Once she got about two feet away from the car, she closed her eyes but kept walking.

"Stop," the voice behind her said. "Just keep your eyes shut. Walk two feet to your left. Stretch your left hand and feel for a car door that's open. Without opening your eyes, slide into the car. Do not worry. People you know are inside. You will be safe. Remember not to open your eyes till you are asked to do so. Stay calm," the voice continued.

Alexis did as instructed. She felt for an open car door, and by keeping her total faith in the mystery voice behind her, she slid inside. The door closed. She heard the passenger door open on the front side and then close quickly. Whoever was driving the car was breathing heavily. She could sense a stench of sweat floating in the air from the front seat. None of that really mattered to her at the moment as the car continued to traverse through the busy rush hour traffic because she sensed a very familiar smell right next to her in the rear seat.

"Alexis Lewis, my life, my love, my everything!" said Jamar and gave Alexis a quick peck on her cheek and a very tight bear hug. The sense of relief compounded with reuniting with Jamar was simply too overwhelming for Alexis, and she started crying.

"Watch those tears now. We can't have you open your eyes yet. Just for a few minutes. We are going to make your suffering go away in just a few minutes, and then you can see Jamar," said Watterson from the passenger seat in the front.

Alexis didn't recognize the voice, but she was also still trying to keep it all together.

"What now, Jamar? What are we doing?" Alexis asked.

"I don't know really. There is a lot to tell you. But first we need to fix those eye cameras. Right, Officer?" Jamar was too excited to share everything.

"Jamar, are you seeing me now? Or are your eyes closed too?"

"I can see my beautiful girl. She is beautiful even with her eyes closed. This is the moment I have been waiting for almost a year now." Jamar was ready to recite a love poem at that very moment.

"So, are your eye cameras taken care of?"

"Yes. Not too long ago," Jamar said.

The car left the city limits and approached a state park. Raymond found a quiet area and parked there. Watterson got out and opened the trunk to pull out his case. He walked up to Alexis's side and opened the door.

"Step out, Alexis. Don't open your eyes yet."

Alexis stepped out of the car slowly. Her shoes touched a piece of rock, and she thought she was going to trip and fall. Watterson held her hand.

"All right. This is going to be quick, but it's going to be a bit painful for a couple of minutes, okay? I am going to make you wear these glasses. Put them on. As soon as I say open, open your eyes and look straight. You will see a flash, a bright one. It will hurt your eyes. If the flash makes your eyes close, open them again immediately. Keep staring. When I remove the glasses, just close your eyes again for one minute and open them again. That will deactivate the cameras." Watterson gave detailed instructions to Alexis on how he was going to take care of the cameras and gave the glasses to her.

Alexis wore the strange-looking blue glasses and waited.

"Open now."

When Alexis opened her eyes and looked straight, a really bright flash lit up her eyes. She clenched her fists and managed to keep her eyes from closing completely. Watterson removed the glasses in a few seconds. As instructed, she closed her eyes again. When she opened her eyes after a minute, the first person she saw was Watterson.

"Hey! I know you," she squealed.

"Shhh! More later in the car. We wait for a few minutes to make sure you have no other eye issues before we head out." Watterson was more focused on "de-gadgeting" her as quickly as possible.

In the meantime, Watterson asked Jamar to get out of the car. He stepped out, walked toward Alexis, and stood next to her.

Alexis's eyes felt almost normal after a couple of minutes. She still couldn't see through the bright light outside, but she was able to finally see Jamar, the light of her life. They both spoke with their eyes for a few seconds. There were tears in both their eyes.

She whispered, "You look good, honey!"

He smiled.

Watterson was busy pulling out a couple of other devious-looking devices from his bag.

"These puppies are supposed to disable the movement-tracking chips on your arms and legs. Never used 'em on anyone before. Guess you are my first guinea pigs." He laughed. "I've also heard they will make you squirm in pain when I use them on you. Don't know if it's going to feel like a needle pick or a sledgehammer thud. Just let me know after you deal with the pain. But it will be quick."

Watterson used the device meant for the arms on Jamar's arms first. As he scanned his arm to locate the multiple chips, he waited for his device to turn green. He pressed the yellow button when it did.

"Ouch!" yelled Jamar.

The device turned green again for a second and then red.

"This means it's done. Clean." He repeated the same process with the other device meant for legs. Jamar felt more pain this time around.

"So, tell me now. Needle prick or sledgehammer?"

"Definitely not a sledgehammer. But more than a needle prick," Jamar said.

"How about we settle for a wooden log?"

"That's funny. Sure."

Watterson used the same two devices on Alexis to de-gadget her as well. Once they both were done, Watterson packed the devices in his bag and signaled them to get back in the car. He offered the water bottle he had to them. Maybe they looked dehydrated after the procedure.

The car was back on the highway in the next ten minutes.

Raymond was tempted to play some music but decided against it. He turned back for a second and looked at Alexis.

"Hey, listen, if you guys want some private time, you may press that sound shield button in front of your seat. It will create a sound shield between the two rows of seats."

"Oh. That's all right. Thanks for letting me know, though." Alexis blushed and waved at Raymond.

"Then it's time to get you up to speed, Alexis. I am kinda the center of this whole plan. Although it is being done for you guys, and you are the heroes of this, I will explain what we are doing now. So, Dr. Watterson here used to be a colleague of Jamar when they were in the air force. When I found out from Jamar that you are in 12000, I reached out to one of my contacts in the precinct to run through the database to see if we could locate any past close contacts of Jamar who are also in our coded network, since Jamar had shared with me what he used to do before all this. By the way, I am Officer Raymond from 16000, Southeast Zone. I am the transfer officer for Jamar. He is under my custody right now, and I am supposed to be transferring him physically to my team waiting for him in my precinct. So, long story short, Watterson showed up in our database. When presented with the plan of pulling you out of the precinct, he came up with this idea of applying for a woman Zero loaner though the shady program that your precinct runs. And that's how he got the message to you."

"Wow. I am indebted to you all, Officer and Dr. Watterson." Alexis's eyes showed gratitude.

The car was now back inside the city, but it was heading to the other end. Neither Alexis nor Jamar knew exactly where they were. After a few minutes of being in rush-hour traffic, Raymond pulled the car into the back parking lot of a huge complex that housed the hospital where Denise would have admitted Nia.

"So, Alexis, the next part of this plan is to pick up Nia. Denise is part of our coded network as well. She will bring Nia here anytime. We can't control her time. But hopefully she doesn't keep us waiting for too long," Watterson said.

"Denise?" Alexis asked with a surprise in her voice.

After about ten minutes, Alexis could see Denise and Nia walking together toward their car. She was about to wave but restrained herself from doing so. Watterson smiled approvingly.

"Good evening, Doctor. Hope this is all you had for me," Denise said.

"What? Oh … yes. Absolutely. We will give a couple of minutes for the family to reunite, and then we will discuss the next steps. Thank you so much. You are amazing," Dr. Watterson said.

When Nia saw Jamar, she was in a state of ecstasy. "Daddy, Daddy, Daddy!"

"Oh, my love. My precious Nia! How I missed you!" Jamar hugged her inside the car while Denise stood outside and gave a thumbs-up to Alexis.

"So, what's going to happen to her?" Alexis asked Watterson about Denise. Watterson could tell Alexis was concerned.

"You mean to Denise? She is going to be fine. She could get fired from this precinct. You know … that may be the worst that could happen to her," Watterson said.

Those ten minutes went by fast, and it was time to say goodbye to Denise. They all waved to her.

Watterson knew getting fired from the precinct was not the worst that could happen to her. There were worse things that could happen, but he hoped she would find an escape route. He had already checked in with a couple of his contacts to find an escape for her.

"What's next, gentlemen?" Alexis asked. She was extremely happy to have her family together, but she wasn't sure if she should celebrate this reunion yet or if there was going to be a twist.

"Unity plan, Alexis," Jamar said.

"That's done. We are here, honey. Now what?"

"Area 808080!," said Watterson with his eyes wide open.

Nia was watching his eyes. "Dad, don't do that. When you do that, you look like you are about to cry!"

"Ha ha … I won't do that again, sweetheart." Jamar planted a gentle kiss on Nia's cheek and winked at her.

"I am totally psyched, Jamar. I am. I never thought we could do this. 808080? With Nia and all? And Officer Raymond, I can't thank you enough. We can't. I have no idea why and how you decided to do this for us."

Raymond nodded and smiled through the rearview mirror. He waved at Nia, and she waved back.

"My navigation unit says eight hours and forty-five minutes. So, lean back and get some sleep. Between me and Dr. Watterson, we plan to drive nonstop. We will stop only once in between for fuel if needed. Does that make sense?" Raymond asked.

"Yes," Jamar said.

"80 … 80 …80 … This is really happening, Jamar!" Alexis held Jamar's hands tight and let her fingers wrap around his.

"Yup," said Jamar and leaned across Nia who was sitting in between them and kissed Alexis on her lips.

808080

Neither Raymond nor Watterson knew what Area 808080 was. Neither should have heard about it or found out about it. But now they knew.

In the wild planning that went into mapping different zones and precincts for ZSG, there were few spots which were considered dead spots. Dead spots, even though they belonged to specific zones on the map, were spots one couldn't easily access, like mountainous slopes, inaccessibile cliffs, swamps, and the like. Dead spots in each zone were clearly marked on the map.

There was one unique thing about one particular dead spot in the Central zone and one in the Midwest zone. They were connected underground through a large cave system. The ZSG patrol teams often visited these dead spots for aerial surveys and land surveys to ensure there was no unlawful inhabitation of the absconding Zeros in these areas—those people who hadn't voluntarily reported to the program. But no one knew about this cave system, and it had been largely undetected except by a few rebel Zeros.

808080 was a 0.5-square-mile cave area that connected these two dead spots between the Central Zone and the Midwest Zone. The cave wasn't entirely devoid of light and water. It had a stream of fresh water originating from a source not too far away and enough open spaces for sunlight to get in. And because of the intricate layouts of the cave structure, the entire area provided a lot of cover for the rebel Zeros who had either escaped from the precincts or never reported for ZSG but managed to abscond.

The population of Area 808080 was now close to one thousand. By then, the inhabitants of 808080, also known as rebels, had developed a steady process to get food and other essential supplies for them—one that involved many risks. In the eight months of its existence, since the first rebel settlement, 808080 had managed to build two specialized fighting units. The units were more a matter of logistical convenience and available skills. There was no single leader commanding 808080 for now, but they needed one. Even though 808080 was originally an escape route and a temporary or permanent hideout, it had now become the headquarters of a rebel army that planned on taking the regime and liberating all Black Americans from ZSG—a freedom revolutionary army. Their mission was clear, and what was still lacking was a clear strategy and a visionary leadership team. The rebels who were living there were living in hopes that they would be able to take over the regime within the next three to five years.

Even before Jamar and family were forcefully caught by the ZSG officers, Jamar had heard of 808080. He had heard how he might be very much needed there should the situation arise. His air force background combined with his general technology and combat skills could make him a potential leader to command the army. So, Jamar always had 808080 in his mind and had even discussed his plans with Alexis. The fighter Alexis was, she was looking forward to joining Jamar at 808080 one day and taking up the case of fighting for the independence of fellow Black Americans. Alexis, for her part, had seen so much tragedy around her that it was not a question of if, but more of when.

When Raymond and Jamar were waiting outside Precinct 12000, Jamar, after much deliberation, decided to share the information about 808080 with Raymond. Jamar pointed at where 808080 was on an electronic map that Raymond had in his car. Even though he had never been there, several months of dreaming about 808080 had made Jamar memorize all access points to the area.

By road, he told Raymond that they would have to drive to a specific point within the boundaries of Central Zone, a spot that wouldn't cause the aerial survey teams to chase them, as it was well within the permitted area for civilian travel. From that spot on, it was going to be a long hike to one of the entrances of the cave.

Raymond, on the other hand, felt like he had found his calling. From the time he witnessed money being exchanged for a human trade to the time he spent inside the car listening to Jamar talk about the sociopolitical changes that were taking place in his country—one that he dearly loved—to that particular moment when he learned about Area 808080 and how there was an opportunity to effect a change. It was a moment he was searching for, one that gave him an opportunity to lift the burden he had been carrying all these months.

He agreed immediately to take Jamar and his family to 808080. He didn't have time to think about the consequences. Once Dr. Watterson was briefed, he too didn't hesitate about participating in this mission. He was another anti-regime activist from within the system, also working hard to set a fraction of the colossal humanitarian damages caused by white Americans right.

Both men clearly understood the indisputable repercussions to their actions if they were caught.

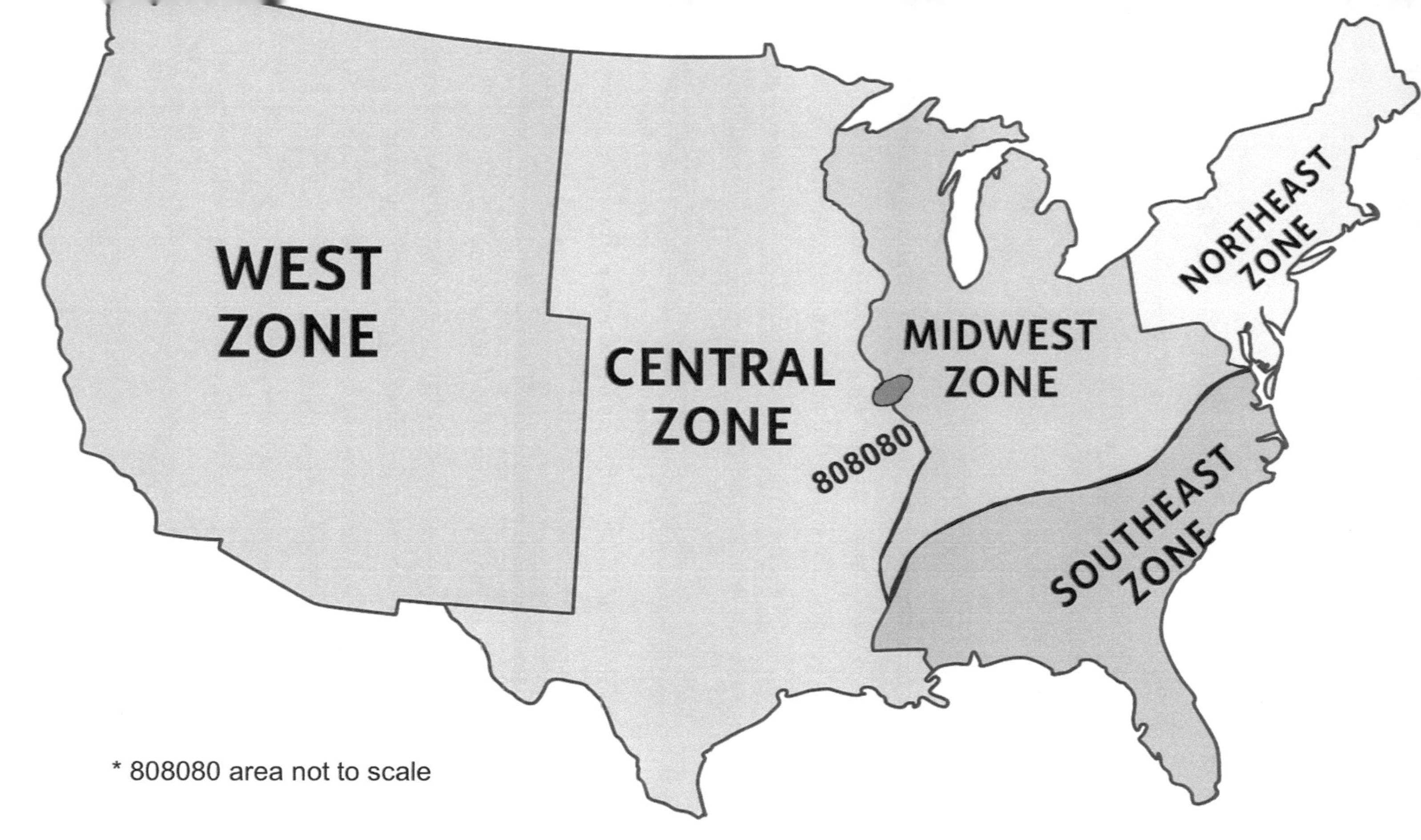

WEST ZONE
CENTRAL ZONE
MIDWEST ZONE
NORTHEAST ZONE
SOUTHEAST ZONE
808080
* 808080 area not to scale

3:47 a.m.

Their car slowly pulled into a corner parking lot of a state park, the farthest one could ago without the surveillance cameras or the aerial survey teams raising a red flag. It was partly cloudy, and the moon was putting up a brave fight with the clouds to share some light.

"Jamar, are you awake? Time to start the trek. You want to get there before sunrise," said Raymond.

Jamar and Alexis got out of the car. Jamar then pulled Nia out. She was fast asleep. Alexis offered to carry her for the first stretch of their hike, as Jamar was the only one who knew anything about where they were going, and he was needed in the front for navigation. They all started to hike eastward in the middle of absolute still darkness. They had just one flashlight, which they used sparingly, relying mostly on the sparse moonlight. It was not a strenuous trek for the most part, just navigating around a few rocks here and there, but it was a long hike, almost 6.5 miles long. It took them two hours and twenty minutes to get to the entrance of the cave.

Jamar pointed at the entrance. "This is it. We should be safe from here, Officer and Doctor, if you want to turn back."

"You don't want us to see what's going on inside? Or are you worried that we would report this back to higher command?"

"Come on now. If I was worried about that, I wouldn't have shared any info about this in the first place."

"Well then, we are going with you. We can't walk back now, as sunrise is in about thirty-five minutes, and the surveillance teams could spot us."

"So …?"

"We are coming with you. We will spend the day and hike back when it gets dark."

Jamar looked at Alexis, who nodded in approval.

All five entered the cave, Area 808080.

After hiking inside the cave for about two hundred meters, Jamar realized that he had no further concrete information as to what to look for, and he was not sure where exactly he was going, although he was sure he was safe and in the right place. Fortunately, within a few seconds, he heard a distant clatter, mostly of men laughing at a distance.

"Help, please! New admission," Jamar yelled.

"Who?" the voice yelled back.

"We are new here. I am Jamar. Jamar Lewis."

"Jamar Lewis? *The* Jamar Lewis?"

They could hear one of the voices approaching them. "What an honor it is to meet you!" The voice was much closer now.

All of a sudden, the tall man stopped abruptly about ten feet away from them. He started to look for something that he could pick up as a weapon to defend himself.

That's when Jamar realized that Raymond was still in his uniform and Watterson was, of course, Watterson, a white man.

"Sorry. They are here to help us. In fact, they helped me get here. And my family too. They are our allies. We can trust them. You are safe."

"Are you sure? Are you sure you are not an informer, Wing Commander Lewis?" the tall man asked with a nervous smile.

"No. Not at all. By the way, how do you know me?"

"Your reputation has reached us before you did, Mr. Lewis.

We've been looking for someone of your caliber to join us and give us some structure. Lead us, command us, prepare us for a real fight."

"I am here then, at your service. Meet my wife, Alexis, and daughter, Nia."

"Hello, ladies. Brave of you both to make the trek with Mr. Lewis."

"I've always wanted to do my part in this fight," Alexis replied.

Nia was wide awake now and she was absorbing what was going on without saying much.

"All right then … you are … I am sorry, I didn't catch your name …" Jamar asked.

"I am Keith. Keith Lamar. Just follow me, gentlemen and ladies. I will find you the best residence quarters inside the cave." And he burst out laughing.

The five of them walked behind Keith. Jamar introduced Raymond and Watterson to Keith, and gave a ten-minute summary of his escape, his unity plan, and their trek to 808080.

When they finally arrived at a specific spot inside the cave which Keith considered to be the residence quarters for Jamar and crew, he stopped and showed them where to go. They all understood what *residence quarters* meant. A few boulders carved like beds with some basic bedding supplies like pillows and blankets. Cozy enough to give some privacy.

"Why don't y'all get some rest now? We will meet after three hours or so. I will bring a few folks with me, and they will help you get oriented here. Maybe you will be able to get a head start on your command plans too. Sounds good, y'all?"

"Absolutely."

After Keith left, they all found their own bedding spots, and without much to say, lay down on their beds.

"So, Officer Raymond, what's next for you? I am sure you are already on the alert system. And you, Doctor Watterson?" Jamar asked while struggling to fall asleep.

"I think we've found our calling, thanks to you, Jamar. We want to be your 808080 transfer agents or supply men. We want to be part of your plan. We could be your face to the outside world for now. I can think of so many ways you could use us. Unless you don't want to hire us. As long as we can, and as long as we don't get caught, we can work from within the system and provide data, people, supplies, anything … whatever we can. We want you to succeed, Commander Jamar," Raymond said.

"You gentlemen are hired then," Jamar said with a mocking command in his voice and continued. "Gentlemen, thank you again for bringing us here. It feels weird that I am actually in the land I had been dreaming about for months — a land that gives me hope. A land where I can feel the promise of one world ending and another world beginning. Our last frontier. And yet, we are nowhere. Our struggle for freedom begins in this no-man's land, where everything is gray and we are all alone. Sorry, I am absorbing it all. I am rambling …"

"No, go on, Jamar! When you get into this deep analytical mode, you seem to make so much more sense," Raymond said as he rubbed his eyes.

"If you say so, Officer. Isn't this a beautiful cave? The cave we fear to enter holds the treasure we seek. That's what they say, right? This cave that hides all its blackness, where white light is sacred, this cave is somehow the place where we get to define the meaning of our lives.

Where our unspoken words and our uncried tears will give rise to stars. So, it doesn't surprise me that I finally feel like a star myself. A distant but a bright star," Jamar said.

Raymond and Watterson were fast asleep.

About ten feet away, Jamar could hear Alexis singing a very familiar Ella Fitzgerald song to put Nia to sleep. They seemed comfortable and cozy on their new boulder bed. Nia was covered in a maroon-and-gray checkered blanket Alexis had picked up from the pile of bedding accessories that were available.

Jamar whispered, "Good night," to them both and closed his eyes.

A splendid mosaic of myriad colors appeared in his gray vision. Jamar, Alexis, and Nia were laughing and chasing a butterfly. It was a beautiful butterfly that transcended borders and times—one that he always saw when he closed his eyes. It was in his gray vision of turbulent waves set in motion by the black-and-white reality of the outside world that Jamar saw the truth—an elusive butterfly that kept their chase real and alive.

The Next Morning

Alexis woke up disturbed. She looked under her neck and checked the bed on which she was sleeping. She didn't find anything abnormal, and she had no idea why felt like she was sleeping on a rock or like someone had thrown a rock at her back. Alexis turned toward her right to check on Nia.

Nia was still sleeping. She had a beautiful smile on her face, even as her eyes were tightly shut. She didn't show any signs of disturbance.

The beauty of childhood innocence … Alexis thought.

It was 7:00 a.m.

Alexis got out of her bed and ran into the shower. She realized that she had very little time to get ready for the rally. She put on a gray T-shirt, one that Jamar loved, and got ready in no time. As she rushed out of her room, she saw her mom at the dining table. Denise was reading something on her phone, and as soon as she saw Alexis come out of her room, she removed her reading glasses and set them on the kitchen counter.

She smiled at Alexis and said, "Good morning, honey!".

"Good morning, Momma! Nia is still asleep. Make sure you check her homework before she goes to school today. And don't forget to pack veggies for her lunch … and I should be back by 2 p.m., but just in case, please have Kimberly pick her up. And at 4 p.m. …"

"I got it, my girl. I got it. You have an important day ahead. Here, I have this coffee made for you. Take this and that muffin over there. Be safe out there, Alexis. Momma loves you. Don't worry about Nia. She will have a good day." Denise gave a tight hug to her daughter and sent her away.

Alexis grabbed the banner standing by the door, which she and Nia had made the previous night. She approached the door and paused for a second, then she turned toward her mom, who was waving at her.

"I love you, Mom!," she said, closed the door gently, and stepped outside onto the street to get a breath of fresh air. She looked up to see the sky, which was making way for the clouds to pass over, and the sun hadn't started shining yet. Alexis started walking briskly with many thoughts running through her mind which she was trying to get organized.

Another day. Another rally.

She had already walked four blocks from home and was now on Fifty-Second Street, far away from the safety and shelter her neighborhood offered her. From a distance, she could see that there were already dozens of people who had gathered for the rally. There were people with banners, with flags, and then there were those with musical instruments. She could feel the energy and the passion from a distance.

A car drove past her. She was so lost in her thoughts that she didn't notice the car till it passed very close to her. The driver in the car, a white female, honked and yelled, "Blue lives matter!" and showed her middle finger at Alexis.

Alexis ignored her and kept walking. She was used to these taunts and abuses. But she was amused at this particular abuse. After all, blue life is a temporary one, a uniform—it was simply a job that comes with certain privilege, while being Black is her life, all Black Americans' lives—that have been cursed for centuries.

She continued walking on these unfamiliar streets. The streets nevertheless had rules, and Alexis, like many Black women, had mastered them. She knew how to be alert about surrounding dangers and when to walk away from predatory pacers. She was used to people giving her circumspect glances, to older white women clutching their purses as she walked past them, to younger white men anxiously smiling at her, and to almost everyone turning back and glancing at her after they walked past her as if to register her physical presence one more time.

The only thought in her mind at that moment, as she continued to walk toward the growing crowd, was about her need to stay strong. She had a responsibility as a parent to teach Nia about acknowledging how the repugnant racist history of the country had led up to shaping the present and why the hard reality for many Black people of never getting a chance to experience the freedom to define themselves mattered.

When she approached the intersection where the rally was about to start, she waved at some known faces and thanked them by cupping her right palm on her heart.

Then she lifted the banner she was carrying.

"JUSTICE FOR JAMAR !!"

❤

"Not everything that is faced can be changed; but nothing can be changed until it is faced."

—*JAMES BALDWIN*

THROUGH HER EYES

The factory floor hummed with the rhythm of machinery, a metallic symphony of gears grinding and pistons pumping. Liam stood at his station, his hands steady and precise as he maneuvered a metal sheet into place beneath a hydraulic press. The hiss of compressed air and the sharp clang of steel on steel echoed around him, but his focus never wavered. This was his world for eight hours a day—a world where a single lapse in concentration could cost him a hand or worse.

It wasn't a glamorous job. Liam knew that. But it was steady, and it paid the bills. The work demanded skill, precision, and a sharp eye for detail—qualities he had honed over years of labor. His colleagues often joked about his "artistic hands," marveling at the way he could guide the smallest components into alignment as if they were extensions of himself. Liam would chuckle along, brushing off the compliments, but he took quiet pride in his craftsmanship. He wasn't passionate about his work, but he respected it. In a way, it was a test of his discipline, of his ability to endure.

Today was no different. The clock on the wall ticked slowly, each second dragging into the next. Liam's muscles ached, a dull throb in his shoulders and back that came from years of repetitive motion. His eyes scanned the control panel, checking the gauges and warning lights. Everything was in order. His hands moved almost instinctively, adjusting levers and tightening bolts with practiced ease.

But his mind was elsewhere.

Clara. Her name drifted into his thoughts like a lifeline, pulling him away from the monotony of the factory. His daughter was the bright spot in his otherwise gray world. At sixteen, she was everything he could have hoped for and more—sharp, curious, and bursting with ideas. Liam often marveled at her ability to find joy in the simplest things. She had an artist's soul, he thought, though she channeled it into her sketches and school projects rather than the heavy blocks of stone he worked with at home.

As he worked, Liam's thoughts wandered to their conversations at the dinner table, on the rare occasions they got to eat together. Clara would excitedly recount her day, her words tumbling out in a rush as she shared her latest project or an amusing anecdote from school. Liam would listen, nodding along, though he often felt out of his depth. The world she described seemed so far removed from his own—a place of ideas and possibilities, where dreams felt attainable. Yet, despite their differences, their bond was unshakable. Clara was his anchor, his reason for pushing through the drudgery of factory life.

A faint smile crossed his face as he imagined their future plans. For years, he had been setting aside a portion of his paycheck, saving for a trip that Clara had always dreamed of. Paris and Florence. She spoke of them as if they were magical realms, places where art came alive, and history whispered through cobblestone streets. Liam didn't share her romanticism, but he loved the way her eyes lit up when she talked about it. He'd promised her they'd go—one day, when there was enough money and time.

The shrill whistle signaling the end of the shift snapped him back to reality. Liam wiped the sweat from his brow and stretched his aching limbs. Another day done. As he walked to the locker room after clocking out, the thought of Clara waiting for him at home brought a flicker of warmth to his chest. He couldn't give her the world, but he could give her himself—his time, his effort, his love. And for now, that was enough.

👁

Clara swung her backpack onto the kitchen counter as she stepped into the small but cozy home she shared with her dad. The familiar scent of wood shavings lingered in the air, a constant reminder of the sculpting studio tucked away in the back of the house. She smiled to herself as she opened the fridge, scanning its contents to piece together a quick dinner.

A grilled cheese sandwich and tomato soup would have to do. It wasn't much, but Clara had perfected the art of simple, comforting meals—a necessity with her dad working long shifts at the factory. As the soup simmered on the stove, she set the table, humming softly to herself. She would leave a plate for him, knowing he'd appreciate the thoughtfulness, even if they couldn't always share meals together. She knew her dad's weekly shift schedule, as she had it carefully marked on her phone calendar.

With dinner prepped, Clara settled at the dining table with her homework. Math problems filled the pages of her notebook, but her mind kept drifting to the upcoming week's activities. The afterschool art club was hosting a showcase on Friday, and Clara had been working tirelessly on a mixed-media project she could not wait to unveil. The club was one of her favorite escapes, a place where she could channel her creativity and connect with like-minded friends.

Her thoughts wandered to her dad. Liam. Her rock. He had been her constant source of support and inspiration, even if he didn't always realize it. Clara often thought about how hard he worked, both at the factory and in his modest sculpting studio. His hands—calloused and strong from years of labor—seemed to transform when he sculpted, becoming instruments of art and grace.

The studio was humble, just a small structure behind the house with a rickety workbench and a few scattered tools. But to Clara, it was magical. She'd spent countless hours watching her dad work, from a distance, mesmerized by the way he brought life to cold blocks of wood or stone or clay. To Liam, sculpting was a hobby—something he'd picked up as an eight-year-old boy, shaping clay into crude figures at the kitchen table. He'd never thought of himself as particularly talented, dismissing his work as amateurish and unworthy of attention. But Clara saw the truth.

"You're a master sculptor, Dad," she'd tell him, her voice full of conviction. "You just haven't shown the world yet."

He'd laugh, shaking his head, but she could see the flicker of pride in his eyes. Occasionally, he'd take on small commissions from neighbors or acquaintances—a garden statue here, a bust there—but it was never about the money. He sculpted because he loved it, because it gave him a sense of peace and fulfillment that the factory never could.

Clara dreamed of a day when her dad's work would be recognized for the masterpieces they were. She wanted to take him to Paris and Florence, to walk with him through the halls of the Louvre and the Uffizi Gallery, to see the awe in his eyes as he stood before the works of Michelangelo and Rodin. She wanted him to believe in his talent the way she did, to see himself as the artist she knew him to be.

The sound of the front door opening snapped Clara out of her thoughts. She jumped up, a wide grin spreading across her face. "Hey, Dad!" she called, rushing to greet him.

Liam stepped inside, weary but smiling as he saw her. "Hey, kiddo. How was school?"

"Good. Dinner's ready," Clara said, taking his lunchbox from him and setting it on the counter.

As they sat down to eat, Clara filled the room with chatter about her day, her excitement about the art showcase, and her plans for the weekend. Liam listened, his exhaustion fading as he soaked in her energy. She was his world, his reason for pushing through the grind of factory life. And though he couldn't give her everything she deserved, he'd keep working, keep sculpting, and keep dreaming of a brighter future for them both.

Liam woke up to an unsettling blur in his right eye. A lattice of faint, shifting patterns danced across his vision. He blinked several times, hoping it was just a trick of light or the remnants of a restless night. But the patterns persisted.

It was a school holiday, so Clara was still asleep when Liam left the house for work. He debated mentioning the issue to her but decided against it. "It'll pass," he muttered to himself, forcing a smile into the bathroom mirror. He needed to get through the day, no matter what.

The drive to the factory was nerve-wracking. Liam relied heavily on his left eye, squinting to make sense of the blurred shapes ahead of him. Several times, he misjudged the distance of oncoming cars or missed a turn until the last second. By the time he arrived at the factory, his shirt clung to his back with sweat.

At work, Liam's hands moved with their usual precision, but his heart pounded each time a machine whirred to life. His partial vision made depth perception difficult, and twice he narrowly avoided mishaps that could have cost him his hands. "You all right, Liam?" a coworker asked during their lunch break. He nodded, feigning a calm he didn't feel. The coworker could sense the nervousness crawling around Liam's body language that day.

The monotonous sounds of the factory seemed louder than usual, almost taunting him. Each clang and hum reminded him of how vital his sight was—not just for this job, but for his entire life. He had always prided himself on his ability to adapt, but this was different. This was terrifying. By the time his shift ended, Liam felt like he had run a marathon.

The drive home was even worse. Darkness blurred the lines further, and the headlights of other cars felt like piercing beams aimed directly at him. When he finally pulled into the driveway, he exhaled deeply, gripping the steering wheel for a moment before heading inside.

Clara greeted him with her usual cheerfulness. "Hey, Dad! Dinner's almost ready." He smiled but kept his responses short. Over the meal, she began to notice his unusual behavior. He avoided looking directly at her and seemed more interested in pushing food around his plate than eating it.

Clara had always been observant. She noticed how his shoulders sagged more than usual, how he seemed to wince when the overhead light flickered. "Dad, are you okay? You're not eating much."

"Just tired, sweetheart," he replied, forcing a weak smile. "Long day at work."

After dinner, Liam retreated to his studio. Clara knew he often sought solace there after a long day, pouring his thoughts into his sculptures. But tonight, something was off. She peeked through the doorway and saw him fumbling, running his hands over tools and materials instead of working with the usual fluidity. He didn't even attempt to touch the special order he had been so passionate about—a commission from a wealthy man who had admired Liam's abstract piece at the city hall. The client had been specific about his request: a blend of a rare metal and an elegant stone, designed to captivate visitors in the foyer of his grand home.

Clara frowned. Her dad's studio, modest as it was, had always been his sanctuary. He'd spend hours here, losing himself in the rhythm of creation. But tonight, he seemed lost in a different way—uncertain, hesitant.

"Dad?" Clara's voice broke the silence. Liam turned toward her, startled. "Is everything okay?"

"Yes," he said quickly, too quickly. He tried to smile but failed to mask the worry in his expression.

Clara stepped closer, her eyes narrowing. "What's going on?"

He sighed, finally sitting down on a nearby stool. "It's nothing. Just … my eyes are acting up. I think I need rest. Tomorrow's Sunday, so I'll take it easy."

But Clara wasn't convinced. She had always been perceptive, and tonight was no exception. "Acting up how?"

Reluctantly, Liam explained the patterns, the blurriness, and how he had struggled through the day. Her face tightened with concern. "You should have told me. We need to see an ophthalmologist."

"Clara, it's not that bad. I just need sleep," he protested weakly.

"No," she said firmly. "We're going tomorrow."

Her tone left no room for argument. Liam hesitated but eventually nodded. He could see the determination in her eyes—the same determination that had carried them through so many challenges before. As they stood there in the dim light of the studio, Liam felt a small, tentative hope bloom within him. Maybe, just maybe, things would be all right.

Clara stepped forward, placing a hand on his shoulder. "We'll figure this out, Dad. Together."

Liam nodded again, feeling a mix of gratitude and guilt. Then he tilted his head toward her shoulder and leaned on it.

He had spent the entire day pretending he was fine, but now, in this moment, he realized he didn't have to face this alone. Clara had his back—she always had. And as daunting as tomorrow seemed, her unwavering support made it just a little less frightening.

The morning brought with it a cold drizzle, matching the somber mood as Liam and Clara sat in the waiting room of the ophthalmologist's clinic. Liam fidgeted with the zipper of his jacket, his mind racing with possibilities. Clara sat beside him, her hands clasped tightly in her lap. She had been the one to insist on the appointment, and though she tried to exude calm, her worried glances at her father betrayed her anxiety.

Dr. Evelyn Monroe, a middle-aged woman with a calm demeanor and an aura of authority, greeted them and led Liam into the examination room. Clara opted to wait outside, giving Liam space but silently praying for good news.

The examination felt endless. Dr. Monroe and her clinic assistants ran a series of tests, shining lights into Liam's eyes, asking him to follow her fingers, pouring multiple eyedrops, photoimaging his eyes, and analyzing images of his retinas. When she finally sat down across from him, her expression was grave.

"Liam," she began gently, "what you're experiencing is a rare condition called central retinal artery occlusion, or CRAO. It's caused by a blockage in the central artery of the retina, which supplies oxygen and nutrients to the eye. In many cases, it results in sudden and severe loss of vision."

Liam's throat went dry. "But … this will go away, right? My vision will come back?"

Dr. Monroe shook her head, her voice soft but firm. "Unfortunately, the damage is usually permanent. It's like a stroke, but in the eye. The patterns and blurriness you've been seeing are due to the cells in your retina dying from lack of oxygen. It's rare to recover from this, and even if we intervene with treatments like hyperbaric oxygen therapy or clot-dissolving drugs, the window for effectiveness has likely passed."

Her words hit him like a punch to the gut. Liam leaned back in the chair, his hands gripping the armrests as he tried to steady himself.

"I … I can't lose my sight. My job depends on it. My life depends on it," he stammered.

Dr. Monroe reached out, placing a hand on his arm. "I understand how devastating this is. There are resources and support groups for people adjusting to vision loss. And you're not completely blind yet—you still have your peripheral vision for now. And your left eye is perfectly all right. That could help you adapt."

Adapt? The word felt hollow, like an insult to everything he had worked so hard to build.

When Liam returned to the waiting room, Clara's face fell at the sight of him. His shoulders were hunched, his eyes red-rimmed, and he looked like a man carrying the weight of the world.

In the car ride home, silence hung heavy between them. Clara glanced at her father from time to time, wanting to say something but unsure of how to breach the fortress of his despair.

That evening, Liam sat on the worn sofa in their living room, staring blankly at the muted television. Clara entered with two mugs of tea, setting one down in front of him.

"Dad," she began, sitting beside him, "what did the doctor say, exactly?"

He hesitated, his fingers tracing the edge of the mug. Finally, he spoke, his voice hoarse. "It's permanent, Clara. My right eye is gone, and the left … it's only a matter of time before it follows."

Clara's breath caught, but she quickly composed herself. When you are the only person your dad has, even a sixteen-year-old mind can conjure up the maturity it needs. "We'll figure it out. There are people who live full lives without their sight. We'll get through this, Dad. And I am not going anywhere."

Liam shook his head, his voice breaking. "You don't understand. It's not just about getting through. My job at the factory … I can't do it without my sight. And sculpting?" He let out a bitter laugh. "That's all about vision. I can't sculpt what I can't see."

Clara placed a reassuring hand on his. "You've always told me that sculpting isn't just about seeing—it's about feeling. About connecting with the material. Maybe this is … I don't know, maybe it's a new way for you to connect."

He gave her a small, grateful smile but didn't reply. After a moment, he spoke again, his tone heavy with regret. "There's a sculpture I started for a client. A wealthy man. He saw my piece at city hall and commissioned me to create something for his home. It's a big opportunity, Clara. He's paying more than I've ever earned for a single piece. If I could finish it … it could change everything for us."

Clara's eyes lit up with determination. "Then you'll finish it."

" I don't know if I can," Liam said, his voice cracking. "I've barely started. The design is intricate. It's supposed to be a blend of metal and stone, but … I can't even see the materials properly, let alone shape them."

"Then we'll figure out a way," she said fiercely. "You've always told me I'm stubborn. I got that from you. We don't give up easily."

Her words sparked a flicker of hope in him. For the first time that day, he allowed himself to believe that maybe, just maybe, they could find a way forward. But as he looked at his daughter's determined face, he felt the weight of responsibility settle even heavier on his shoulders.

They had a long road ahead, but at least they weren't walking it alone.

Clara woke up to the faint sound of rain tapping against her window and the weight of the previous day pressing on her chest. She lay in bed for a moment, staring at the ceiling, before making a decision. She wasn't going to school today—not when her dad needed her.

Downstairs, the house was quiet except for the occasional creak of the wooden floors under her feet. She padded into the kitchen, tying her hair into a loose bun, and set about making coffee. The scent of freshly brewed beans filled the room, followed by the comforting sizzle of eggs in a pan.

"Good morning, Chef Clara," came a groggy voice from the doorway.

Clara turned to see her dad leaning against the frame, his hair disheveled, his eyes heavy with exhaustion. "Morning, Dad. Coffee's ready. Sit."

Liam raised an eyebrow. "Skipping school, are we?"

"Yep," she said nonchalantly, sliding a plate of eggs and toast in front of him. "Don't even try to argue."

He chuckled softly, sitting down. "I see how it is. You're the boss now."

"Always have been," she quipped, pouring herself a cup of coffee and joining him at the table.

For a while, they ate in silence, the quiet punctuated by the clinking of forks on plates. Then Clara broke the stillness. "You're calling in sick today. Actually, for the whole week."

Liam frowned, setting his fork down. "Clara, I can't just take a week off. You know how tight things are. And Jerry will have my head if—"

"Jerry can deal with it," Clara interrupted firmly. "You need this time. You can't risk getting hurt at work, especially now."

Liam hesitated, his gaze dropping to his plate. "It's not that simple."

"It is," she said, grabbing his phone and holding it out to him. "Call him. Right now."

With a sigh, Liam took the phone and dialed his supervisor. The conversation went about as he'd expected—Jerry's voice boomed through the receiver, demanding to know how Liam could be so irresponsible. Liam muttered something about a health issue, and after a few more minutes of yelling, Jerry begrudgingly agreed to let him take the week off.

When Liam hung up, he looked at Clara, exasperated. "Happy now?"

"Very," she said with a grin.

He shook his head, unable to suppress a small smile. "You're impossible."

"I get that from you," she shot back.

They lingered at the table, sipping their coffee. Clara's expression grew more serious. "Dad, I've been thinking. About the sculpture."

"What about it?"

"I want to help you finish it," she said, her tone steady.

Liam froze, the mug halfway to his lips. "Clara, I don't think that's … you …"

"Before you say no," she cut him off, "just hear me out. I know I have never sculpted before, but I can be your hands. Or … your eyes, I guess. You can guide me, and we can do it together."

"Clara, sculpting isn't something you just pick up in a week," he said, shaking his head. "It takes years of practice. And you … well, let's just say fine art hasn't exactly been your thing."

She laughed, knowing exactly what he was referring to. "You mean the piccolo? Or the trumpet? Or maybe the violin?"

"All of them," he said, chuckling. "You gave up on each one faster than I thought possible. We used to joke that music and you had a mutual agreement to stay out of each other's way."

"And yet, here I am, volunteering for something even harder," she said with a smile. "But seriously, Dad. I have evolved over the years. You hear me talk about the mixed-media project at school, don't you? I know it sounds crazy, but this is important. Not just for you. For us. You always tell me how sculpting is more about feeling than seeing. Well, you still have that feeling. And I have two perfectly good eyes. Together, we can do this."

Liam looked at her, his heart swelling with both pride and apprehension. "Clara, this isn't just any project. It's the most intricate piece I've ever been commissioned to make. The client is expecting something extraordinary."

"Then let's make something extraordinary," she said simply.

He sighed, rubbing his temples. "What if we fail? What if it's not good enough?"

"Then we'll learn from it and move on," Clara said firmly. "But you always told me that we don't let fear stop us. That we try, no matter what. Remember when I was scared to ride my bike without training wheels, and you said—"

"You can't learn to balance if you're too afraid to fall," he finished, smiling despite himself.

"Exactly," she said. "So, let's do this. Together. Don't be afraid to fall, Dad!"

Liam stared at her for a long moment, the memories of her childhood flooding back—her first steps, her scraped knees, the way she'd always looked up at him with that same determined glint in her eye.

"All right," he said finally. "We'll do it. But it's going to take a lot of work. We will need a plan."

Clara grinned, already pulling a notepad from the kitchen counter. "Then let's make one. I'm way ahead of you."

They spent the next hour sketching out a timeline, dividing the work into manageable sections. Liam explained the process in detail—how to shape the metal, polish the stone, and merge the two seamlessly. Clara listened intently, taking notes and asking questions.

As they worked, the kitchen filled with laughter and stories. They reminisced about Clara's childhood, her failed attempts at music, and the way her mom used to sing while cooking dinner.

"I wish Mom could see this," Clara said softly, her smile tinged with sadness.

"She would be proud of you," Liam said, his voice thick with emotion. "Of us."

By the time they finished, the rain had stopped, and the sun was breaking through the clouds. Liam looked at the plan they had laid out and felt a spark of something he hadn't felt in days: hope.

"Seven days," Clara said, tapping the notepad. "We've got this."

Liam nodded, a small smile playing on his lips. "Seven days."

For the first time since his diagnosis, he believed it might actually be possible. Together, they were stronger than the obstacles before them.

The studio was tucked behind the house, a standalone structure with weathered wooden walls and tall windows that let in streams of natural light. Clara had always thought of it as her dad's secret lair, a place she rarely ventured into. Today, as Liam led her inside, she realized she'd never really seen him in his element.

Liam paused just inside the doorway, his fingers brushing against the wall to find the light switch. "This is it," he said, his voice filled with both pride and hesitation.

The studio always felt mystical to Clara—an unassuming building with four walls of magic, a place where she didn't feel she belonged, and it was just a few steps from their house, through the kitchen patio door. Clara had seen her dad disappear into it countless times, but the door was rarely open to anyone else. Today, it was her turn to step inside and see what had been hidden in plain sight for all these years.

As Liam pushed the door open, a faint creak echoed, and they stepped into his world. The scent hit Clara immediately—a mix of sawdust, stone, and something metallic, like the sharp tang of tools freshly used. Sunlight filtered through the dusty windows, creating streaks of light that illuminated the organized chaos of the room.

Every inch of the space seemed to tell a story. To the left, shelves held blocks of stone in varying stages of transformation, from raw, jagged slabs to smooth, polished pieces awaiting their final touches. On the right, neatly arranged tools hung on pegboards—chisels, mallets, files, and instruments whose purposes Clara could only guess. A large wooden workbench stretched across the back wall, its surface scarred and stained from years of labor.

"Well," Liam said, gesturing broadly, "this is it. The heart and soul of your old man's hobby—no, scratch that—his obsession. Welcome to the studio."

Clara turned in a slow circle, taking it all in. "It's … not what I expected."

Liam smirked. "And what exactly were you expecting? A sterile art gallery?"

"No, but—wow," she said, stepping further inside. "There's so much stuff in here!"

"Stuff?" he repeated with mock offense. "These, young lady, are the tools of the trade. And if you're serious about helping me, you will need to know every single one of them."

He led her to the first workbench, running his fingers along its edge as though reacquainting himself with an old friend. "This is where it starts. These are chisels—see the way they're lined up, smallest to largest?"

Clara nodded, picking one up. It was heavier than it looked, its wooden handle smooth and worn. "What do these do?"

"They're for carving stone," Liam explained. "Each one has a different purpose. The big ones, like this, are for rough shaping, getting the basic form. The smaller ones are for detail work, the kind of precision that turns a block of stone into something alive."

Clara turned the chisel in her hand. "How do you even control this? It seems so … final."

"That's the trick," Liam said with a grin. "Sculpting is all about patience and control. You don't fight the material; you work with it. Every tap of the mallet matters. Too hard, and you ruin it. Too soft, and nothing happens."

He reached out, feeling for a mallet. "This is your best friend when working with stone. You'll use it to guide the chisel, one tap at a time. Want to try?"

Clara hesitated, then nodded. Liam handed her the mallet and guided her to a small practice piece of stone. "All right," he said, positioning her hand on the chisel, "hold it steady. Now, tap the top with the mallet—gently."

She did as he said, flinching slightly at the sound of the mallet striking the chisel. A tiny sliver of stone flaked away. "Did I just … sculpt?"

"Technically, yes," Liam said, laughing. "But don't get too excited. That was the easy part."

He moved them to the next station, where an array of sandpapers and polishing tools were neatly organized. "Once you've got your shape, this is where the magic happens. Polishing. It's slow, tedious work, but it's what makes the difference between a decent piece and something extraordinary. You start with coarse grit to smooth out the rough edges, then move to finer grits until the surface feels like silk."

Clara ran her fingers over a finished piece nearby. Its surface was so smooth it reflected the light like water. "This is insane. I can't believe you do all of this."

"And we're not done yet," Liam said, leading her to another corner of the studio. "Metalwork. That's where things get tricky. You see those tools over there? That's the welding setup. It's for joining metal pieces together, adding structure or embellishments to the sculpture. Welding is a whole art form in itself, and it's as much about precision as it is about creativity."

Clara looked at the welding tools with wide eyes. "You can weld too? Is there anything you don't do?"

"I don't play the piccolo," Liam said with a grin.

Clara burst out laughing. "Touché."

"Then there is the wood workbench right in the middle. But we don't need it for this sculpture." Liam pointed at the workbench, and even without his guidance, it was quite obvious to Clara that was where woodwork happened.

Finally, Liam brought her to a large object covered with a cloth. He hesitated, his hand hovering over the fabric. "And this," he said, his voice softening, "is what we're here for."

He pulled the cloth back, revealing the sculpture beneath. Clara's breath caught.

It wasn't finished, but even in its incomplete state, the piece was breathtaking. The stone base was rough and solid, grounding the sculpture. Above it, spiraling tendrils of metal twisted upward, as though reaching for something beyond.

"This is the project," Liam said. "The client wanted something that represents transformation. For me, this is it—the balance between chaos and order, between past and future. The stone at the base—that's the foundation, the things we can't change. The metal? That's us, always moving, always adapting."

Liam spent another five whole minutes explaining his vision for the sculpture and showed her sketches that he had meticulously drawn to scale in his special notebook.

Clara stepped closer, running her fingers lightly over the stone. "It's incredible, Dad. I mean it. I've never seen you talk about something like this before."

Liam smiled faintly. "It's personal. It's not just for the client. It's for us. It's for you."

Clara looked at him, her eyes shining. "We are going to finish this. Together."

He nodded, his expression a mix of determination and vulnerability. "All right," he said. "Let's make some magic."

For the next three nights, the studio became their sanctuary. Clara would rush home from school, her backpack barely touching the floor before she joined Liam in the quiet, fragrant space of his workshop. The faint smell of stone dust and the metallic tang of tools greeted her like old friends, welcoming her into this new world. The routine was grueling but exhilarating: hours spent shaping, smoothing, and refining the sculpture, often stretching past midnight into the early hours of the morning.

The first evening, Clara approached the incomplete frame with trepidation. It loomed before her, an untamed mess of stone and metal, rough edges sticking out like unsolved problems. She turned to Liam, who sat in his chair, his clouded eyes seemingly gazing past the structure.

"Where do I even start?" she asked, her voice tinged with doubt.

"The base," Liam said with certainty. "It's the foundation of everything. Without it, the whole piece collapses. Take the rasp. It's hanging on the second hook to your left—and even out the stone. Run your fingers along it. Feel for where it's uneven."

Clara retrieved the rasp, her fingers brushing against its textured handle. She knelt beside the stone, placing her hands on its surface. "It's cold," she murmured.

"It'll warm up as you work with it," Liam replied with a knowing smile. "Now, use the rasp. Gentle strokes. Let the stone guide you—it'll tell you what it needs."

Her first attempts were clumsy, the rasp grating against the stone with a jarring screech. "I'm terrible at this," she muttered.

"Every sculptor is terrible at the beginning," Liam assured her. "The key is persistence. Keep going."

Slowly, she found a rhythm. The rasp moved back and forth, shaving off tiny bits of stone. The studio filled with the soft sound of dust falling to the ground, and Clara began to lose herself in the process. Hours passed as she worked, pausing only to step back and assess her progress.

When the base was finally smooth, Liam nodded approvingly. "You've done well. Tomorrow, we'll tackle the metal. That's where the real challenge begins."

The next evening, Clara returned to the studio with a mix of excitement and apprehension. She greeted Liam, who was already seated and waiting. "Ready for the next step?" he asked.

"As I'll ever be," she replied, tying her hair back.

"Metal is tricky," Liam began. "It doesn't forgive mistakes easily. You have to be precise. First, we'll heat it. There's a torch on the workbench to your right. Light it carefully and let the flame steady before you begin."

Clara picked up the torch, her hands trembling slightly. She turned the knob and struck the flint, the sudden hiss of the flame startling her.

"Good," Liam said. "Now, bring it close to the brass tendril on the left—not too close, just enough to make it pliable. Watch the color. When it glows a dull red, you'll know it's ready."

The metal responded to the heat, softening as the flame danced over it. Clara used pliers to bend it into shape, her arms straining with the effort. "This is harder than it looks," she said through gritted teeth.

"It's a dance," Liam explained. "You lead, but you also listen. Metal has its own will. If you try to force it, it'll fight back. We are using brass and bronze for this sculpture."

They worked late into the night, alternating between heating, bending, and letting the metals cool. Liam's instructions were precise, his voice calm and steady despite the challenges. "Now let it rest," he said. "Metal has a memory—it needs time to set."

Clara nodded, her hands aching but her spirits high. "This is starting to feel like a workout," she joked.

"It's a workout for the soul," Liam replied with a chuckle.

By the third evening, Clara had grown more confident. She suggested intertwining the metal tendrils, creating a sense of tension and connection.

"That's not what I had in mind," Liam said, his tone hesitant.

"But it could work," Clara argued. "Look—if we weave them together, it'll create movement, like they're pulling toward and away from each other."

Clara quickly grabbed the notebook and turned to a fresh page and drew her vision with her pen.

Liam was not quite impressed. He paused, then nodded. "Show me. Pick a few small pieces and create a sample of your intertwining magic."

Clara didn't hesitate. She seemed to have picked up the basic skills needed to create four tendrils very quickly, using heat and other techniques. When Liam got to see what she created in a couple of hours, he was quite impressed.

"Go on then, young lady! I like your confidence." Liam was hiding the proud smile that tried to sneak out.

Clara spent hours bending the metal into intricate loops and spirals, each piece requiring careful adjustment and cooling. She worked until her fingers were raw, her imagination running wild.

By Saturday morning, exhaustion and excitement mingled as Clara entered the studio for the final push. She retrieved the clay from its storage shelf, kneading it with determination.

"Clay is forgiving," Liam said. "It's where you can be bold. Let your instincts take over. Remember, we are using clay for aesthetics in this sculpture. Clay shouldn't stand out and instead should blend in with the metal. To bring out some contrast and balance over the intertwining tendrils you have created."

Clara began shaping the clay, adding delicate textures and bold curves. Liam described his original vision. "I wanted it to represent struggle and resilience as part of the transformation concept. A push and pull between forces—but always moving forward."

Clara nodded, adding her own interpretation. "It feels like life— messy and complicated, but beautiful when you step back and see the whole picture."

They worked together until the sculpture was complete, the studio filled with the soft light of afternoon.

"It's not what I imagined," Liam said, his voice thick with emotion. "It's better."

Clara smiled, her hands still dusted with stone and metal shavings. "We did this, Dad. Together."

The two stood in silence, the sculpture casting long shadows in the fading light. It wasn't just a work of art—it was a testament to their bond, their resilience, and their shared creativity.

The morning dawned with a quiet buzz of nerves and excitement. Liam and Clara carefully secured the sculpture in the back of their truck, wrapping it meticulously in layers of blankets and straps. The creation felt heavier than it was, as though it carried the weight of their journey.

"You've triple-checked it's secure, right?" Clara asked, her voice laced with both concern and anticipation.

"For the fourth time, yes," Liam replied, smiling faintly. "It's not going anywhere."

The drive to Mr. Kensington's estate was quieter than either of them expected. Clara drove while Liam sat in the passenger seat, his fingers tracing invisible patterns on his jeans.

"Do you think he'll like it?" Liam finally asked, breaking the silence.

"He'll love it," Clara said firmly. "And if he doesn't, he's got terrible taste."

Liam chuckled. "You've got your mother's way with words."

When they arrived, the estate loomed before them, a grand spectacle of wealth and opulence. Wrought-iron gates swung open to reveal manicured lawns, a winding driveway, and a mansion that looked like it belonged in a period drama. Clara couldn't help but gawk as she parked the truck.

"Are we delivering art or entering a palace?" she muttered.

Mr. Kensington greeted them at the entrance, his tailored suit and gold-rimmed glasses giving him an air of polished sophistication.

"Ah, Liam!" he said, shaking his hand warmly. "And this must be your daughter. I've heard so much about you both."

Clara nodded, smiling politely. "It's a pleasure to meet you, Mr. Kensington."

"I must say," Kensington continued, "I've been looking forward to this all week. I've kept myself from peeking at the sculpture—you've kept it quite the mystery!"

Liam smiled, steadying his breath. "Well, I hope it lives up to your expectations."

The unveiling ceremony was set in the sprawling garden behind the mansion, where a pedestal had been prepared for the sculpture. Guests milled about, sipping champagne and chatting as a soft string quartet played in the background. The crowd was a mix of local art connoisseurs, community leaders, wealthy neighbors, and a few members of the press.

Clara helped Liam carefully carry the sculpture, still cloaked in its protective covering, to the pedestal. As they set it down, she could feel the weight of everyone's gaze.

"Breathe, Dad," she whispered.

When the time came, Mr. Kensington took the small stage set up near the pedestal. He raised a glass to the crowd, his booming voice silencing the chatter. "Ladies and gentlemen, thank you all for joining me today. As many of you know, I've long been a patron of the arts, and it's rare to find a piece—or an artist—that truly moves me. Particularly an artist who belongs to this community—our community. But today, I believe we are about to witness something extraordinary. Liam Callahan has crafted a sculpture that promises to be nothing short of breathtaking."

The audience applauded politely, their interest piqued.

Kensington gestured toward Liam. "Now, without further ado, let's unveil this masterpiece. *Transformation.*"

Clara gently guided Liam forward, whispering directions to him as they approached the pedestal. His hands found the cloth covering the sculpture, and he paused for a moment, as if saying goodbye to a secret he'd held for so long.

With a single, fluid motion, he pulled the cloth away.

The gasp that followed was nearly audible over the music. Conversations stopped mid-sentence. Glasses paused halfway to lips.

The sculpture stood tall and radiant, its interplay of stone and metal giving it a life of its own. The metallic arcs seemed to dance in the sunlight, while the carved stone base grounded it with a sense of permanence. The abstraction was purposeful yet evocative, inviting the viewer to find their own interpretation of the concept.

For Mr. Kensington, it was a moment of stunned silence. He stepped closer, his mouth slightly open. "My God," he murmured. "Liam, this is … it's beyond anything I could have imagined."

The crowd began to applaud, the sound growing louder as people approached to admire the sculpture up close. Words like "mesmerizing," "genius," and "unparalleled" floated through the air.

Kensington turned back to Liam, his expression one of awe. "You've outdone yourself, truly. This is not just a sculpture—it's a statement, a testament to the power of art. I love it."

Liam's voice was steady, though his hands were clasped tightly behind his back. "I'm glad it resonates with you."

Guests began to approach Liam, offering their congratulations and probing him with questions about his inspiration and technique. Clara stayed close, whispering cues when needed, ensuring he navigated the conversations without revealing his condition.

One guest, a prominent gallery owner, exclaimed, "Mr. Callahan, you must showcase this at our next exhibition! It's too magnificent to keep here alone!"

Another chimed in, "Do you take commissions? I have a garden that would be perfect for one of your works."

Kensington, watching all this, leaned toward Liam. "It seems you've created quite the sensation. I hope you're ready for the spotlight."

As the evening wound down, Kensington handed Liam an envelope. "Here's your payment, and let me just say—it's worth every penny. I'd also like to commission you for another piece. Something even larger, if you're up for the challenge."

Liam took the envelope, his fingers trembling slightly. "Thank you, Mr. Kensington. I'm honored."

The ride home was filled with a quiet sense of accomplishment. Clara glanced at her dad, who was unusually still, holding the envelope tightly.

"You okay, Dad?" she asked.

"Better than okay," he said softly. "For the first time in a long while, I feel … complete."

As they pulled into the driveway, Clara's phone buzzed. She stepped out to take the call, recognizing the number immediately.

"Miss Callahan, this is Dr. Monroe," the ophthalmologist said. "I wanted to let you know that we've had a breakthrough. There's a new surgical procedure that could restore part of your father's vision. It's not guaranteed, but it's promising. Can you bring him in next week to discuss this?"

Clara's heart raced, but she forced herself to remain calm. "Thank you, Dr. Monroe. I'll bring him in."

She ended the call and turned to see Liam unloading their tools, his expression peaceful.

"Everything okay?" he asked.

Clara smiled, nodding. "Yeah, just a friend checking in."

As they walked into the house, Liam paused by the door and turned to Clara. "You know, I thought losing my sight would be the end of everything. But tonight, I realized something. Life isn't just about what we see—it's about what we create, what we share. And I think I can live the rest of my life through your eyes."

Clara hugged him tightly, her throat tight with emotion. No words were spoken as they stepped inside, the warm light of their home wrapping around them. The future remained uncertain, but for now, they had this—a triumph born of struggle, a bond that nothing could break.

BONDS BEYOND TIME

The old man stood at his gate, leaning lightly on his cane, his sharp blue eyes scanning the quiet street. His hands, weathered with age, rested on the wrought iron bars that had seen decades of seasons pass. The street was quiet, save for the occasional rustle of leaves as the evening breeze carried the faint scent of pine. It was his favorite time of the day—that golden hour when the sun dipped low and bathed everything in a soft, amber glow.

At eighty-one, solitude had become both a comfort and a burden. Mr. Carter had lived in the same house for nearly half a century. He knew every crack in the pavement, every tree that lined the street, and every bird that perched on the telephone wires. Yet, he knew few of the people who passed by these days. The neighborhood had changed over the years; the families he had once known had moved away, replaced by strangers with busy lives and unfamiliar faces.

As he leaned there, savoring the evening's tranquility, a movement caught his eye. A young boy appeared at the far end of the street, a leash dangling from his hand. At the other end of the leash was a golden retriever, its tail wagging with unrestrained enthusiasm. The dog seemed to lead the way, occasionally pulling at the boy's grip, eager to explore the scents and sights of the evening.

The boy, in contrast, moved with a certain hesitancy. His head was slightly bowed, his gaze fixed on the pavement as though it held secrets only he could see. His small frame was dwarfed by the over-sized hoodie he wore, and his sneakers made soft scuffing sounds against the sidewalk.

The dog, oblivious to the boy's demeanor, suddenly perked up, its ears twitching. It had spotted Mr. Carter at the gate. With a joyous bark, the golden retriever bounded forward, nearly pulling the boy off balance. The leash slipped from his hand, and the dog bolted straight to the gate, its tail wagging furiously.

Mr. Carter chuckled, crouching down to meet the exuberant animal. "Well, hello there," he said, his voice warm but tinged with the raspy wear of age. He reached through the bars, his fingers finding the dog's soft fur. "Aren't you a friendly one?"

The boy hurried after his dog, his steps quickening until he reached the gate. He stopped a few feet away, his dark eyes flicking nervously between the old man and his canine companion.

"Sorry," the boy mumbled, his voice barely above a whisper. He tugged lightly at the leash, but the dog refused to budge, now fully engrossed in Mr. Carter's affectionate pats.

"No need to apologize," Mr. Carter said, straightening up with some effort. "He's a good dog. What's his name?"

The boy hesitated, his fingers twisting the loose end of the leash. "Max," he said finally.

"Max," Mr. Carter repeated with a smile. "A fine name for a fine dog." He gave the retriever one last pat before stepping back. "And what about you, young man? Do you have a name?"

The boy's gaze dropped to the ground, and for a moment, Mr. Carter thought he might not answer. Then, almost inaudibly, he said, "Ethan."

"Ethan," the old man said, nodding as though committing it to memory. "Well, Ethan, it's a pleasure to meet you and Max."

Ethan nodded but didn't say anything more. He gave the leash another gentle tug, and this time, Max relented, though not without a wistful glance back at the old man. As they walked away, Ethan cast a quick look over his shoulder, his expression a mix of curiosity and caution.

Mr. Carter watched them until they disappeared around the corner. A faint smile lingered on his lips as he turned back toward his house. For the first time in a long while, the evening felt a little less empty.

Over the next few days, Ethan and Max's evening walks became a part of Mr. Carter's routine. He would wait by his gate at the same time each evening, leaning on his cane and looking out for the familiar figures at the far end of the street. The golden retriever, ever eager, would often spot him first, tugging at Ethan's leash with newfound enthusiasm.

It wasn't long before Ethan began to slow his steps as they approached Mr. Carter's gate. The boy was still shy, still hesitant, but Max's uncontainable excitement seemed to act as a bridge between them. Mr. Carter's warm smile and gentle demeanor helped too. It wasn't just Max who enjoyed these visits—Ethan had started to look forward to them, though he was careful not to show it.

One evening, as the autumn air carried the scent of woodsmoke, Ethan found himself lingering at the gate longer than usual. Mr. Carter had pulled a squeaky toy out of his pocket, much to Max's delight. The dog pounced at the toy, his paws skidding on the pavement as he chased it back and forth through the bars of the gate.

"Does he always have this much energy?" Mr. Carter asked, chuckling as Max let out a series of happy barks.

Ethan shrugged. "Most of the time. But he gets tired after a while."

"Good thing," Mr. Carter said with a wink. "Otherwise, you'd never get any rest."

The boy's lips twitched into a small smile—the first Mr. Carter had seen. Encouraged, the old man continued. "You know, I used to have a dog when I was about your age. His name was Rusty. He was smaller than Max but just as stubborn."

"What kind of dog was he?" Ethan asked, his voice soft but curious.

"A terrier mix," Mr. Carter replied, his eyes growing distant. "He used to chase squirrels like it was his life's mission. Never caught one, though."

Ethan's smile widened slightly. "Max tries to catch birds. He's not very good at it."

"Smart birds," Mr. Carter said with a grin. "Or maybe Max just likes the chase more than the catch."

For a few minutes, they stood there, exchanging small stories about their dogs. Ethan's initial caution seemed to melt away, replaced by a tentative sense of comfort. Max, meanwhile, busied himself with the squeaky toy, gnawing at it with the single-minded focus only dogs possess.

"You're welcome to stop by anytime," Mr. Carter said after a while. "Max seems to enjoy the company, and I … well, I've got plenty of treats and toys to spare."

Ethan looked up at him, his dark eyes thoughtful. "Maybe. If it's okay with my parents."

"Of course," Mr. Carter said quickly. "I wouldn't want to cause any trouble."

The boy nodded but didn't say anything more. He gave Max's leash a gentle tug, signaling it was time to leave. As they walked away, Mr. Carter called out, "Good night, Ethan. Good night, Max."

Ethan hesitated for a moment before turning back. "Good night, Mr. Carter," he said quietly, his voice barely carrying over the distance.

From then on, Ethan and Max visited every day. Mr. Carter would leave the gate open, and Ethan would walk onto the porch, where Mr. Carter would be standing. At first, they stayed only for a few minutes, just long enough for Max to collect his treat and play with a new toy. But as the days passed, the visits grew longer. Mr. Carter began to keep a small stash of dog toys by the wall lining the porch—bright tennis balls, ropes, and the occasional squeaky bone. For Ethan, he kept a jar of homemade oatmeal cookies on hand, in case the boy ever felt brave enough to accept one.

By the second week, Ethan's caution had been replaced by something resembling trust. He began to share snippets of his day—small, inconsequential details about school, the weather, or a funny thing Max had done. Mr. Carter listened intently, never interrupting, letting the boy set the pace of their conversations.

One particularly crisp evening, as the sky turned a deep shade of orange, Ethan surprised Mr. Carter by asking a question of his own. "Why do you always wait by the gate?"

Mr. Carter smiled, the lines around his eyes crinkling. "Well, I suppose I enjoy the company. The days get a bit quiet when you live alone. And besides," he added, glancing at Max, "you two are much better company than the pigeons in my back yard."

Ethan laughed softly, the sound carrying a warmth that lingered in the cool evening air. For the first time in a long while, Mr. Carter felt the heaviness of his solitude lift, replaced by the quiet joy of connection.

⧻

As the third week began, the visits had become a highlight of Mr. Carter's day. He had always been a man of routine, but this new addition—the sound of Max's excited barking, the sight of Ethan's small, hesitant smile—had given his life a new sense of purpose. He found himself browsing the pet aisle at the local store more often than usual, picking out treats and toys he thought Max might like.

Ethan too seemed to be changing. His usually quiet demeanor had brightened, and his parents had noticed. They didn't press him for details, but they were grateful for whatever was bringing him out of his shell. The boy who once kept to himself now hummed as he set the table or walked Max around the block.

The weather had turned a bit too cold for Ethan to be walking without his gloves these days. But he did not want that to prevent his evening meetings with Mr. Carter. One cold November evening, as they sat on the front steps of Mr. Carter's house, Ethan opened up about his struggles with math homework. "I just don't get fractions," he admitted, scratching Max behind the ears.

"Ah, fractions," Mr. Carter said, nodding. "They used to confuse me too. But you know what helped me? Thinking of them like slices of pie."

Ethan tilted his head. "Pie?"

"Sure. If you have one pie and you cut it into four pieces, each piece is a quarter. It's much easier to understand when you're thinking about dessert," he said with a wink.

Ethan giggled. "Maybe I'll try that."

They spent the next half hour going over Ethan's math problems, with Mr. Carter turning each fraction into a slice of imaginary pie or cake or an oatmeal cookie that was readily available. By the time Ethan stood to leave, he seemed more confident—and a little more willing to tackle his homework.

As they waved goodbye, Mr. Carter leaned on his cane and watched them disappear down the street. The crisp evening air was filled with the faint sound of Max's excited barking and Ethan's soft voice, and for the first time in years, Mr. Carter felt truly content.

The days turned into weeks, and Ethan's evening walks with Max to Mr. Carter's house became a routine. For Mr. Carter, those precious hours filled his days with joy. For Ethan, they became the highlight of his afternoons. The quiet, shy boy had begun to open up, and Mr. Carter's gentle patience seemed to work wonders.

It was a late fall evening, and the sun had started to set early. During his regular walk, Ethan approached the gate with Max tugging at the leash, his tail wagging furiously. Mr. Carter was already waiting with a bag of treats and a bright-red rubber ball he had picked up that morning.

"Good evening, Ethan! Good evening, Max!" Mr. Carter greeted them warmly.

Max barked in excitement, wagging his tail so vigorously it looked like he might take off.

"Hi, Mr. Carter," Ethan replied, his voice louder and more confident than it had been the first week.

"Come in, come in! I've got something new for Max," Mr. Carter said, opening the gate wide.

Ethan hesitated for a moment, as he always did, before stepping through. But Max had no such reservations and darted forward, nuzzling Mr. Carter's leg before sniffing at the treat bag.

"No manners, that dog," Ethan said, grinning shyly.

"Nonsense! He's a connoisseur of fine treats." Mr. Carter chuckled, pulling out a treat and tossing it to Max. "Catch!" Max caught it in midair with an impressive snap of his jaws.

Ethan laughed, and it was the kind of laugh that seemed to surprise even him. It lit up his face, and for a moment, Mr. Carter felt a warmth that made his old house feel a bit livelier than he had seen in almost a decade.

⊪

Inside the cozy living room, Ethan sat on the couch with Max sprawled at his feet. Mr. Carter handed Ethan a mug of hot chocolate and settled into his armchair.

"So, Ethan, how was school today?" Mr. Carter asked casually, leaning back and sipping his tea.

Ethan's shoulders tensed slightly, and he stared into his mug. "It was okay," he said, but his tone lacked conviction.

Mr. Carter noticed but didn't press. Instead, he let the silence hang for a moment before shifting the topic. "Do you know what I used to do when I was your age?"

Ethan's curiosity got the better of him. "What?" he asked, glancing up.

"I'd spend hours building model airplanes," Mr. Carter said. "I wasn't much older than you when I built my first one. Got it to fly for about thirty seconds before it nosedived into my mother's rosebushes."

Ethan smiled faintly. "Thirty seconds is pretty good, I guess."

"Oh, it was spectacular," Mr. Carter said, his eyes twinkling. "But one of the young rosebushes didn't survive, and neither did my allowance that month."

Ethan giggled, the tension in his shoulders easing. "Did you build more after that?"

"Of course! I got better with every one I built. Life's a bit like that, you know. You try, you fail, and then you try again. Each time, you get a little better."

‖≠

As the days went by, Ethan started opening up in small increments. It was Max, as always, who first sensed the boy's unease. One evening, while Mr. Carter tossed the new red ball for Max to chase, Ethan sat unusually quiet on the porch steps.

"You're awfully quiet today, young man," Mr. Carter said gently, sitting down beside him. "What's on your mind?"

Ethan shrugged. "Nothing."

"Ah, nothing. The heaviest word there is," Mr. Carter said with a knowing smile. "If I had a nickel for every time someone said 'nothing' when they really meant 'something,' I'd be richer than all the kings and queens in the storybooks."

Ethan didn't say anything at first, but Mr. Carter waited, his expression open and patient. Finally, Ethan glanced over at him.

"There's this kid at school," Ethan began, his voice barely above a whisper. "He's mean to me."

"I see," Mr. Carter said, nodding. "What does he do?"

Ethan hesitated. "He calls me names. Pushes me sometimes. But the worst part is …" He trailed off, staring at his hands.

"The worst part is?" Mr. Carter prompted gently.

"He knows something about me," Ethan said. "Something I don't want anyone to know. He said he'll tell everyone if I say anything to the teacher."

Mr. Carter's expression didn't change, but inside, his heart ached for the boy. He placed a comforting hand on Ethan's shoulder.

"That's a tough spot to be in," he said. "I'm sorry you're going through this. But you know, Ethan, bullies rely on fear. They win by making you believe you have no choices."

"But I don't have a choice," Ethan said, his voice trembling.

"There's always a choice," Mr. Carter said firmly. "You just need a plan. And I think we can come up with one together."

Ethan's eyes widened. "Together?"

"Of course," Mr. Carter said. "That's what friends are for, isn't it?"

For the first time that evening, Ethan smiled. It was small, but it was genuine.

⫢

The rest of the evening was spent brainstorming. Mr. Carter was careful not to push too hard, letting Ethan take the lead as much as possible.

"What does Max do when he wants something he's not supposed to have?" Mr. Carter asked at one point.

Ethan looked puzzled. "He … distracts me?"

"Exactly," Mr. Carter said. "Sometimes the best way to deal with a bully is to outsmart them. Let's think about ways we can distract this boy—or maybe even turn the tables on him, without getting you into trouble."

They talked late into the evening, their conversation punctuated by bursts of laughter as Max repeatedly interrupted by dropping the red ball onto their laps. By the time Ethan and Max left, the boy's spirits had lifted noticeably.

Mr. Carter watched them disappear down the street, his heart lighter than it had been in years. He had no doubt that they were on the path to solving Ethan's problem. And perhaps, along the way, Ethan was helping him solve a problem of his own—the quiet loneliness that had settled over his life like a fog.

As he closed the door and turned out the porch light, Mr. Carter smiled to himself. "What is that strange feeling?" he asked himself because he felt like he truly belonged to something after many years. And that something was Ethan and Max.

Ethan sat cross-legged on his bedroom floor, staring intently at the piece of paper in front of him. Scribbled on it were ideas and phrases Mr. Carter had suggested when they discussed how to handle Ethan's problem with Brian, the school bully. Mr. Carter's voice echoed in his mind. *Sometimes, the best way to deal with someone like Brian is to take away his power—his ability to intimidate you. Remember, it's about confidence, Ethan.*"

The plan was simple yet daring. Ethan had decided to subtly confront Brian by flipping the script. Instead of showing fear, he would use humor and quick thinking to challenge Brian without escalating the situation. But the real key lay in exposing Brian's threats in a way that defused their potency. Ethan's heart raced as he mentally rehearsed every step, bolstered by the trust and encouragement Mr. Carter had instilled in him.

The next day at school, Ethan saw Brian lingering near the lockers, his usual smirk plastered across his face. Ethan took a deep breath and approached him, clutching his lunchbox tightly. Brian turned and immediately began to sneer.

"Hey, Ethan! Ready to hand over your cookies again? Or do I need to remind you of our little ... secret?"

Ethan forced a small smile and tilted his head. "You know, Brian, I've been thinking about that."

Brian's smirk faltered slightly. "Thinking about what?"

"The secret," Ethan said nonchalantly, leaning casually against the lockers. "It's not really that big of a deal, is it? I mean, you could tell people, but honestly, it's kind of funny if you think about it."

Brian frowned. "Funny? What are you talking about?"

Ethan chuckled softly. "Well, who cares if I tripped in gym class and fell into the equipment cart? Everyone trips sometimes. If you tell people, I'll just tell them how you're obsessed with it. Maybe they'll start to wonder why you care so much about something so silly."

Brian's face flushed. He hadn't expected Ethan to turn the situation around so calmly. "Uh ... whatever," he mumbled, shoving his hands into his pockets. "You're still a loser."

Ethan smiled wider. "Maybe, but at least I'm a loser who doesn't spend all day worrying about other people's gym class mishaps. Later, Brian!"

Brian, ruffled but unfazed, came back with his second line

of attack. "You know what Ethan? I have another secret. That drawing …"

Before Brian could finish his sentence, Ethan piped in and said, "Be my guest. Jack has already seen it and he actually likes it. Boo!"

Brian's face was red now. He didn't know what came over Ethan and how he had transformed. This was a new Ethan—one he had never seen before. His body language showed he had been insulted. He shrugged his shoulders and said again, "Uh … whatever," and quietly walked away.

Ethan walked away confidently, his heart pounding with adrenaline and triumph. For the first time, he felt a spark of pride in standing up for himself—all thanks to Mr. Carter's advice and belief in him.

That evening, Ethan could hardly contain his excitement as he and Max walked down the familiar path to Mr. Carter's house. Max wagged his tail enthusiastically, sensing Ethan's good mood.

Mr. Carter was already waiting by the gate, his usual warm smile in place. "Evening, Ethan. You look like a man on a mission. What's the news?"

Ethan grinned from ear to ear. "It worked, Mr. Carter! Your plan worked!"

Mr. Carter's eyes twinkled with pride. "Did it now? Come on in and tell me all about it."

Once they were settled in the cozy living room, with Max happily gnawing on a treat, Ethan recounted the events at school in vivid detail. He mimicked Brian's reaction and his own newfound confidence, eliciting a hearty laugh from Mr. Carter.

"You handled it brilliantly, Ethan," Mr. Carter said. "By taking control of the situation, you showed Brian he couldn't hold anything over you. That takes courage."

Ethan blushed slightly but felt a warm glow of pride. "I couldn't have done it without you. You gave me the idea and … I don't know, just made me feel like I could actually do it."

Mr. Carter leaned forward. "Ethan, all I did was remind you of what was already inside you. You have more strength and cleverness than you realize. It's just about believing in yourself."

They spent the rest of the evening talking and laughing, with Ethan sharing more about his school life and Mr. Carter recounting humorous stories from his own childhood. Mr. Carter told him about a time when he had to outsmart a bully of his own in grade school by pretending to befriend him and then cleverly avoiding conflict altogether. Ethan listened intently, marveling at how similar their experiences seemed.

"You know, Ethan," Mr. Carter said, "when I was your age, I used to think the people who picked on me were the strongest. But over time, I learned that real strength isn't about being the loudest or the toughest. It's about being smart, kind, and not letting others dictate how you feel about yourself."

Ethan nodded, feeling a newfound admiration for his older friend. "I guess I never thought about it that way. But you're right. Standing up to Brian wasn't just about making him stop. It was about proving to myself that I could do it."

Mr. Carter smiled warmly. "Exactly. And you should be proud of yourself, Ethan. You've taken a big step today."

As the evening stretched on, their conversation meandered to lighter topics. Ethan asked about Mr. Carter's favorite hobbies, and Mr. Carter regaled him with tales of his gardening adventures, complete with mishaps involving overenthusiastic squirrels and bunnies. In turn, Ethan shared his aspirations of building a treehouse one day, a dream he'd always kept to himself.

"A treehouse, huh?" Mr. Carter said with a grin. "You know, I used to build forts with my friends when I was your age. Maybe one day we could sketch out some ideas for your treehouse. I've still got a few tricks up my sleeve."

Ethan's face lit up. "Really? That would be awesome!"

Max, as if sensing the joyful energy in the room, leapt up and barked playfully, his tail wagging furiously. The three of them laughed, the room filled with a sense of warmth and connection that felt almost magical.

As the sky outside turned a deep indigo, Ethan finally stood to leave. "Thanks, Mr. Carter," he said sincerely. "For everything."

Mr. Carter smiled and patted Ethan's shoulder. "You're always welcome here, Ethan. And remember, you've got a friend in me—and Max, of course."

Ethan walked home that night with a lighter heart and a brighter outlook, feeling as though he'd gained not just confidence but a true mentor and friend in Mr. Carter. And in his pocket, tucked away for safekeeping, was a small note Mr. Carter had given him: *The strongest people aren't those who show strength in front of us, but those who win battles we know nothing about.*

As he reached his house, Ethan looked back in the direction of Mr. Carter's home, the glow of the porch light still visible. He smiled to himself, knowing that this friendship had become something truly special. Tomorrow, he thought, would be another good day.

Ethan had been unusually happy over the past few days. His parents, Sarah and David, noticed the spring in his step, the frequent humming as he worked on his homework, and the way his face lit up whenever Max nudged him for a pat. It was a delightful transformation, but it also left them curious. They exchanged glances across the dinner table, silently agreeing it was time to ask Ethan what had changed.

"Ethan, you've been looking so cheerful lately," Sarah said, placing a hand on his shoulder. "Did something good happen at school?"

Ethan looked up from his plate, his fork pausing in midair. He hesitated, unsure how to start. Max, lying at his feet, seemed to sense his uncertainty and gave a small, encouraging bark.

"Well … sort of," Ethan began, his cheeks turning a faint pink. "Actually, a lot of good things happened."

David leaned forward, his curiosity piqued. "Really? Like what?"

Ethan set his fork down and took a deep breath. "You know how I used to be quiet all the time? How I didn't want to talk about stuff that bothered me?" He glanced at his mom, then his dad. They both nodded, their expressions soft with encouragement.

"There was this kid at school," Ethan continued. "Brian. He was kind of a bully."

Sarah's face tightened with concern. "A bully? Ethan, why didn't you tell us?"

Ethan shrugged, looking down. "I was scared. Brian knew something about me, and he said he'd tell everyone if I tattled on him. I didn't know what to do."

David frowned, his protective instincts kicking in. "What did he know? And how bad was it?"

Ethan's voice dropped. "It wasn't really bad, but it was embarrassing. He saw me tripping and falling in gym class one day. And another day, he saw me drawing in my notebook—a picture of Max and me wearing superhero costumes. It was an awful drawing. He said it was stupid and babyish. He said if I told anyone about him bullying me, he'd show everyone my drawing and share the story of my gym mishap."

Sarah's heart ached as she reached out to touch Ethan's hand. "Oh, honey, I'm so sorry you went through that."

Ethan smiled faintly. "It's okay now. I'm not scared anymore. I figured out how to handle it."

David exchanged a puzzled glance with Sarah. "What changed?"

Ethan's face brightened, and he leaned forward, his enthusiasm spilling out. "Mr. Carter helped me. He's the old man who lives down the street. Max really likes him, and we started visiting him during our evening walks. At first, I didn't talk much, but Mr. Carter's really nice. He's kind of like a grandpa."

Sarah tilted her head. "Mr. Carter? I think I may have caught a glimpse of him a few times. Older man, gray hair, always waving to everyone?"

Ethan nodded. "Yeah, that's him! He's really smart too. I told him about Brian and the drawing and the gym, and he came up with this plan. He said I should show the drawing to my best friend first. That way, if Brian tried to embarrass me, it wouldn't work because I wouldn't be ashamed anymore. And then also confront Brian about the gym incident directly and let him know that he was free to share it with whoever he wanted, cause it didn't bother me anymore. "

David raised his eyebrows. "That's … actually really clever."

Ethan beamed. "It worked, too! I showed the drawing to Jack, and he thought it was awesome. He even asked if I could draw him and his dog as superheroes. So, when Brian tried to make fun of me, I just laughed and told him Jack already liked it. Brian didn't know what to say."

Sarah's eyes welled up with pride. "Ethan, that's amazing. I'm so proud of you."

David nodded in agreement. "You faced your fear and came out stronger. That's not easy to do."

Ethan's smile grew wider. "I couldn't have done it without Mr. Carter. He's the best. He listens, he gives great advice, and he even lets me help him in his garden. And Max loves him too."

Max, as if on cue, wagged his tail and barked softly, earning a chuckle from everyone at the table.

"We need to thank Mr. Carter," Sarah said. "He's clearly made a big difference in your life."

Ethan's eyes sparkled. "Can we invite him over for dinner? I think he'd like that."

David smiled. "Absolutely. Let's set it up."

As the family finished their meal, they marveled at how much Ethan had grown in such a short time. The boy who once kept his struggles to himself was now opening up, solving problems, and forging meaningful connections—all thanks to an old man, a wise heart, and the love of a dog named Max.

Ethan and Max had settled into a comforting routine of visiting Mr. Carter every evening. As the days passed and autumn turned into winter, their bond only deepened, and Ethan began to look forward to these moments more than anything else. Max, as always, was the bridge between them, bounding ahead on their walks and nudging the old man's hand for affection as soon as they arrived.

One December evening, Ethan and Max found Mr. Carter sitting on his porch, a wool blanket draped over his knees. He was sipping tea from a chipped ceramic mug, his gaze distant as if lost in memories. Max trotted up to him, nudging his hand, and Mr. Carter smiled faintly, scratching the dog's ears.

"You're always the first to greet me, aren't you, Max?" he murmured.

Ethan climbed the porch steps, carrying a small bouquet of wildflowers he'd picked along the way. "These are for you, Mr. Carter," he said shyly, handing them over.

Mr. Carter's face softened as he accepted the flowers. "Why, thank you, Ethan. These are lovely. You're quite the thoughtful young man."

They sat together on the porch, with Max lying contentedly at their feet. For a while, they simply enjoyed the stillness of the evening, the occasional chirp of crickets filling the silence. Then Ethan spoke. "Mr. Carter, do you ever get lonely?" he asked, his voice tentative.

The old man hesitated, his fingers tightening slightly around his mug. "Sometimes," he admitted. "It's hard not to, living alone. But Max and you … you've made my days much brighter."

Ethan smiled, feeling a warm glow of pride. "You've made my days better too," he said. "Before we met, I didn't really talk to anyone except Max and my parents. I didn't think anyone would understand me."

Mr. Carter looked at him, his eyes filled with a mix of sadness and affection. "I understand that feeling, Ethan. Sometimes it's easier to keep to yourself than to risk being misunderstood."

Ethan tilted his head. "Did you always live alone?"

Mr. Carter's gaze drifted to the horizon. "Not always. There was a time when my house was full of laughter. My wife … she loved to bake, and the kitchen always smelled of something sweet. And my daughter … she had a laugh that could light up the whole street."

Ethan's heart ached at the wistfulness in Mr. Carter's voice. "What happened to them?"

Mr. Carter hesitated, his voice dropping to a near whisper. "Life has a way of taking things away. My wife passed on many years ago. My daughter … she moved away, and we lost touch."

Ethan didn't know what to say, so he reached out and placed his hand gently on Mr. Carter's arm. "I'm sorry," he said softly.

The old man smiled faintly, patting Ethan's hand. "Thank you, son. But don't be sad for me. I've had my share of happiness too. I am eighty-one. And now, I have you and Max to keep me company."

Max, sensing the somber mood, rose and rested his head on Mr. Carter's knee, looking up at him with soulful eyes. Mr. Carter chuckled, stroking the dog's head. "You always know how to cheer me up, don't you, Max?"

Ethan watched the interaction, feeling a swell of gratitude for the bond they all shared. After a moment, he cleared his throat. "Um, Mr. Carter? My parents want to meet you. They're really happy about how much better I've been feeling, and I told them it's because of you."

Mr. Carter looked at him, surprised. "Me? I'm not sure I've done anything special."

Ethan shook his head. "You've done a lot. And they want to thank you. They … they invited you to come over for dinner."

The old man's expression turned uncertain, and he glanced away.

"Dinner? I … I don't know, Ethan. It's been a long time since I've been to someone's house."

Ethan leaned forward earnestly. "Please, Mr. Carter? It would mean a lot to me. And to Max too!"

Max barked in agreement, wagging his tail. Mr. Carter chuckled, shaking his head. "Well, I suppose it's hard to say no when both of you are so persuasive. All right, I'll come."

Ethan grinned, practically bouncing in his seat. "Great! How about Saturday evening? My mom makes the best lasagna, and maybe I will ask her to bake an apple pie too."

Mr. Carter's eyes twinkled. "Saturday it is, then. But only if Max promises not to steal my pie."

Ethan laughed. "Deal!"

As they sat together, the weight of Mr. Carter's past seemed to lighten, replaced by the warmth of companionship. Max rested his head on Ethan's lap, and the three of them watched the sun dip below the horizon, content in each other's presence. The promise of a shared meal and new memories filled the air with quiet anticipation.

Ethan's parents were abuzz with excitement as the day of the dinner approached. The house had been cleaned from top to bottom, the dining table polished to a shine, and Ethan's mother had brought out the family's special dinnerware—reserved for only the most meaningful occasions.

"Ethan, we want this to be perfect," his mother said, tying her apron tightly around her waist. "You've got to tell us—what does Mr. Carter like to eat?"

Ethan paused, scratching his head. "I … don't know for sure," he admitted. "But … I've noticed some things."

His parents leaned in, eager to hear more. Ethan began narrating what he'd observed from his visits to Mr. Carter's home. "He has a lot of tea bags—different kinds. So, maybe he likes tea? And I've seen a bowl of apples on his kitchen counter. I think he likes fruit. He's always sharing treats with Max, so I bet he likes simple snacks too."

Ethan thought harder. "There's always a loaf of bread in his kitchen, and once, I saw him making soup. It smelled really nice, like chicken and herbs. And then, I told him you will make my favorite lasagna."

Ethan's father nodded. "Soup sounds like a good idea. What else?"

"He also mentioned once that he loved homemade apple pie when he was younger," Ethan added thoughtfully.

His mother smiled. "Perfect. We'll make apple pie for dessert. Now, let's divide and conquer."

The family got to work. Ethan's father took charge of the soup, chopping vegetables, chicken, and seasoning the broth with care. His mother focused on lasagna, baking the pie, expertly rolling out the crust while humming a cheerful tune. Ethan was put in charge of making a fruit salad and setting the table.

Max, meanwhile, was a whirlwind of energy, sniffing the air and wagging his tail furiously every time a tantalizing aroma wafted through the kitchen. At one point, he even attempted to snatch an apple from the counter, causing Ethan to laugh and gently scold him.

"Max, you'll have your share later," Ethan promised, giving him a treat to keep him occupied.

As evening approached, the table was set with steaming bowls of soup, three-cheese lasagna, a fresh fruit salad, warm bread rolls, and, of course, the golden, fragrant apple pie. Everything looked and smelled wonderful. Ethan's parents exchanged a satisfied glance.

"I think we're ready," his father said.

At precisely 6:00 p.m., the doorbell rang. Ethan ran to open it, Max close on his heels. Standing there, dressed neatly but still with an air of modesty, was Mr. Carter. He held a small bouquet of flowers and a bag of dog treats.

"Good evening, Ethan," Mr. Carter greeted warmly.

Ethan beamed. "Come in! Max has been waiting for you all day."

As Mr. Carter stepped inside, Ethan's parents came to greet him. The moment they saw him, a look of astonishment crossed their faces. Ethan's mother gasped softly, her hand flying to her mouth.

"Oh, my goodness … it's you," she whispered, her voice trembling.

Mr. Carter's smile faltered slightly as he looked at her, then at Ethan's father, who appeared equally stunned. Recognition flickered in his eyes, followed by a mix of emotions—surprise, hesitation, and a hint of sadness.

"It's been a long time," Mr. Carter said softly.

Ethan glanced between them, confused. "Wait … you know each other?"

His mother nodded, her voice filled with emotion. "Yes, Ethan. We know Mr. Carter. He … he was a part of our lives a long time ago."

Ethan's father stepped forward, offering his hand. "It's good to meet you, Mr. Carter," he said sincerely.

Mr. Carter hesitated for a moment before shaking his hand. "It's a pleasure to meet you too."

The tension in the room was palpable, but it was quickly broken by Max, who nudged Mr. Carter with his nose and wagged his tail, as if sensing that everything would be all right. Ethan's mother smiled through her tears.

"Please, come in. Dinner is ready," she said, leading him to the dining room.

As they sat down to eat, the air began to fill with warmth and laughter. The past could wait for a while; tonight was about reunion, old and new friendships, and the joy of being together.

As the dinner carried on, Ethan's parents, Sarah and David, leaned into the poignant story unfolding at their dining table. Mr. Carter—revealed as Mr. William, a name that resonated with both nostalgia and gravity—began to unveil the reasons behind his transformation and the decisions that had led him to become the solitary figure Ethan had met. Max, sensing the emotional charge in the air, lay quietly under the table, his watchful eyes moving between Ethan and Mr. William, as though guarding their bond.

Mr. William began cautiously, his voice low and deliberate. "I was not always Mr. Carter," he said. "Carter was my mother's maiden name. I chose it years ago when I needed to start over."

Sarah's hand trembled slightly as she gripped her fork. Her face carried a mixture of recognition and surprise. "William … I can't believe it's really you. We thought—" She paused, her voice catching. "We thought we'd never see you again."

David looked at Sarah, his brow furrowed in confusion. "You actually knew each other?"

Sarah nodded slowly, her eyes moist. "Yes, David. William and I … we were neighbors when I was a teenager. He was the sort of like a father I never had. Always looking out for me." She turned to Mr. William. "You vanished without a trace. What happened?"

Mr. William sighed, his gaze fixed on the flickering candlelight. "Life happened. Choices happened. After my wife passed, I … couldn't stay. The memories in that town were too heavy to bear. I sold everything, changed my name, and moved here. I didn't want to be found—not even by the people I cared about most." Mr. William began to choke up.

Ethan, sitting wide-eyed between his parents and Mr. Carter, found himself piecing together fragments of the conversation. "You mean … you left because you were sad?" he asked softly.

Mr. Carter smiled gently at Ethan. "Yes, Ethan. Very sad. Sometimes, when you lose the only people you love, the pain can feel like it's too much to carry. It felt like I had only two options. And I was not going to take the easy option out. So, I thought disappearing would help me heal. But, as I've learned over the years, it's connections like ours—like the one I have with you and Max—that truly heal a broken heart."

David leaned forward, his voice filled with curiosity. "You've lived here all this time? How did we never cross paths before now?"

"I kept to myself. Besides, age does this wonderful thing of changing our appearances," William admitted. "But then Max and Ethan changed everything. I can't explain it, but the day Max came up to me, wagging his tail and nudging my hand, something shifted. It was like … fate."

Sarah wiped a tear from her cheek and smiled. "Fate indeed. And to think, after all these years, you're sitting here at our table. It feels surreal."

The conversation took on a philosophical tone as they delved deeper into the idea of destiny and serendipity. Mr. Carter spoke of how he had spent years reflecting on his past choices and how meeting Ethan had reignited a part of him he thought was long gone.

"You know," Mr. Carter said, looking at Ethan, "I didn't think I had much left to give. But you proved me wrong after everything I gave to my wife, my daughter, and your mom. Your kindness, your courage—it reminded me that even in our darkest moments, there's always a chance to find light."

Ethan beamed, his cheeks flushed with pride. "And you helped me too, Mr. Carter … I mean, Mr. William. You taught me how to stand up for myself and believe in who I am."

David reached across the table and placed a hand on William's shoulder. "You've done more for our son than we could ever thank you for. You've given him confidence, a friend, and a role model. We're truly grateful."

Mr. William shook his head humbly. "Ethan did the hard part. All I did was listen. I guess this was meant to be."

As the evening progressed, the atmosphere grew warmer, filled with laughter, shared memories, and heartfelt exchanges. Sarah recounted stories of her childhood, painting vivid pictures of a time when Mr. William had been a constant presence in her life. Mr. William, in turn, shared glimpses of his late wife, his estranged daughter, and the joy they had once shared, his voice tinged with both sorrow and gratitude.

Max, not one to be left out, eventually made his way to Mr. William's lap, eliciting a chuckle from everyone at the table. "This dog," Mr. William said, scratching Max behind the ears, "has been the bridge between us all. He's got a heart bigger than any of ours."

As the evening drew to a close, the family felt an unspoken bond growing stronger between them. The reunion, though unexpected, had brought clarity, closure, and a sense of renewal. Before leaving, Mr. William stood and looked at the family he had unknowingly reconnected with.

"Thank you," he said, his voice filled with emotion, "for welcoming me, for forgiving me, and for reminding me of what truly matters."

Sarah hugged him tightly, her eyes shimmering with tears. "You're family, William. You've always been family." Sarah gently wiped tears rolling down her cheeks.

Ethan clung to Mr. William's hand as he walked him to the door. "You'll come back, right?" Ethan asked, his voice filled with hope.

"Of course," Mr. William replied with a smile. "This isn't goodbye. It's just the beginning."

As Mr. William stepped into the cool night air, he felt a profound sense of peace. The journey that had begun with a simple friendship with a boy and his dog had come full circle, bringing him back to a place of belonging. And as he walked home under the starlit sky, he couldn't help but feel that his late wife, watching from somewhere beyond, was smiling too.

REROUTING

The morning sun poured golden light over the lush, rain-kissed greenery of Kochi as the Subramaniam family loaded their maroon sedan. It was the perfect weekend for a family outing, or so everyone hoped. Their destination was the Edakkal Caves in Wayanad, a historic site rich with ancient petroglyphs, promising both adventure and learning.

"Do we really have to go so early?" complained thirteen-year-old Karthik, slumping into the back seat with a resigned pout. His sister Meera, a bubbly eight-year-old, cheerfully ignored his grumpiness as she climbed in beside him, clutching her favorite sketchbook. Meera had vowed to sketch the "first cave drawing" she saw.

"Stop whining," said Anitha, their mother, as she adjusted her Tibetan flower print scarf. Her tone carried the dual authority of a schoolteacher and a mother who had dealt with endless teenage sulks. "You'll thank us later for taking you to see something educational instead of letting you stare at your phone all day."

Karthik rolled his eyes. "I could learn about the caves on YouTube, Amma."

"Enough of your back talk," said Sridhar, their father, as he started the engine. The car's hum was a comforting prelude to the hours of winding roads ahead. "We planned this trip so we can enjoy some family time together. Now behave."

Despite the groans and sighs, the family's spirits lifted as they left the bustling streets of Kochi behind and began their ascent into the misty hills of Wayanad. The air grew cooler, the greenery denser, and the scenery more breathtaking with every kilometer. Anitha unpacked a tiffin box of hot idlis and coconut chutney, passing them around to keep everyone's energy up. Even Karthik managed a half-smile as he munched on an idli, staring out the window at the passing coffee plantations.

As they neared Wayanad, Sridhar glanced at the dashboard GPS and noticed a blinking message: "Route recalculating." He frowned slightly but said nothing, trusting Google Maps to adjust. The road they were on seemed quieter than expected, with no other vehicles in sight. Instead, the sedan trundled along narrow paths lined with towering trees, their dense foliage casting long shadows.

"Are we taking a shortcut?" Anitha asked, glancing at her husband.

"The app says this is the fastest route," Sridhar replied, his eyes narrowing as the road began to narrow. The asphalt turned patchy, with gravel crunching beneath the tires. "It should save us twenty minutes."

Karthik leaned forward, his curiosity piqued. "This looks like the kind of place where a tiger could jump out."

"Don't say such things!" Meera protested, clutching her sketch-book tightly.

Anitha gave Sridhar a worried glance. "Are you sure this is right? It doesn't feel like a well-used road at all."

Sridhar's confidence wavered, but he, like most men who are ashamed to admit they are lost, masked it with a reassuring smile. "It's fine. These apps are usually reliable."

The road continued to deteriorate, the gravel now giving way to dirt. Bushes encroached on the path, brushing against the sides of the car. The eerie silence of the forest was broken only by the occasional chirping of birds and the rustling of leaves in the breeze.

"I don't see any signboards," Anitha muttered, craning her neck. "What if we're going the wrong way?"

Before Sridhar could answer, the car jolted violently. A loud thud echoed as the vehicle came to an abrupt halt.

"What happened?" Anitha exclaimed, her voice rising in panic.

"I think we hit something," Sridhar said, his knuckles tightening on the steering wheel. He threw the car into park and stepped out to investigate.

The rest of the family followed hesitantly, their shoes crunching against the dirt road. Meera clung to her mother's shirt as they approached the front of the car. There, wedged under the bumper, was a large tree root that had pushed through the dirt, its gnarled surface looking as though it had been waiting for years to catch an unsuspecting traveler.

"The tire's busted," Sridhar groaned, crouching to inspect the damage. "And the road ahead doesn't look any better."

Anitha's hand instinctively went to her forehead. "So, now what? There's no signal here, and we haven't seen another vehicle for ages."

"Can't we just turn back?" Karthik asked, his earlier bravado gone.

"Not with a flat tire," Sridhar said grimly.

The family stood there for a moment, surrounded by towering trees and an unsettling quiet that seemed to close in around them. Above, the sun's rays filtered weakly through the canopy, casting fragmented patterns on the forest floor. For the first time that day, a sense of unease crept over them.

"We're stuck," Sridhar said finally, his voice heavy.

And with that realization, the Subramaniams found themselves not at the doorstep of the ancient Edakkal Caves, but at the mercy of a forest that seemed determined to keep its secrets.

The sun hung low over the winding roads of the Western Ghats as Priya and Anjali rolled down the windows of their sleek hatchback, letting the cool mountain breeze tussle their hair. The sisters had been planning this hiking trip for six months, a much-needed escape from their routine lives in Goa, which wasn't all that boring, but everyone needed a change. Priya, the older of the two at thirty-two, was a no-nonsense corporate lawyer who rarely took time off. Anjali, five years younger and a self-proclaimed free spirit, ran a travel vlog, always chasing the next adventure.

"I still can't believe you convinced me to do this," Priya said, glancing at her sister. She adjusted her sunglasses, her tone carrying the slightest edge of annoyance—and affection. "You know I'm not a 'roughing it' kind of person."

"Oh, please, you'll love it," Anjali chirped, balancing her phone on her knee as she flipped through their planned itinerary. "Fresh air, beautiful views, no emails. Trust me, Didi, you'll thank me later. Besides, you need this break more than I do."

Priya gave a skeptical snort. "I'll thank you when we get there without any detours."

"Relax," Anjali replied breezily. "Google Maps says we're on track. We should be at the trailhead in less than an hour."

The car climbed steadily higher into the hills, the dense greenery of the Ghats wrapping around them like a warm embrace. Every now and then, Anjali would squeal in delight at a particularly scenic view, leaning precariously out of the window to snap a photo and shoot video. Priya, ever the cautious one, gripped the steering wheel tighter and muttered about seatbelt safety.

Despite Priya's reservations, the sisters' excitement was palpable. This was more than just a hiking trip; it was a chance to reconnect. Their busy lives had kept them apart for too long, and this shared adventure felt like a step toward reclaiming the bond they'd once had.

"Remember when we used to go trekking in the Western Ghats with Appa?" Anjali asked, her voice tinged with nostalgia. "He'd make us count all the different birds we saw."

Priya smiled at the memory. "And you'd always make up names for the ones you didn't know. 'Yellow-belly squawker,' wasn't it?"

Anjali laughed, the sound echoing through the car. "I was creative!"

Their laughter filled the car as they continued their ascent, but the cheerful atmosphere dimmed slightly when Priya noticed the maps app and GPS acting up.

"Anjali, why does it keep saying 'Recalculating route'?" Priya asked, frowning at the dashboard display.

Anjali leaned over to inspect the map. "It's probably recalibrating because of patchy satellite connection. These mountain roads can be tricky for navigation apps. Just follow this road; it'll sort itself out."

Priya's grip on the wheel tightened as the road began to narrow, the asphalt giving way to gravel. The surrounding forest seemed to grow thicker, the towering trees casting long shadows over their path.

"Are you sure this is the right way?" Priya asked, a note of worry creeping into her voice.

"Yes, yes, keep going," Anjali said, waving a dismissive hand. "We'll be fine."

The reassurance was short-lived. Moments later, the gravel road turned into a steep decline, the car's tires struggling to maintain traction. Priya slammed on the brakes, but the car skidded, the loose gravel sending it careening down the slope.

"Hold on!" Priya shouted, her voice barely audible over the screeching of tires and the sisters' panicked screams.

The car slid for what felt like an eternity before coming to an abrupt halt in a small valley, cushioned by a thicket of bushes. For a few seconds, there was only silence, broken by the distant chirping of crickets.

"Are you okay?" Priya asked, her voice trembling as she turned to her sister.

Anjali nodded, her face pale but determined. "Yeah. You?"

"Just … shaken," Priya admitted, her hands still gripping the wheel. She exhaled sharply and unclipped her seat belt. "Let's get out of here. Thank God for the seat belts!"

The sisters climbed out of the car, their legs wobbling as they took in their surroundings. The car's front bumper was crumpled, and one of the tires was flat, but it had somehow avoided serious damage. The same couldn't be said for their path forward; the valley was surrounded by dense forest, with no clear way back to the road.

"Well," Anjali said, brushing dirt off her jeans, "that was … exciting."

Priya shot her a look. "If your idea of exciting is almost dying, then sure."

Anjali grinned, trying to lighten the mood. "Hey, Didi, look on the bright side. We're alive, and this will make a great story for my vlog."

Priya shook her head, but a faint smile tugged at her lips. "Let's focus on getting out of this mess first."

The sisters gathered their backpacks, checking for any supplies they might need. Anjali found a small first-aid kit and handed it to Priya, who tended to a shallow cut on her arm. They both had minor bruises but nothing serious.

"Ready?" Priya asked, adjusting the straps of her bag.

Anjali nodded, her enthusiasm undimmed. "Ready."

With the car abandoned and no cell phone signal to call for help, the sisters began their climb out of the valley, determined to find their way back to the main road. As they scaled the steep incline, the bond between them felt stronger than it had in years. They didn't know what lay ahead, but they knew they'd face it together.

The forest around Sridhar and his family was growing darker by the minute. With each passing second, the air seemed to grow heavier, the chirping of birds giving way to the hum of crickets and the occasional distant hoot of an owl or two. Sridhar, clutching his flashlight tightly, kept his focus on the barely visible trail ahead. His wife, Anitha, followed closely, holding their son, Karthik, by the hand, while their daughter, Meera, walked behind, dragging her feet.

"Appa, how much longer?" Meera asked, her voice breaking with exhaustion. "My legs hurt."

"Not far," Sridhar replied, though the doubt in his voice was clear.

Anitha, sensing the children's growing unease, tried to sound cheerful. "Let's think of this as an adventure," she said. "Like the treasure hunts you two used to love."

"Except there's no treasure, Amma," Karthik said, sulking.

"Finding water will be our treasure," Sridhar said, stopping to wipe his brow. "I'm sure I heard a stream nearby. We just need to keep going a little longer."

The family trudged on, the dense canopy above blocking out the last traces of daylight. The ground was uneven, littered with roots and fallen leaves that made every step precarious. When they finally broke through a cluster of bushes and spotted the stream, a collective sigh of relief escaped their lips.

The stream was narrow but clear, its waters shimmering in the fading light. Sridhar dropped to his knees, scooping up the cool water to splash on his face. "Finally," he said. "This will keep us going."

Anitha handed an empty water bottle to Meera. "Fill this up carefully, and don't lean too far over."

"Is this water safe to drink, Amma? We don't have a filter," said a genuinely concerned Meera.

Seeing her mother's cold stare, Meera obeyed, crouching by the stream's edge. The moment she dipped the bottle into the water, a rustling sound came from the undergrowth nearby. She froze, her heart pounding.

Then she saw it—a sleek, dark shape slithering through the grass. "Snake!" she screamed, dropping the bottle and scrambling backward.

Sridhar rushed to her side, pulling her away from the stream. His flashlight beam swept over the bushes, catching a fleeting glimpse of the snake's tail as it disappeared into the forest.

"It's gone," he said, his voice steady but firm. "It won't bother us if we leave it alone."

"Can we go now?" Meera asked, her voice trembling.

"We need to rest here for a bit," Sridhar said. "We're all exhausted, and we need the water."

Anitha pulled Meera into a reassuring hug. "It's okay, sweetheart. Appa's right. We'll rest here, and then we'll figure out our next steps."

On the other side of the forest, Anjali and Priya were navigating their own ordeal. The sisters had managed to climb out of the small valley where their car had landed, but the journey up had left them scraped and bruised.

"You okay?" Anjali asked, glancing at her younger sister as they sat on a fallen log to catch their breath.

Priya inspected a shallow cut on her palm. "I'll live," she said, wincing as she wiped away the dirt. "But this definitely wasn't the adventure I had in mind."

Anjali tried to lighten the mood. "Hey, you can't call it a real adventure unless there's a bit of danger, right?"

"Remind me of that when we're not stranded in the middle of nowhere," Priya said, rolling her eyes. "This was supposed to be a fun hike. Six months of planning, and now this."

Anjali reached over and gave her a nudge. "Come on. We'll laugh about this someday."

"Yeah, when we're not on the verge of being eaten by leopards or bitten by snakes," Priya muttered.

The sisters stood and resumed their trek, following the faint sound of running water. The forest around them felt alive, every rustle and crackle making their nerves jangle. As they drew closer to the stream, Priya's unease began to fade. The sound of the water was soothing, a small reminder of civilization.

But then, a distant shriek cut through the stillness. Both sisters froze.

"What was that?" Priya whispered, her voice barely audible.

"Didi, it sure sounded like someone's scream. A human!" Anjali said, her expression turning serious. "It came from over there."

"Are you sure we should check it out?" Priya asked. "It could be … I don't know, anything."

"Exactly. It could be someone who needs help," Anjali said, already moving toward the sound.

Priya hesitated but reluctantly followed, muttering under her breath about bad decisions.

When the sisters emerged by the stream, the sight that greeted them was both startling and relieving. A family of four was huddled by the water's edge, their faces weary but unmistakably human.

"Hello?" Anjali called out cautiously, raising her hands to show she meant no harm. The light from her phone was enough to catch the family's attention.

The family turned toward her, their expressions shifting from alarm to relief. Sridhar stood and stepped forward, his flashlight casting a beam over the newcomers.

"Thank God," he said. "We thought we were the only ones out here."

"We thought the same," Priya said, stepping closer. "We've been lost for hours."

"So have we," Anitha said, her voice heavy with fatigue. "Our car broke down, and there's no signal."

"Ours slid down a hill," Anjali said. "It's totaled."

As introductions were made, the tension eased slightly. Anjali, ever practical, rummaged through her backpack and pulled out a small tent. "It's not big enough for all of us, but we can squeeze in," she said.

"Thank you," Anitha said, her gratitude evident. "We have some snacks to share."

The group worked together to set up the tent and arrange a makeshift camp by the stream. Inside the cramped shelter, they exchanged their stories. Meera and Karthik listened wide-eyed as Anjali described their car's terrifying descent into the valley. Priya, meanwhile, recounted how the GPS had led them astray.

"Wait," Sridhar said, leaning forward. "You said your Google Maps app messed up just before you entered the forest?"

"Yes," Priya said. "It started glitching right when we reached that fork in the road."

"That's the same spot where ours messed up," Sridhar said, his brows furrowing. "It was working fine until then."

Priya's mind raced. "What if it wasn't just a coincidence?" she said slowly. "What if something interfered with the GPS at that spot?"

The group fell silent, the implications of her words sinking in. Outside, the forest seemed to hold its breath, its darkness pressing in around them. Somewhere in the distance, an animal howled, its cry echoing through the trees.

"Whatever it is," Anjali said, breaking the silence, "we'll figure it out together. For now, let's focus on making it through the night."

The group fell silent, the realization adding a layer of unease to their situation. Above them, the forest canopy darkened as night crept in. Anjali, ever prepared, began setting up the minimalistic bedding she'd brought for their hiking trip.

"It's not big enough for all of us," she admitted, "but we'll make do."

"I have some snacks," Anitha offered, pulling out packets of murukku and plantain chips. The modest meal brought a semblance of comfort to the weary travelers as they huddled together, sharing stories and pooling their resources.

As the stars began to peek through the darkening sky, the shared ordeal created an unspoken bond between the two groups. Yet, the mystery of their simultaneous misfortune lingered in the air, casting a shadow over the newfound camaraderie.

The two families huddled together under the dim glow of their flashlights. Sridhar, ever practical, reminded everyone, "Let us not waste the batteries. We'll need them later. Who knows how many more nights we are going to be in this together?"

Anjali, already rummaging through her hiking backpack, pulled out a compact fire-starting kit. "We'll set up a campfire. It'll keep us warm and give us light," she suggested. Sridhar and Karthik didn't have to go too far to collect firewood. Soon, the flickering flames cast long shadows on the surrounding trees, adding a sense of intimacy to their impromptu campsite.

They introduced themselves properly for the first time. "I'm Dr. Anitha Subramaniam," said the mother, her voice steady despite the fatigue. "This is my husband, Sridhar, our son, Karthik, and our daughter, Meera."

"I'm Anjali, and this is my sister Priya," said Anjali, smiling warmly. "We're from Goa."

"Wow, a doctor!" Anjali exclaimed, impressed. "And Mr. Sridhar, what do you do?"

"I'm an advocate," Sridhar replied. "Though, right now, I'm just a worried father."

"We're all in this together," Anjali reassured him. "We'll get through it."

As the fire crackled, Anitha shared tips for quick meals on busy days. "Sometimes, between work and family, I barely have time to cook," she admitted. "But an Instant Pot and some precut veggies are lifesavers. A simple dal-chawal with a pickle can feel like a feast."

"That's brilliant!" Priya said, jotting down notes in her journal. "I'll try that when I get back home. But can we please not talk about food right now? I am hungry." She giggled.

Meera and Karthik, meanwhile, sat beside Priya, who was pointing out constellations in the clear night sky. "That one's Orion," Priya said, tracing the pattern with her finger. "And there's the Big Dipper."

"Wow," Meera said, her eyes wide with wonder. "You know so much!"

"I love stargazing," Priya replied. "It's like a treasure map in the sky."

Sridhar, seated next to Anjali, opened up about his fears. "As a father, my biggest worry is not being able to protect my family. Getting lost like this feels like a failure."

"Don't be so hard on yourself, Mr. Sridhar," Anjali said gently. "You've kept everyone calm and together. That's what matters."

The group talked for a while longer, the fire casting a warm glow over their faces. Eventually, exhaustion set in, and they settled down for the night, cramped but thankful for the small tent Anjali had brought. The families drifted off to sleep, lulled by the distant hum of the forest.

Sridhar woke early the next morning to find Priya already awake, her flashlight propped up on a rock as she scribbled on a sheet of paper. Curious, he walked over. "Priya, what are you working on so early?"

Priya looked up, her expression thoughtful. "I've been thinking about the Google Maps glitch," she said, tapping her pen against the paper. "It doesn't seem random. The fact that both our families ended up lost at the same spot feels too coincidental."

Sridhar frowned. "You think it was intentional?"

"Maybe," Priya said cautiously. "I'm not sure, but something doesn't add up. It's like someone deliberately altered the route."

Sridhar's brows knitted. "That's … unsettling. So, what do we do now?"

"We follow the stream," Priya said confidently. "Water always leads to civilization—a village, a settlement, something."

"Makes sense," Sridhar said, nodding. "Let's wait for everyone to wake up and then get moving."

As the first rays of sunlight pierced through the dense canopy, the families stirred, ready to face the day. Priya's discovery lingered in Sridhar's mind as they prepared to navigate their way out of the forest, their spirits bolstered by a sense of purpose and solidarity.

The families set off early, their spirits cautiously optimistic as they followed the stream. The morning sunlight filtered through the tree-tops, casting dappled shadows on the ground. The forest was alive with the sounds of birdsong and rustling leaves, but an underlying tension lingered.

As they walked, Meera skipped ahead, her curiosity piqued by every splash of water and flutter of wings. Priya kept pace with her, pointing out interesting plants and tiny insects. "Look at this!" Priya said, holding up a vibrant red flower. "It's a type of orchid."

"It's so pretty," Meera said, carefully touching a petal.

Sridhar and Anitha followed closely, talking softly about the day ahead. Karthik trudged behind, occasionally poking at the ground with a stick.

"Wait, what's that?" Anjali's voice broke through the hum of the forest. She had stopped abruptly, pointing at something glinting in the stream ahead.

The group gathered around as Anjali knelt to inspect the shiny object. It was partially buried in the silt, its edges rusted and worn. She pulled it out with some effort, revealing an old, corroded metal sign.

"Let's clean it," Anitha suggested, grabbing a wet cloth from her bag. As they wiped away the grime, faded letters emerged:

DANGER: DO NOT ENTER. UNSTABLE GROUND.

The words were barely legible, the sign's edges jagged from years of erosion.

"This looks like it has been here for decades," Sridhar said, examining the metal. "The question is, why?"

"This whole route might have been abandoned," Priya said, her voice tinged with unease. "Maybe Google Maps wasn't glitching. What if someone—or something—deliberately led us here?"

"But why?" Anitha asked, frowning. "What would anyone gain from sending us to a dangerous place?"

"Could just be an error," Sridhar said, though his tone was uncertain. "Technology isn't perfect."

"Or," Priya countered, "it's intentional. Someone could be exploiting a glitch in the system."

The group fell silent, the sound of the stream filling the void. The sign felt like an ominous warning—a relic of past dangers that might still lurk nearby.

As they continued downstream, the forest seemed to shift subtly. Broken branches appeared in their path, some with jagged edges that suggested they had been snapped recently. Karthik pointed to a nearby rock, its surface etched with strange markings.

"They look like arrows," Karthik said, tracing the lines with his finger. "But they point in opposite directions."

"It's confusing on purpose," Priya said. "Someone doesn't want us to know where we're going."

The rhythmic sound returned faintly, a low thudding that seemed to echo through the trees. "Do you hear that?" Anjali whispered, her voice tense.

"It's like drums," Meera said, clinging to her mother's arm.

"Stay close," Sridhar instructed, his voice firm, "and keep moving."

The group quickened their pace, focusing on the stream as their guide. Anitha handed out snacks from her bag, urging everyone to stay hydrated. The children's earlier chatter had given way to quiet determination.

"We need to stick to the plan," Sridhar said. "Follow the water, no matter what."

The sun began to dip lower in the sky, casting long shadows that danced ominously on the forest floor. Every snap of a twig or rustle of leaves set their nerves on edge. The sense of being watched grew stronger, an invisible presence that made their skin crawl.

"We'll make it," Anjali said, her voice steady despite the unease in her eyes. "Just keep moving."

The families pressed on, their footsteps blending with the sound of the stream and the faint, haunting rhythm that seemed to follow them.

The sight of the small building nestled among the trees brought an overwhelming sense of relief to both families. It was a modest structure, with weathered wooden walls and a slanted roof. A faint wisp of smoke curled from a chimney, signaling life within.

"We made it!" Meera exclaimed, gripping her father's hand tightly.

"Finally," Anitha said, her voice a mix of exhaustion and gratitude. "Let's hope someone here can help us."

The group approached the building cautiously, unsure of what to expect. It wasn't quite dark yet. Anjali knocked on the wooden door, the sound echoing in the still forest. A moment later, the door creaked open, revealing a man in his fifties with sharp, alert eyes and a rugged appearance. He was dressed in khaki, his badge identifying him as a forest ranger. He spoke like he may have been asleep when he heard the knock on the door.

"Well, this is unexpected," the ranger said, eyeing the weary group. "Come in."

The families stepped inside, grateful for the warmth of the small fire-place. The ranger gestured for them to sit on a bench while he poured water into metal cups. The cabin area was very modest. A table, a chair, and an old wooden bench were the only furniture they could see.

"Who are you all? How did you get here? Tell me what happened," he said, sitting down across from them.

Sridhar took the lead, recounting how they had followed Google Maps only to end up stranded in the forest. Anjali added their story, explaining how their car had slid into a small valley. The children chimed in occasionally, describing the strange signs and eerie sounds they had encountered.

The ranger listened intently, his expression unreadable. When they finished, he leaned back in his chair and sighed.

"What can I say? You're lucky," the ranger said finally. "This forest is not just any forest. It's part of what was once a protected tribal land. A faction of the tribe still lives deep inside, avoiding all contact with outsiders."

"The sounds and signs we saw as we hiked along the stream," Priya said, leaning forward. "That was them, wasn't it?"

The ranger nodded. "They have lived here for generations, and they have their own ways of keeping people out. The warnings and those rhythmic sounds are part of their deterrent."

"But how did we even get here?" Anitha asked. "The road was on Google Maps."

"That road," the ranger said, his tone somber, "The road you were on was never meant to be public. It's an old access path that somehow made its way into digital maps. We've been trying to get it removed, but it's not easy."

"Were we ever in real danger?" Sridhar asked, his voice filled with concern.

The ranger shook his head. "Not real danger. The tribe doesn't harm people unless they feel directly threatened. But they don't want visitors, either. They want absolutely no contact with the outside world. You were lucky they chose to guide you away rather than confront you."

"Guide us away?" Karthik asked, his curiosity piqued.

"Those arrows you saw," the ranger explained. "They weren't meant to confuse you. They were meant to lead you back toward the stream—and eventually, out of the forest."

"Why not just meet us and tell us to leave?" Anjali asked.

"It's not their way," the ranger said. "They've been avoiding outsiders for decades. It is a matter of trust and tradition."

The group fell silent, absorbing the revelation. The weight of their unintentional intrusion into the tribe's sacred land settled heavily on them.

There was a sense of relief in all their faces. Karthik even broke a smile.

"What should we do now?" Priya asked, breaking the silence.

The ranger stood and began gathering supplies. "First, I'll help you get back to the main road. But there's something I need to ask of you."

"Of course," Anitha said immediately. "What is it?"

"Don't share what you've seen or the route you took," the ranger said firmly. "The tribe's privacy needs to be respected. The more people hear about this place, the more likely it is that someone will come looking for them. And that's the last thing they want."

The families exchanged glances, nodding in agreement. "We understand," Sridhar said. "We won't tell anyone."

"Good," the ranger said. "Now let's find a way to get you all out of here safely."

As the families quietly looked at each other, the ranger's words lingered in their minds. The forest, once a source of fear and confusion, now felt like a place of profound mystery and quiet resilience. Sridhar stood up as if he needed to stretch. The rest of them followed, and they all stepped outside, ready to plan their next course of action with a newfound respect for the land and the people who called it home.

After the emotional relief of reaching the ranger's outpost and finding out about the tribes, the families began to focus on practical matters—retrieving their cars. While they rested near the small wooden cabin, Sridhar approached the ranger, the man they were speaking to, a man named Rajesh, with the query on everyone's mind.

"What about our cars? My wife and I—we need them to get back home," Sridhar said, worry evident in his voice. "And the sisters' car … well, it seems it's totaled, but …"

Rajesh held up a hand to reassure him. "Don't worry. I have a pretty good idea of where your car might be. These forest paths are old and not well-mapped, but I've seen a few cases like yours. We'll send a rescue team out to locate and repair it."

He turned to Anjali and Priya. "As for your vehicle, I'll make some calls and see what we can do. Unfortunately, it sounds like it might be beyond repair, but we'll try to at least retrieve your belongings."

Priya nodded, grateful. "Thank you. Just knowing someone is looking into it helps."

Rajesh took down their contact information and assured them they would be updated once their vehicles were found. "For now, relax. It'll take some time for the team to mobilize. You're safe here."

The group walked back into the ranger station and settled into the waiting area, a simple but comfortable spot near the ranger's main office. There was cot made of coconut coir, a pillow, a blanket, and another bench. Karthik and Meera asked their parents if they could walk outside the cabin, and then they busied themselves exploring the area around the outpost, though they stayed within sight. Anitha unpacked a few remaining snacks to share, creating a sense of calm despite the uncertainty.

It was Priya who broke the quiet moment. "I've been thinking about something," she said, leaning forward to get everyone's attention. Her voice carried the familiar spark of someone who'd uncovered a theory they couldn't wait to share.

"Thinking about what?" asked Sridhar, intrigued.

"About how we got lost in the first place," Priya began. "I've been piecing things together, and I don't think it was just a random Google Maps glitch. I think the tribe living here may have manipulated the maps themselves."

The others stared at her in surprise. Even the usually calm Anjali raised her eyebrows. "Manipulated the maps? How would they even do that?"

Priya adjusted her glasses and continued. "Well, think about it. Both of our families ended up lost at almost the exact same point. That's too much of a coincidence. And when you add in the misleading markings on the rocks and the sounds that led us in circles … it feels deliberate."

"But why would they do that?" Anitha asked, a mix of curiosity and skepticism in her voice.

"To protect their territory," Priya said matter-of-factly. "I am only making an intelligent guess here based on the information Rajesh, the ranger, shared with us. If they know how to mislead digital maps, they can keep people away from their land without having to confront them directly. It's actually quite clever."

Meera, ever the inquisitive one, chimed in. "But how could they even change Google Maps? Isn't that, like, super hard to do?"

Priya shrugged. "Not necessarily. If they have someone with the right technical skills—a rogue programmer, maybe—it's possible to feed false data into the system. It's the same principle hackers use to spoof locations. The markings and sounds were just the extra layer of misdirection. It very well could be someone outside working for the tribe."

Sridhar leaned back, his expression contemplative. "It does make sense," he admitted. "But it's also … disturbing. If they can do this, how many other people might have been affected?"

From the next room, the faint murmur of Rajesh's voice on the phone could be heard. Unbeknownst to the group, he had paused mid-conversation, his head tilted slightly toward the door. A small smile played on his lips as he eavesdropped on the discussion.

"Regardless of how they did it," Anjali said, "we're here now. And honestly, if it's a way to protect their way of life, I can't say I blame them."

The group fell into a thoughtful silence, their earlier panic replaced by a mix of curiosity and respect for the tribe's ingenuity. Outside, the sun began its descent, casting long shadows across the dense forest.

As the evening wore on, Rajesh returned to the group. "The rescue team is on their way," he said. "They'll call me once they've located your car, Mr. Subramaniam. And for the sisters, I'll update you as soon as I hear anything."

"Thank you," Sridhar said sincerely. "For everything."

Rajesh nodded. "It's my job. You're lucky you found the stream. It's one of the safest routes out of the forest."

As night fell, the group remained by the fire, their conversation gradually shifting to lighter topics. But Priya's theory lingered in the air, a puzzle waiting to be unraveled.

The next morning, the families were finally on the road again, driving in the Subramaniams' car. Sridhar was behind the wheel, carefully navigating the winding roads that led them away from the forest and back toward civilization. The sisters sat in the back seat, their expressions a mix of relief and resignation. They had just been informed by the ranger that their car, too damaged and inaccessible, would have to be dealt with through insurance. While they were understandably disappointed, their spirits remained high, buoyed by the adventure they now shared.

"You know, this whole thing is going to make for one epic story," Anjali said, leaning forward slightly. "People aren't going to believe it when I tell them."

"You're planning to include it in your vlog?" Meera asked, twisting in her seat to face her.

"Only if you're all okay with it," Anjali replied. "I have enough photos and video clips to work with, but I'll keep things anonymous if you prefer."

"No, I think it's fine," Anitha said with a smile. "It's not every day you get lost in a forest and come out with new friends."

"Friends we'll keep in touch with," Priya added, glancing at her sister with a nod.

Karthik, who had been quiet most of the drive, spoke up. "I'll probably tell all my classmates about this. They'll think it's so cool."

"Just make sure you don't exaggerate too much," Sridhar teased. "You know how kids can't resist making a snake sighting sound like a battle with a cobra."

The group chuckled, and then Priya took the opportunity to elaborate on her theory.

"So, here's what I've pieced together," she began, her voice gaining an edge of excitement. "The GPS mishap wasn't random. If you think about it, all the signs were there—literally."

"What do you mean?" Anitha asked, intrigued.

"The old warning sign we found in the stream," Priya explained. "It might have been put there decades ago, but the fact that it's still around tells me this area has been carefully maintained. The tribe is actively protecting it. The broken branches, the markings on the rocks, and even the rhythmic sounds we heard—those were all intentional. And like I said, they are probably getting some outside help."

"But how does that connect to the maps glitching?" Sridhar asked.

"It is very clear to me now," Priya said. "If you wanted to keep people away from your territory, what's the most effective way to do it in this day and age? Technology. Messing with the mapping system might seem complicated, but it's possible if you have the right knowledge. Those markings on the rocks could be signals—landmarks used by the tribe to confuse GPS navigation."

"And GPS jammers," Anjali added thoughtfully. "It's not impossible for them to have old or repurposed tech that creates interference. That would explain the constant rerouting on our phones."

"It's a fascinating theory," Anitha chimed in, "and it explains why we both got lost in nearly the same place. The tribe might've redirected us to keep us from venturing deeper into their land."

"Or," Meera added with a smile, "maybe they just didn't want us at all."

Everyone laughed, the tension from the last two days melting away. The conversation continued, each member of the group recalling moments they'd overlooked but now saw as part of a deliberate effort to protect the forest.

"The ranger did hint at this," Anitha said. "He said they're protective of their land because of what happened with loggers and tourists in the past. Can you blame them?"

"Not at all," Sridhar agreed. "If anything, it's impressive how resourceful they've been. It's a reminder that not everything can be explained through our lens of logic and convenience."

Eventually, the car reached a small bus stop near the entrance to Edakkal Caves. Sridhar pulled over, and the sisters began gathering their belongings.

"Thank you so much for the ride," Priya said, extending her hand to Sridhar. "We really owe you one."

"Don't mention it," Sridhar replied, shaking her hand warmly. "Just promise to stay in touch."

Anjali gave each member of the family a hug. "I'll send you the link when the vlog is up," she said. "And if you're ever in Goa, let us know. We'll show you around. Beaches, sunsets, and great food. You'll love it!"

"Same goes for Kochi," Anitha replied with a smile. "We'd love to have you."

The sisters waved one last time as they headed toward the bus stop. The Subramaniams watched them go, feeling a mix of relief and gratitude for the unexpected friendship they'd forged. As the car pulled back onto the road, the family couldn't help but marvel at how a series of wrong turns had led them to an adventure they would never forget.

A SHADOW LOVE DANCE

In Lirith, where shadows told truths no one dared to speak, Kaelina's shadow, empty and unresponsive, made her the most silent of them all. She was the third and the youngest of the siblings. Kaelina was also the only shadowless member of her family, making her worthless in the eyes of Lirithians and her own family. The three sisters lived with their aunt and uncle, to whom they owed everything since their parents' death.

Althea and Camilla, twenty-two and twenty, respectively, were practicing with their aunt and uncle to become scholars of shadow enchantment. While Kaelina, the most ridiculed sibling, was treated more as an experiment or a specimen than a member of the family. Althea and Camilla could not do anything to protect their sister, so they joined their cousins, aunts, uncles, and the people of Lirith in labeling Kaelina a curse and someone who was born to bring bad luck to the family. Once, Kaelina even overheard her aunt and uncle's conversation in which the aunt blamed her for her parents' death.

"'The day she was born with a pale shadow, my sister knew it would be the end of them!" the aunt said with a certain disgusted look on her face.

"Look at her face. Does anyone even want to look at her face? Doom and gloom is written all over it," she continued.

"Come on! Kaelina did not choose to be born this way. There is probably some explanation to it." Her uncle paused, with a lot more consideration for Kaelina.

"Are you going to spend the rest of your life trying to solve it? Or are you going to ensure our promotion at the school is guaranteed?" The aunt was stirring a pot of stew in a fit of anger.

"All right, I get it. But whatever it be, should we treat her like an untouchable in our house? She is just seventeen, a young girl who is probably confused enough already."

"I am not going to have this conversation with you again. That girl is a bad omen. She is a curse for the family. Maybe for the whole of Lirith. Her breath screams death. The only reason I am feeding her and giving space in my house is because we need her. We need to study her. We are the only scholars in the world of shadow enchantment who have access to a subject like this. Do you hear me?" the aunt asked.

"I do. I do," the uncle mumbled and walked away from the kitchen.

Kaelina coiled into a fetal position and tried to cuddle a doll her mother had knitted when she was very young. She did not remember her childhood all that well, since her parents died when she was only nine. She rarely slept at night because everyone was home, and she was worried that she could be taken away to the Ivanor Castle for good.

Although no one in her family had any firsthand knowledge of the castle, legend had it that Ivanor Castle was a secret fortress where the shadowkeepers kept people like Kaelina for centuries. The castle had cryogenic powers to keep people in frozen state forever. The people who stayed frozen inside the castle had their minds fully awake while just their bodies froze. In other words, Ivanor Castle symbolized eternal torture.

Kaelina's parents were once prominent, but their status diminished when she was born with a blank shadow. Her parents were two out of a total of ten people in Lirith who could read the ancient Pryllis script. Since almost all the local literature, shadow enchantment scriptures and fables, and other old religious books were all written in Pryllis, Lirithians were always in need of Pryllis experts like Kaelina's parents. They held them in high regard and were considered noble. But after Kaelina was born, something changed. And her parents, embarrassed by the stigma associated with no shadow, pressured her to stay out of sight, while her relatives and older cousins mocked her relentlessly.

It took her eight years to understand why her parents made her stay out of Lirithians' sight as much as they could and why they never took her out along with her older siblings when the family went to plays, musicals, and picnics, and why she was always asked to stay in a room at the back of their house. It took her eight years to realize that her life was destined to be on the fringes.

In the luminous city of Lirith, shadows held the secrets of everyone's soul. Each Lirithian had a shadow that carried the person's unique emotional code. Every emotion—joy, anger, fear, love, hate, sadness—cast its unique hues and movements into the shadows that followed each citizen. People's social status and relationships were often dictated by the beauty and vibrancy of their shadows. But for seventeen-year-old Kaelina, her shadow was blank—a pale and formless void, devoid of any movement or color.

Kaelina was old enough to feel the pain caused by being the outcast of Lirith and her own family. That was when she understood why she was the subject of whispered rumors and mistrust. Blank shadows were rare in Lirith, and most in Lirith considered them an ill omen. Despite her quiet resolve, Kaelina was consumed by loneliness and a burning curiosity about why her shadow was different. Before she could do something about it, her parents died in a forest fire, and no one could tell the sisters what really happened and why the parents were where they were during the fire. It was simply understood that their aunt and uncle, who were childless, would inherit all of Kaelina's parents' wealth to become the guardians of these sisters.

Ardyn was an eighteen-year-old single child born into a family of Guardians. His parents were the Guardians of Shadow for North Lirith and were also high-ranking members of the upper council that governed Lirith. Coming from a prestigious and an affluent family, Ardyn lived on top of a small hill, far away from the hustle and bustle of city life, and where all the council members had their residences. The Shadowkeepers Council controlled Lirith, and under the leadership of its chairman, they maintained the shadow enchantment as a pillar of the city's identity. Ardyn grew up under immense pressure to uphold the legacy of his family, but he harbored doubts about the fairness of the shadow enchantment system.

Ardyn was a direct descendant of one of the original Shadowmakers, a truth his family had carefully hidden for generations. His vibrant, uncontrollable shadow was a result of this lineage, making him a constant source of curiosity and fear in the city. His family, by choosing to live in quiet luxury, avoided attention toward Ardyn, while ensuring their secrets about their lineage remained buried.

Ardyn was always torn between loyalty to his family and his growing belief that the enchantment might be flawed or unjust. His charm and composure masked his inner turmoil. He was burdened by a sense of responsibility he didn't fully understand, haunted by the knowledge that his family may have caused the city's curse.

At the age of twelve, Ardyn met a palace security guard and knew immediately that he was shadowless, which the guard was trying to keep secret for years. But this discovery led to Ardyn getting exposed to an underground shadowless community, a group of Lirithians who had rejected the enchantment and lived outside the city's structured society without the knowledge of the majority of Lirithians. Through this community, Ardyn learned about the growing resistance against the council and their committed fight against shadow enchantment. This community of rebels had been trying to expose the shadow enchantment as a form of control rather than freedom.

Ardyn was always a resourceful boy with passion, and despite his parents' direct connection to the council, he was raised with a strong sense of justice, but he struggled with bitterness and mistrust toward the city of Lirith and its inhabitants. He was as much a mystery as his shadow. Though his emotions played out beautifully in the flickering patterns of his shadow, he hid behind a mask of detachment.

Every week, he would sneak out of his house at midnight to take part in the shadowless community ritual. This ritual consisted of the rebels sitting around a fire and reading pages from the Holy Enchantment book, which provided the guiding principles for the citizens of Lirith—those who believed and followed the Enchantment. A member of the community would read out a page and ask the others to discuss the dangers of what was discussed in that page. Then they would engage in an open discussion on any new discoveries the community members may have had and analyze any unassessed enchantment-nullifying techniques. Ardyn was fascinated by the wealth of knowledge the rebels possessed about the enchantment—often more than that of shawdowkeeprs themselves. But more importantly, he enjoyed the freedom of being with a group of people who did not care about their shadows and lived life as they wished. The common connection the group had was what pulled Ardyn to the community week after week, while he was seeking his own answer.

It was during one such meeting when Ardyn revealed to the rebel community something he had not even shared with his parents before. He revealed that his shadow would "dance alone" for as long as he could remember, untethered by his control, searching for something—or someone. Whenever he noticed his shadow dancing without his control, in order to camouflage the untethered nature of it all, he would simply follow the shadow and pretend to dance.

"You should go to the Archives one of these days, Ardyn!" an elder member shouted.

"Yeah. You should. If you go there on a Sunday when there is a full moon, you are likely to meet people who may open your minds more," another rebel piped in.

"What happens at the Archives?" Ardyn asked.

"Well, that's the place where all the scholars of enchantment come to share their discoveries. You see, they don't let anyone inside the wisdom hall unless you are a registered scholar with the Archives. But you, with your parents' credentials, should have access. Go there. Find what is being discussed. For decades, we have been trying to create spells to break the enchantment, to no avail. I am afraid we have exhausted all our means. We need access to new knowledge. You could help us get the key," the elder member replied.

Ardyn nodded and asked, "When is the next full moon Sunday?"

"You are lucky boy. It's in four days!" another member with a long black beard said.

The Archives loomed like a solemn guardian at the edge of Lirith, its towering spires entwined with creeping ivy and bathed in the silvery glow of the full moon. Inside, its labyrinthine halls whispered with centuries of accumulated knowledge, the air heavy with the scent of aged parchment and polished stone. Tonight, the Wisdom Hall was alive with anticipation, the murmur of scholars mingling with the low hum of enchantment.

Kaelina followed her aunt and uncle, her footsteps hesitant as they ascended the spiral staircase that led to the hall. Though she had been here before, she had never crossed the threshold of the Wisdom Hall, a chamber reserved for the most erudite minds and their prized discoveries. Tonight, she was the specimen—the subject of a new theory her aunt and uncle were eager to present. Her blank shadow—or lack thereof—was to be dissected in front of prying eyes and scribbling quills.

The hall itself was a marvel. Its vaulted ceiling shimmered with enchanted constellations, the stars shifting and winking as if alive. Shelves of ancient tomes lined the walls, interspersed with glowing sigils that pulsed faintly in rhythm with the Scholars' Crest engraved on the floor. At the center of the hall stood a circular dais, where theories and findings would be unveiled under the scrutiny of the gathered scholars.

Kaelina lingered near the edge, her gaze fixed on her shadow. Or rather, the faint outline that pretended to be one. Unlike the vibrant, animated shadows of those around her, hers was dull, thin, and static. A reminder of her difference. Her failure.

As the scholars filed in, a figure slipped through the heavy oak doors unnoticed. Ardyn—his Council badge tucked discreetly into his coat pocket—moved with practiced ease, his vivid shadow flowing like liquid at his heels. The Wisdom Hall was breathtaking, but Ardyn had little time to admire it. He kept his head low, weaving through the crowd, his heart pounding as he sought the dais.

Kaelina's eyes drifted to the floor, her stomach twisting into knots as her aunt began speaking to the gathering. She barely listened, too preoccupied with the whispers of judgment she imagined behind her. But then, something changed. Her shadow flickered.

She froze.

For a moment, she thought it was her imagination. But no—her shadow moved again, elongating unnaturally, reaching toward … another. Her breath caught as she watched it dance with a vivid, fluid figure that had appeared beside it. The other shadow moved with confidence and grace, intertwining with hers like it had been waiting for this moment.

Her gaze snapped upward, scanning the room for the source of this anomaly. That's when she saw him.

Standing near the edge of the hall, half-shrouded in the dim light, was a boy. His dark hair fell messily over his forehead, and his sharp features were framed by an expression of quiet determination. But it was his eyes that held her. They were piercing yet warm, brimming with curiosity and something unspoken—something that made her pulse race.

Ardyn had felt it too—the moment their shadows connected. His vivid shadow, usually so hard to control, had drifted toward hers like a moth to flame. And now, as his gaze met hers across the crowded hall, he felt an inexplicable pull. She was striking in a way that caught him off guard—her wide, dark eyes shimmering with a mix of fear and wonder, her auburn hair catching the light like threads of copper. She looked as though she belonged to a secret the world wasn't ready to know.

For a heartbeat, the rest of the room disappeared. It was just the two of them, their shadows dancing in a silent, forbidden language.

Kaelina's heart pounded as her aunt's voice droned on. She forced herself to look away, but her shadow betrayed her, continuing its intricate dance. She risked another glance at the boy and was startled to find him still watching her.

And then he smiled. It was subtle, almost imperceptible, but it was enough to send a shiver down her spine.

Ardyn knew he couldn't stay long without arousing suspicion, but he couldn't leave without ensuring this girl—this mystery—would meet him again. He reached into his coat pocket and withdrew a small slip of parchment. Shielded by the folds of his cloak, he scribbled a hasty message and, with a flick of his wrist, sent his shadow spiraling toward hers. The shadows met, merged, and for a moment, carried his message.

Kaelina felt a tickle at her feet and looked down to see the parchment materialize near her shoes. She glanced up in panic, but no one else seemed to notice. With trembling hands, she picked it up and unfolded it.

Tonight. Midnight. The Moonbridge.

Her eyes darted back to the boy, but he was already slipping out of the hall, his shadow retreating with him. The door clicked shut, and Kaelina felt a strange emptiness where his presence had been.

Her aunt's voice pulled her back to the present, but her mind was elsewhere. Midnight. The Moonbridge. Her fingers tightened around the note as a thrill of fear and excitement coursed through her.

For the first time in her life, her shadow had danced. And she wasn't about to let that be the end of it.

Kaelina's heart pounded as she tiptoed across the creaky wooden floors of her aunt's house. The faint snores of Althea and Camilla drifted through the walls, steady and undisturbed. She paused at the door, her hand trembling over the latch. The cool night air seeped through the cracks, brushing her flushed cheeks as if urging her forward.

Her shadow stretched faintly behind her in the dim glow of the moonlight streaming through the window. It wasn't much of a shadow, but it was hers—and tonight, for the first time, it had danced.

Slipping out, she shut the door as quietly as possible and took a deep breath of the crisp night air. Her pulse quickened, and she felt a bubbling excitement that she hadn't known in years. She pulled her shawl tighter around her shoulders and set off toward the Moonbridge.

The city was quiet, the cobblestone streets glistening faintly with dew. Every sound—her footsteps, the rustling of leaves, even the distant hoot of an owl—seemed magnified in the stillness. But Kaelina didn't feel fear; she felt alive, her heart racing with a thrilling mix of nerves and anticipation.

By the time she reached the Moonbridge, she could see him—a

lone figure standing in the center, silhouetted against the silver glow of the moon. His shadow stretched long and vivid across the stone, curling and swaying faintly as though it were waiting for her. She slowed her steps, suddenly self-conscious, and clutched the edges of her shawl tightly.

Ardyn turned as she approached, his face breaking into a soft smile. "You came," he said, his voice warm but slightly tentative.

Kaelina's breath caught at the sight of him. In the moonlight, his features were sharp yet gentle, his dark eyes gleaming with an intensity that made her stomach flutter. She nodded, her voice momentarily lost.

"I wasn't sure if you would," he continued, stepping closer. His shadow flowed toward hers, a vivid streak meeting her faint outline like a greeting.

"I wasn't sure I should," she finally managed, her lips curving into a small smile. "But then again, I've never been very good at doing what I'm supposed to."

He chuckled, the sound low and comforting. "I'll take that as a compliment."

They stood there for a moment, the silence between them comfortable but charged. Kaelina could feel her heart racing, her pulse echoing in her ears. The chill of the night made her shiver slightly, and Ardyn noticed.

"Here," he said, shrugging off his coat and draping it over her shoulders. "I can't have you freezing before we've even started talking."

Kaelina blinked at him, startled by the gesture. "Thank you," she murmured, clutching the coat close. It smelled faintly of pine and something earthy, something that was distinctly him.

"So," he said, leaning casually against the stone railing of the bridge. "Why did they bring you to the Archives? You didn't look particularly thrilled to be there."

Kaelina hesitated, her fingers playing with the edge of the coat. "I didn't have much choice. My aunt and uncle … they're scholars. They think I'm some sort of anomaly. A curiosity worth studying."

"Because of your shadow?" he asked gently.

She nodded, her eyes fixed on the ground. "They think I'm a curse. And maybe they're right. My shadow has always been this way—weak, pale, almost nonexistent. People in Lirith … they …" She trailed off, her voice trembling.

Ardyn straightened, his gaze softening. "Hey," he said, stepping closer, "you're not a curse. Whoever told you that doesn't understand you. They're afraid of what they don't know."

Kaelina looked up at him, her eyes glistening with unshed tears. "You don't even know me."

"Maybe not," he admitted, "but I know what it's like to feel different. To feel like you don't belong."

She tilted her head, curiosity flickering across her face. "What do you mean?"

He hesitated, glancing away for a moment. "My shadow … it's not normal either. It's … too vivid, too wild. It moves on its own sometimes, like it has a mind of its own. It's one of the reasons I … I can't be what people expect me to be."

Kaelina frowned, her fear momentarily forgotten. "That sounds … beautiful," she said softly.

He laughed, a hint of bitterness in the sound. "*Beautiful* isn't exactly what people call it."

They fell silent again, their shadows entwining at their feet. Kaelina's heart swelled with something she couldn't quite name, a mix of hope and connection and the undeniable pull she felt toward him.

"When our shadows crossed," she said, her voice barely above a whisper, "something happened. I felt … something. Did you?"

He nodded, his gaze locking with hers. "I did. It was like … magic. Like they were meant to find each other."

Her cheeks flushed, and she looked away, but not before he caught the small smile playing at her lips.

"Kaelina," he said softly, his voice drawing her attention back to him, "I want to show you something. Something that might help you understand you're not alone."

"What is it?" she asked, her curiosity piqued.

"There's a group of us," he said, his voice low. "The Shadowless. We're trying to figure out the truth behind the enchantment. We meet in secret, and I think … I think you should come."

Her eyes widened. "Me? Why?"

"Because I think you're stronger than you realize. And because …" He hesitated, his voice softening. "Because I want to see you again."

Kaelina's heart skipped a beat. She looked up at him, her expression a mix of wonder and disbelief. "The same place?"

He nodded. "Midnight. Two nights from now."

She smiled, a spark of excitement lighting up her face. "I'll be here."

As they stood there, the chill of the night forgotten, their shadows danced together in the moonlight, weaving a story of connection, hope, and something that felt very much like destiny.

Kaelina sat at the long dining table, tracing idle patterns on the worn wood as her sisters chattered on about mundane things. Althea, the eldest, was perched at the head of the table, her posture straight and authoritative as always. Camilla, the middle sister, leaned back lazily in her chair, a cup of herbal tea cradled in her hands. They paid little attention to Kaelina, save for the occasional dismissive glance.

"Did you hear about the new decree?" Camilla asked, her tone laced with superiority. "The Council's cracking down on unregistered shadows. It's about time they tightened the leash."

"You'd think they'd have better things to do," Althea replied with a languid shrug. "Half the city's starving, and they're worried about shadows?"

Kaelina's fingers froze mid-pattern. She kept her gaze down, feigning disinterest, though her heart raced at the mention of the Council. She could feel Camilla's eyes boring into her.

"What do you think, Kaelina?" Camilla's voice was sharp, almost accusatory. "Or are you too preoccupied with your …" she waved a hand dismissively, "little musings to care?"

Kaelina clenched her fists under the table but forced her voice to remain steady. "I don't see why it matters what I think. You've already decided what's right."

Althea chuckled, a soft, mocking sound. "Oh, don't take it so personally. Camilla's just trying to include you. You should be grateful."

Grateful. The word echoed bitterly in Kaelina's mind. She pushed back her chair abruptly, the legs scraping against the floor. "I'm tired. I think I'll go to bed."

"Good idea," Camilla said, her tone clipped. "An early night might do you some good."

Kaelina didn't reply. She walked to her room, her footsteps measured, even as her pulse thundered in her ears. Her room was small and windowless, tucked away in the corner of the house—a place where her sisters could forget she existed. She closed the door quietly and leaned against it, exhaling a shaky breath.

Her mind was already elsewhere. She glanced at the small clock on her bedside table. Midnight was still an hour away, but she couldn't afford to wait too long. Camilla had a habit of checking in unannounced, and Kaelina needed to be sure her sisters were asleep.

The house was silent. Kaelina had waited until the faint sounds of Camilla's and Althea's breaths became steady and rhythmic. She slipped on her cloak, pulling the hood low over her face. Her heart pounded as she crept to the door, wincing at every creak of the floorboards.

Once outside, the cool night air hit her, sharp and bracing. The moon hung low in the sky, casting an ethereal glow over the empty streets. Kaelina pulled her cloak tighter around herself and began walking briskly toward Moonbridge.

Her excitement built with every step. She couldn't deny the giddy anticipation bubbling within her. She'd never felt this way before, and it terrified and thrilled her in equal measure. The thought of seeing Ardyn again—his intense eyes, his quiet confidence—sent a rush of warmth through her.

Ardyn was already there when she arrived, leaning casually against the stone railing of the bridge. The moonlight caught the sharp angles of his face, and his shadow danced lightly beside him, flickering like a restless flame.

"You made it," he said, straightening as she approached.

"I'm not sure I should have," she replied, a teasing lilt in her voice. "But here I am."

He smiled, a soft, genuine expression that made her heart skip a beat. "Come on. There's something I want to show you."

He led her down a narrow path that wound its way to the riverbank. The air grew cooler as they descended, and Kaelina could hear the gentle rush of water in the distance. The path was bordered by tall trees, their branches arching overhead to form a natural canopy.

"Is this the shortcut you mentioned?" she asked, her voice hushed in the stillness.

"It's one of them," he replied. "But it's more than that. It's a place where the noise of the world fades away."

Kaelina glanced at him, noting the way his features softened in the moonlight. "You've been coming here for a while, haven't you?"

He nodded. "Ever since I found the community. It's a place where people like us … belong."

"People like us?" she echoed, her voice barely above a whisper.

He stopped walking and turned to face her. "People who don't fit into the perfect mold the Council wants to impose. People with shadows that don't conform."

Kaelina hesitated. "I don't even know what my shadow is," she admitted. "It's just … blank. Empty. A void."

"Maybe that's its strength," he said quietly. "Maybe it's waiting for the right moment to show its true power."

They resumed walking, the path opening up to a small clearing. A circle of figures sat around a fire, their faces illuminated by the flickering flames. Kaelina recognized the elder from their first meeting, his weathered features stern yet kind. The others looked up as they approached, their expressions curious but welcoming.

"This is Kaelina," Ardyn said, his voice steady. "She's ... one of us."

The elder nodded. "Welcome, child. We've heard of you. Your parents were brave souls."

Kaelina swallowed hard, unsure how to respond. She felt Ardyn's hand brush against hers, a subtle gesture of reassurance.

"We have much to discuss," the elder continued. "But first, let us hear what brings you here."

Ardyn and Kaelina recounted their experience in the Wisdom Hall, their voices intertwining as they described the strange magic that occurred when their shadows crossed. The elder listened intently, his brow furrowed in thought.

"The Void and the Balance," he murmured at last. "Rarely do they find each other. But when they do, it is said that great change follows."

Kaelina's heart raced. "What does it mean? What are we supposed to do?"

"That is for you to discover," the elder said. "But together, you may hold the key to breaking the enchantment."

Kaelina exchanged a glance with Ardyn, a mixture of fear and determination in her eyes. Whatever lay ahead, she knew she couldn't face it alone.

Ardyn held Kaelina's hand and whispered, "I am the Balance to your Void!"

Kaelina's heart pounded. "How do you know this?"

The elder gestured to the fire. "Sit. There are things you need to understand."

Kaelina and Ardyn joined the circle as the elder began to speak. "Long ago, the Shadowmakers crafted the Enchantment to reveal people's true emotions. But it came at a cost. They tied the shadows to their own immortality. As long as the shadows exist, so do they."

Kaelina shivered. "So, breaking the Enchantment …"

"Would end their reign," the elder finished, "and free us all. But one thing this community has been searching for is a hidden place. A hidden vault where they save books, materials, and more. Maybe there's something there that can help us. I believe that something that will have the answer to what we are looking for."

Kaelina stood near the elder of the Shadowless community, her voice steady despite the racing thoughts swirling in her mind. The firelight illuminated her pale features, and she glanced at Ardyn, drawing courage from his silent support. The rest of the community waited patiently, their curiosity evident as they leaned in to hear her plan.

"The place you're referring to," Kaelina began, "I've overheard my aunt and sisters talk about it. They call it the Vault of Origins. It's not just hidden; it's sealed and protected by layers of enchantments, but there's a key—a physical object and a set of instructions on how to bypass the enchantments." She paused, her fingers nervously twisting the hem of her cloak. "Both of these are in my sisters' possession."

The elder nodded slowly. "And you believe you can retrieve these?"

Kaelina's gaze hardened, determination flickering in her eyes. "Yes. Althea and Camilla have always underestimated me. They don't think I'm capable of anything significant. That's my advantage."

A woman from the circle, her silver-streaked hair tied in a loose braid, spoke up. "And how do you plan to take these items without alerting them? If they realize what's missing, it could put all of us in danger."

Kaelina hesitated, then drew a deep breath. "Camilla is meticulous—she keeps the key in a locked chest in her room. But I've seen where she hides the chest key: under a loose floorboard by her bed. As for the instructions, Althea carries them in a journal she keeps in her satchel. She's careless with it at night, leaving it on the table in the main hall before going to bed."

Ardyn frowned. "It sounds risky. What if they wake up?"

Kaelina tilted her head, a wry smile playing on her lips. "They won't. My sisters' evenings are always filled with wine and their endless discussions about the Council's affairs. By the time they're done, they sleep like the dead."

The elder's expression remained thoughtful, his brow furrowed. "Even if you succeed, you'll need to be careful with the Vault of Origins itself. If the enchantments are as strong as we suspect, you'll need more than just the key and instructions. You'll need intuition and caution."

Kaelina nodded. "That's why I need Ardyn with me. If his shadow truly represents Balance, it might be the key to navigating the enchantments without triggering them. Together, we can do this."

The elder exchanged a glance with Ardyn, who gave a resolute nod. "Then it seems the two of you are bound to this path. But remember, Kaelina, this isn't just about unlocking a door. The Vault holds truths that could shatter everything you've known. Be prepared for what you might find."

Kaelina's jaw tightened. "I've lived in shadows my whole life, elder. It's time I understand why."

The elder's eyes lit up. "If you can find a way inside, it could be the key we've been searching for."

Kaelina nodded, determination building within her. "I'll find a way."

Ardyn placed a hand on her shoulder, his touch warm and steady. "We'll do it together."

The elder smiled faintly. "Be careful, both of you. The Shadow-makers will stop at nothing to protect their secrets."

The circle fell into a contemplative silence, the fire crackling softly in the background. Finally, the elder leaned forward, his voice carrying the weight of his years. "May the void and balance guide you both. We will await your return."

Kaelina and Ardyn shared a final glance, the unspoken bond between them stronger than ever. As the meeting dispersed, Kaelina's mind raced ahead to the task before her, a mixture of fear and excitement bubbling within her. The Vault of Origins awaited—and with it, answers she had long been denied.

Kaelina met Ardyn's gaze, her heart thundering. In that moment, she felt a spark of hope. Together, they might just stand a chance.

Kaelina paced the length of her windowless corner room, the faint glow of the moon sneaking through a gap in the curtain. Her sisters, Althea and Camilla, were in the study—as usual, poring over maps and whispering cryptic instructions about their upcoming trips. Kaelina had overheard enough to know they possessed the access key and the secret procedure to reach the vault. Tonight was the night she would find out where they kept it.

She stepped lightly into the hallway, careful not to let the wooden floorboards creak. Through the half-open study door, she caught fragments of their conversation.

"The map will reset at dawn. We need to ensure no one else knows how to find it," Althea said sharply.

"Of course," Camilla replied. "And the key stays in its usual place. No need to complicate things."

Kaelina suppressed a grin. "Usual place," she repeated silently. Perfect.

Feigning innocence, she pushed the door open wider. "What are you two whispering about this time?"

Both women stiffened. Althea's eyes narrowed. "Nothing you need to concern yourself with, Kaelina. Don't you have chores to finish?"

"Chores? You mean the ones you leave for me while you hide away in here?" Kaelina shot back, her voice laced with feigned irritation. "Fine. I'll leave you to your secrets."

She turned on her heel and stormed out, slamming the door for good measure. In her periphery, she caught the flicker of annoyance on Althea's face. That would keep them distracted.

Kaelina crept down the hall and into her sisters' shared room. She began searching methodically. The dresser, the jewelry box, under the bed. Nothing. Then her gaze fell on the wardrobe. She opened it cautiously and rifled through the neatly hung garments. Her fingers brushed against something solid. She pulled it out: a small, ornate box with a lock.

"This has to be it," she whispered. She reached into her pocket and produced a thin piece of wire she had smuggled from the kitchen. With nimble hands, she picked the lock. Inside was the access key, a thin metallic disc engraved with symbols, and a parchment detailing the secret procedure to unlock the vault.

Beside the key was a folded map, its surface alive with shifting lines and glowing markers. Kaelina marveled at it, realizing this was the "live map" her sisters had referenced. She unfolded it carefully and committed the shifting coordinates to memory, tracing the patterns with her finger.

"The city center," she murmured. "The vault's door is there tonight."

A noise in the hallway jolted her. She hastily returned everything to the box except the key, which she pocketed, and slipped out of the room.

At the Moonbridge, Ardyn was waiting, his figure silhouetted against the silvery glow of the water. "Did you get it?" he asked, urgency in his voice.

Kaelina held up the key. "And more." She explained the live map and the procedure to unlock the vault. "It's in the city center tonight, but we have to be quick. It moves at dawn."

Ardyn nodded, his expression a mix of awe and determination. "Let's go."

The city center was quiet, the usual bustle replaced by eerie stillness. Kaelina led the way, the map's shifting coordinates vivid in her mind.

They stopped at an unremarkable stone wall. Kaelina ran her fingers over its surface, searching for the hidden mechanism. Finally, she found a groove and inserted the key.

"Here goes nothing," she whispered, twisting the key.

The wall shimmered and dissolved, revealing a narrow passageway.

"Stay close," Ardyn said as they stepped inside.

The air grew cooler as they descended, the passage widening into a cavernous room filled with shelves that stretched infinitely upward. At the center was a massive hourglass, its sand frozen mid-fall.

"Time," Ardyn breathed. "It's stopped."

Kaelina nodded, her eyes scanning the shelves. The place felt alive, the hum of dormant energy vibrating through her. The shelves were laden with scrolls, books, and peculiar artifacts encased in glass. She reached out to touch one, a silver orb that shimmered with faint blue light, but Ardyn grabbed her hand.

"We can't risk activating anything," he cautioned, his voice low.

They pressed on, their footsteps echoing in the vastness. Strange symbols glowed faintly on the floor, and the walls seemed to shift when viewed from the corner of the eye.

Suddenly, Ardyn paused and pointed. "Look."

A floating pedestal held a crystal mirror. Its surface rippled like water, showing fragments of memories as they walked past. Kaelina froze when she saw a flash of her childhood—her mother's face, stern yet loving, whispering in Pryllis. The mirror darkened as they moved away.

"This place … it's testing us," Kaelina said, her voice barely above a whisper.

"Then we'd better pass," Ardyn replied, his hand brushing hers as they moved forward.

Finally, Kaelina spotted it: a weathered tome with the title written in Pryllis.

She grabbed it, but the cover wouldn't budge. Frustrated, she remembered her uncle's words about the books inside the vault. "They open only to those who understand their secrets," he had said.

Kaelina placed her hand on the cover and began reciting the Pryllis script aloud. The book glowed faintly, then unlocked.

"It worked," she whispered, flipping it open. She devoured the pages, translating aloud for Ardyn.

"The Shadowmakers tied their immortality to the enchantment," she read. "Breaking it will end their reign, but it is not without cost."

As they reached the final pages, Kaelina's breath hitched. Two signatures stared back at her: her parents'.

"They were trying to end it," she said, her voice trembling. "All this time, I thought they served the Shadowkeepers."

Ardyn placed a reassuring hand on her shoulder. "They would be proud of you."

They spent hours crafting shorthand notes and encoding the book's knowledge into songs and poems. When they finally emerged, the city center was as still as when they had entered.

🕵️

The shadowless community listened intently as Kaelina and Ardyn recited their findings. The elder's eyes shone with pride. "Thank you," he said, embracing them both.

Kaelina's voice trembled as she asked, "Are the Shadowmakers still alive?"

The elder's expression grew somber. "They exist as mist atop a mountain beyond Lirith. Break the enchantment, and they will cease to be."

He explained the book's instructions for the Shadow Dance, the ritual requiring Kaelina and Ardyn to unite their powers during a rare astronomical event. "But it comes with a price," he warned. "Kaelina, you risk losing your emotions. Ardyn, you may become trapped in the void."

Kaelina turned to Ardyn, her gaze searching his. "Are you sure about this?"

Ardyn took her hands in his, his voice steady. "I'm with you, no matter what."

They exchanged a glance, their determination unwavering. "We'll do it," Kaelina said.

The elder outlined the plan for the Mega Masquerade Ball, a ruse to gather all Lirithians under the guise of celebrating the enchantment. "We must secure the council's approval first," he added, his tone grave.

Kaelina and Ardyn exchanged a glance before stepping forward. "We can present the idea to them," Kaelina volunteered, "but convincing them might be a challenge."

"The council communicates through the Hall of Echoes," the elder said. "You'll need to submit a proposal using the Prism Orb. It conveys ideas directly to their consciousness, but the orb reflects doubts and inconsistencies, so your argument must be flawless. One important thing to note is that the orb requests go to them anonymously."

Kaelina nodded, already formulating her pitch. "That will work in our favor, wouldn't it? We'll emphasize the unity and cultural importance of the event."

Ardyn added, "And we'll play up the allure—masks, mystery, and celebration of Lirith's heritage. It's the perfect cover."

The elder handed them the Prism Orb, its surface gleaming with shifting colors. "Be persuasive," he said. "The council is skeptical of gatherings this large, especially during these times."

The next morning, Kaelina and Ardyn stood before the Orb in a secluded chamber. Kaelina took a deep breath and began. "Honored council, we propose a Mega Masquerade Ball to honor the enchantment and foster unity. The event will reinvigorate our people's pride and bring everyone together in harmony."

As she spoke, the Orb emitted a soft glow, but when Ardyn added, "This will also strengthen our defenses against external threats," the light flickered briefly, signaling doubt.

"Careful," Kaelina whispered. She quickly interjected, "The ball will also serve as a reminder of our shared history, keeping Lirith's spirit alive."

The Orb steadied, and after a tense pause, its surface turned a radiant green, indicating the council's approval.

Relieved, they returned to the shadowless community to strategize. "How do we ensure everyone attends?" Ardyn asked.

"The masks," Kaelina said thoughtfully. "We'll craft enchanted invitations that compel curiosity. The masks will be sent as part of the invite, ensuring everyone feels obligated to participate."

"And for those reluctant to attend?" one of the elders asked.

"We'll add a hint of allure," Ardyn said with a sly grin. "The promise of uncovering a mystery about Lirith's future—something no one will want to miss."

The room buzzed with approval. "It's risky," Kaelina admitted to Ardyn later that evening, "but it just might work."

Ardyn reached for her hand, their fingers intertwining. "We're in this together. Risk is part of the adventure, isn't it?"

Kaelina smiled, her resolve strengthening. "Then let's make it unforgettable." There was a twinkle in her eye, and Ardyn noticed it. He couldn't sleep that night, as all he could think of was this beautiful girl who had taken over his life and how he couldn't get enough of Kaelina's presence.

To ensure widespread attendance, Kaelina and Ardyn devised a multilayered plan. Every minute she got to spend with Ardyn planning the ball was important for Kaelina to break the curse. But she also realized that she truly enjoyed spending time with Ardyn, and how much she had been smitten by Ardyn's captivating smile and loving care.

They decided to dispatch enchanted messages through an ancient network of luminescent scrolls known to reach every household in Lirith. These scrolls would unfold with a burst of light, projecting a holographic invitation detailing the ball's allure and importance. Additionally, emissaries from the shadowless community, skilled in persuasion and cloaked in mystery, would travel to the most remote corners of Lirith to personally deliver masks and invitations to key families.

Kaelina suggested involving local bards and performers to create excitement. "Let them sing of the Mega Masquerade Ball in every village square," she proposed. "The songs will plant curiosity and anticipation in the hearts of even the most reclusive."

Ardyn added, "We'll also need a compelling story—a legend, perhaps—that ties the ball to Lirith's heritage. Something that makes attendance feel like an honor, a duty even."

As they finalized the details, Kaelina couldn't help but feel a mix of nervousness and exhilaration. Ardyn, sensing her unease, placed a hand on her shoulder. "We're doing this for Lirith," he said gently. "Together."

Kaelina smiled, bolstered by his unwavering support. The secret meeting place where they were with the shadowless community buzzed with approval as their plan took shape, weaving unity, intrigue, and purpose into a single irresistible event.

Kaelina paced the dimly lit balcony of the Moonbridge Tower, her cloak swirling in the cool night breeze. Below her, the city of Lirith shimmered faintly, the flickering glow of shadowed lanterns casting dancing shapes on the cobblestone streets. Somewhere in the distance, Ardyn's voice called her name. She turned to see him ascending the spiral staircase, his expression a mix of weariness and determination.

"You're late," Kaelina said, a teasing edge in her tone, though her eyes betrayed her relief at seeing him.

Ardyn sighed, brushing back his windswept hair. "I was cornered by another group of dissenters. The unrest is worse than we feared. They're saying they want to keep their shadows, that they're a part of who they are."

Kaelina folded her arms. "I overheard the same sentiment in the market earlier. They believe losing their shadows means losing their identity."

"And do they have a point?" Ardyn asked softly, stepping closer to her.

Kaelina hesitated, gazing out at the city. "Maybe. But what good is identity if it's tied to the very thing keeping us enslaved? The enchantment needs to be broken, no matter the cost."

At the word "cost," they both fell silent. The immensity of what lay ahead pressed down on them like an unseen weight.

Ardyn broke the silence first. "Have you thought about it? The risks?"

Kaelina turned to face him fully. "How could I not? I've replayed it a hundred times in my mind. If I lose my emotions—" She paused, her voice faltering. "If I become a hollow shell of who I am, what will be left of me?"

"You'll still be you," Ardyn said firmly, his voice filled with conviction. "Your strength, your courage—those are the things that define you, Kaelina. Not the enchantment."

She smiled faintly, but her eyes searched his. "And you? What if you're trapped in the void forever? Ardyn, I can't bear the thought of losing you."

He reached out, brushing a strand of hair from her face. "I've accepted the risk. I'd face the void a thousand times if it meant freeing Lirith." He hesitated, then added softly, "And if it meant saving you."

Kaelina's heart ached at his words. She took his hand in hers, holding it tightly. "You're too noble for your own good, Ardyn. But there's something I need to know."

He tilted his head, his expression curious. "What is it?"

She drew in a deep breath, her grip on his hand tightening. "I discovered something today. About your parents."

Ardyn's expression froze. "What did you discover?"

"That they're high-ranking members of the Shadowkeepers Council," she said, her voice quiet but steady. "Why didn't you tell me?"

Ardyn stepped back, his face a mask of conflicted emotions. "Kaelina, I—" He stopped, exhaling sharply. "I didn't tell you because I didn't want you to think I was like them. I've spent my entire life trying to undo the damage they've caused. I didn't want their sins to taint … us."

Kaelina's gaze softened, though her voice remained firm. "I understand why you kept it from me, but Ardyn, I need to know—should I be worried? Can I trust you?"

Ardyn's eyes burned with intensity as he stepped closer, cupping her face with both hands. "Kaelina, look at me. You have my heart, my loyalty, my everything. I love you with all my breath and bone. I would never betray you. I would burn every bridge, sever every tie, and defy even my own blood for you. For Lirith."

Her breath caught in her throat at the raw emotion in his voice. "Do you mean that?"

"With every fiber of my being," he said, his voice unwavering. "And if that's not enough, tell me what I need to do to earn your trust. I'll do anything."

Tears welled in her eyes, but she smiled through them. "You've already done enough, Ardyn. More than enough."

He exhaled in relief, his forehead resting against hers. "Then we risk it. For the city. For us."

"For Lirith," Kaelina whispered, her voice filled with both determination and love.

They stood there for a moment, the world fading away as they held on to each other—the hug tightening. Then, as if the city itself sighed in response, a gust of wind swept past them, carrying with it the faint whispers of the restless shadows below.

Kaelina took a deep breath and stepped back, her hand still entwined with Ardyn's. "Let's make this count."

Ardyn nodded, his eyes never leaving hers. "Together."

The day had arrived. The city of Lirith, bathed in the soft light of twilight, seemed to pulse with anticipation. From the cobblestone streets to the towering spires, banners of deep indigo and shimmering gold fluttered in the cool breeze. The council's emblem, a silhouette of two intertwined shadows, was painted across the city square—a mark of both unity and division. The air hummed with the symphony of bustling preparation and murmured excitement.

The rebel committee's daring campaign had worked. Posters and whispered words in the alleys had spread the call for change, while the council, eager to maintain control, had ironically amplified the ball's significance. They framed it as a celebration of tradition, an homage to the mystic bond between shadows and their bearers. The people of Lirith, whether out of loyalty, curiosity, or rebellion, gathered in unprecedented numbers at the central square, eager to witness the Shadow Ball.

The Square

The central square had been transformed. Lanterns enchanted to emit a kaleidoscope of colors floated in the air, casting prismatic patterns on the cobblestones. The council spared no expense in security. Masked enforcers patrolled the perimeter, their sleek black uniforms blending with the shadows. Yet their presence did little to quell the electric energy of the crowd.

At the heart of the square, an ornate stage rose, its floor made of polished obsidian that seemed to drink in the light. Around it, an intricate labyrinth of mirrors and ivy created a mesmerizing backdrop, designed to reflect the dancers and their shadows in infinite patterns. The faint hum of violins tuning added to the charged atmosphere, their notes rising and falling like whispered secrets.

The dancers who would perform were chosen weeks ago. To participate, pairs had to visit the council office to collect a yellow card, each bearing a unique number. Three weeks before the ball, the council displayed the selected numbers on the city center's notice board, drawing eager crowds as people jostled to see if their fates aligned with the event.

Among the ten chosen pairs was Ardyn, who had quietly ensured his selection using his council connections. The act wasn't without risk, but Ardyn's resolve had hardened. This was his only chance to set things right—for Kaelina, for Lirith, and for himself.

Kaelina's Preparation

At their home, Kaelina's aunt and uncle, for once, did not scold or dismiss her. Instead, they seemed strangely hopeful, their tones softer than usual.

"This may be a good day for you, child," her aunt said, adjusting her own new dress. "If the curse is to be cleansed, the ball is your best hope."

Kaelina nodded, her heart heavy yet fluttering with an unnameable feeling. She retrieved her mother's dress from the cedar chest—a gown of midnight blue with tiny stars embroidered along the hem. Time had not been kind to it; the edges were frayed, and the fabric bore the faint scent of lavender and age. Despite its flaws, Kaelina wore it with pride, letting her auburn hair fall in loose waves over her shoulders. Her sisters, clad in new dresses of vibrant silks, scoffed but said nothing. Deep down, even they felt the weight of the evening.

The Ball Begins

As the first musical notes drifted into the night air, the crowd hushed. The ten chosen pairs, their faces hidden behind ornate masks, stepped onto the obsidian stage. Kaelina and Ardyn stood among them, their hands brushing briefly as they took their places. Her mask, delicate and silver, framed her eyes like the wings of a butterfly. His, stark and angular, mirrored the silhouette of a raven.

The music swelled—a haunting melody of violins, cellos, and drums that seemed to resonate with the heartbeat of the city. The dancers began to move, their shadows stretching and merging on the obsidian floor, creating shapes that seemed almost alive. The air grew thick with magic, an ancient power stirring as the dance progressed.

The Astronomical Moment

As the night deepened, the moment approached. The celestial alignment, foretold by the Shadowkeepers, brought the moon and stars into exact symmetry. A silver beam of moonlight pierced the square, illuminating the dancers. Kaelina and Ardyn, moving in perfect harmony, felt the weight of their task.

When their shadows crossed, a ripple of energy surged through the stage. The obsidian floor shimmered, colors exploding across its surface like liquid fire. The crowd gasped as an otherworldly transformation unfolded; the once-muted hues of Lirith sprang to life. Reds, golds, and violets painted the city, banishing its perpetual grayness. The people felt an overwhelming rush of emotions—joy, sorrow, love, hope—each more vivid than the last.

High above, on the distant peak where the Shadowmakers were said to dwell, the mist began to churn. Thunder rolled across the sky, and a landslide rumbled down the mountainside. But the people of Lirith, enraptured by the transformation below, paid no mind. For the first time in generations, they felt truly alive.

Kaelina and Ardyn, standing at the center of the storm of light and shadow, turned to face each other. The masks that had concealed their identities slipped away, revealing their bare faces to the crowd. For a moment, silence reigned.

Ardyn took Kaelina's hands, his voice steady but filled with emotion. "For Lirith. For us."

Kaelina nodded, tears glistening in her eyes. "For us."

As the crowd watched, the two leaned in, their lips meeting in a kiss that seemed to seal the city's newfound freedom. A wave of warmth and light spread outward, washing over the onlookers. Even Kaelina's aunt, uncle, and sisters felt their hearts soften, their resentments fading into the ether.

A New Dawn

When the kiss ended, the crowd erupted into cheers. No one—not the council, not the Shadowkeepers, not even Ardyn's parents—felt anger or betrayal. Instead, they were overwhelmed by a sense of liberation, a freedom they had never known.

For Kaelina and Ardyn, the curse had been broken. They stood together, hand in hand, as the people of Lirith celebrated a new beginning, their shadows no longer a burden but a testament to their humanity.

♟♟

Kaelina and Ardyn sat close together on the hill where the mists of the Shadowmakers once swirled. The night was unusually quiet, save for the occasional murmur of the wind through the trees. Below them, the city of Lirith glowed softly, no longer adorned with the erratic brilliance of dancing shadows but with the steady, warm light of lanterns swaying in the breeze. The stars above seemed brighter, freer, as if even they had been liberated from some invisible burden.

Kaelina leaned back on her hands, her eyes scanning the horizon where the remnants of the mountain blended into the sky. "Do you miss them? The shadows?"

Ardyn tilted his head, the corner of his mouth curling into a faint smile. "Maybe. But this feels ... real." He gestured toward the city below. "Every light, every flicker—it's chosen. Not stolen."

Kaelina smiled, her gaze fixed on the stars. "It's strange, isn't it? For so long, the shadows were part of who we were. Now, without them, it feels like ..." She paused, searching for the right words.

"Like we're finally breathing," Ardyn finished for her, his voice soft.

Kaelina turned to him, her golden eyes reflecting the starlight. "And you? Do you feel lighter?"

He reached out and brushed a stray lock of hair from her face, letting his fingers linger for a moment. "I feel ... free. Like I can finally be something more than what I was born into. And maybe even worthy of you."

"You were always worthy," she whispered, her voice catching slightly. "I didn't just fall in love with the part of you that fought for Lirith. I fell in love with the Ardyn who sees the world differently. Who makes me believe in things I thought were impossible."

For a moment, silence stretched between them, but it was a comfortable silence, one that carried the weight of everything they'd endured and the hope of what lay ahead.

Ardyn's hand slipped into hers, their fingers intertwining as naturally as if they'd been meant to fit together. "You know," he said, his voice carrying a playful lilt now, "we're heroes now. I think that means we get to make the rules."

Kaelina laughed, the sound carrying over the hill. "Oh, is that how it works? Should I start calling you *Lord Ardyn*?"

He feigned a thoughtful expression. "Hmm, no. How about *Ardyn, the fearless romantic?*"

She rolled her eyes, her smile widening. "Let's not push it."

Their laughter died down, replaced by the rhythmic symphony of the night. Ardyn glanced at her, his expression serious now. "Do you ever think about what comes next? After all of this?"

Kaelina leaned her head on his shoulder, sighing. "Every day. But for the first time, I'm not afraid of it. Whatever it is, we'll face it together."

Ardyn looked up at the stars, their light soft but unwavering. "Together," he echoed.

After a long pause, Kaelina murmured, almost to herself, "Do you think the stars ever feel alone?"

Ardyn turned to her, his expression thoughtful. "Maybe. But they shine brightest when they're not trying to hide behind anything.

Maybe that's the lesson, Kaelina. The light doesn't need the shadow to be beautiful."

Kaelina lifted her head, meeting his gaze, and in that moment, the world seemed to hold its breath. "Then let's promise each other something," she said.

"Anything," he replied without hesitation.

"No more hiding. Not from the world, and not from each other."

Ardyn brought her hand to his lips, pressing a gentle kiss to her knuckles. "I promise."

And as they sat there, the wind carrying the faint hum of the city's newfound joy, Kaelina spoke the last words of the night, her voice filled with wonder and certainty: "The stars were always there, Ardyn. We just needed to see them."

The two of them sat in silence after that, their hands clasped, their hearts light. Above them, the sky stretched endlessly, full of promise.

ACKNOWLEDGMENTS

The journey of writing a collection like this is not a solitary one, and I am deeply grateful to the many individuals who have supported me along the way.

First, my sincere thanks to my editor, Joe Pierson, whose insightful feedback and guidance helped shape these stories into their final form. His expertise and patience were invaluable throughout this process. I would also like to thank the talented designer, David Ter-Avanesyan, whose exceptional creativity helped to give this book a cohesive and striking visual presence.

I am incredibly fortunate to have had the support of a wonderful group of beta readers, who gave me their time, feedback, and encouragement throughout the creation of this collection. While I won't name each of them individually, their input has been crucial in helping me refine these stories and stay true to the spirit of each one.

The stories within these pages span nearly a decade, with the earliest written about nine years ago and the most recent just three months old. I'm grateful to the stories themselves, which have evolved alongside me, reflecting shifting moods, curiosities, and creative experiments. Each of these stories was written at a different moment in my journey as a writer, and I hope that the diversity of voices, language, and genres will resonate with readers as much as they have with me.

To my family, your support is unwavering and boundless. My deepest gratitude to my wife, Kameshwari, whose constant encouragement and insightful feedback have been a source of strength and inspiration. To my children, Nakul and Rachna, who bring laughter and joy into my life, even during the most intense writing sessions. And to Tayga and Monk, my loyal canine companions, whose presence has always made my workspace warmer.

I am especially grateful to my amma (mom) and appa (dad), whose love and support have shaped me throughout my life. Their encouragement during my younger years laid the foundation for my creative journey, and their belief in me has been a constant source of strength as I've grown both as a writer and as a person.

To all those mentioned here and to the many others who have shaped my life in ways too numerous to list, thank you. Your support has been a constant throughout this journey, and I am forever grateful.